Never Had Ian Glimpsed a Greater Beauty.

Her perfect oval face and alabaster skin were tinted with a pinkness that grew as their eyes held. Large blue eyes stared at him openly and artlessly for a moment. Just before she looked away, he saw the pink tint rise up her forehead to the edge of her upswept, glossy wheat-colored hair.

God help him, tonight he might find himself seated next to this alluring vision. But he wouldn't let her cause him to forget the real purpose of his life.

And he would never again allow himself to be tossed into the tumultuous sea others called love.

Dear Reader,

We, the editors of Tapestry Romances, are committed to bringing you two outstanding original romantic historical novels each and every month.

From Kentucky in the 1850s to the court of Louis XIII, from the deck of a pirate ship within sight of Gibraltar to a mining camp high in the Sierra Nevadas, our heroines experience life and love, romance and adventure.

Our aim is to give you the kind of historical romances that you want to read. We would enjoy hearing your thoughts about this book and all future Tapestry Romances. Please write to us at the address below.

The Editors
Tapestry Romances
POCKET BOOKS
1230 Avenue of the Americas
Box TAP
New York, N.Y. 10020

Gilded Hearts

Johanna Hill

A TAPESTRY BOOK
PUBLISHED BY POCKET BOOKS NEW YORK

To my parents,
and Ann Vigliotti and Dana Bryan—once again.
Thank you.

An *Original* publication of TAPESTRY BOOKS

 A Tapestry Book published by
POCKET BOOKS, a division of Simon & Schuster, Inc.
1230 Avenue of the Americas, New York, N.Y. 10020

ISBN 978-1-4516-8803-0

First Tapestry Books printing December, 1984

10 9 8 7 6 5 4 3 2 1

Printed in the U.S.A.

Chapter One

"DOESN'T CLARICE LOOK LOVELY!" DAPHNE EXCLAIMED in a whisper to her sister, Julia, seated beside her. They watched their twenty-five-year-old cousin, Clarice Davenport Appleton, and Freddy Stewart Courtney standing before the minister at the altar. The minister was about to pronounce them man and wife.

Julia Davenport smiled in assent but she was too moved to speak. Freddy lifted the veil from Clarice's upturned face and kissed her as the organ chords reverberated through the church. Julia gazed at the stained-glass windows glimmering above the altar. Although weddings were as common as balls and dinner parties, Julia found herself feeling sentimental this evening.

The newlyweds began their promenade to the front of the church, where a horse-drawn carriage awaited them. The carriage would carry them the half-dozen blocks north, to the Appletons' Fifth Avenue mansion.

There would commence the dinner for the immediate family and friends, which would precede a ball at which over three hundred of society's best were expected.

Julia wondered if the snow that had hung so heavily in the silvery dusk sky had begun to fall. She hoped so, for she loved the way a light snowfall softened the edges of the city streets and gave a magical look to the park that bordered Fifth Avenue on the west. As a child, Julia had believed snowfall the work of angels painting the earth, just as she herself spread a wash of colors on paper at her drawing table in the nursery.

Clarice turned in Julia's direction, looking so radiant that Julia could not prevent the trickle of tears rolling down her cheeks. Julia felt a communion with her shy cousin as their eyes met and held for a moment. Clarice's plain face and hefty body seemed transformed into loveliness, more by her happiness than by the delicate lines of her satin-and-lace wedding gown, Julia decided. Even Freddy looked almost dashing.

For the first time in her twenty-three years, Julia envisioned herself dressed in white lace, walking proudly down the aisle, her hand entwined with that of her new husband. Yet, as clearly as she could picture herself, the man beside her remained an unfocused, attractive figure whose face eluded recognition. While Julia acknowledged that she'd been blessed with a fair amount of physical beauty in face, form and coloring, she wondered if she would glow with half the inner beauty emanating from Clarice. For Julia knew that if true love did not manifest itself during the next year or so, she would have to make a suitable marriage, which her mother had been pressing her to do for the past three years. Twice Julia had been engaged; twice she had broken the engagements. Fond as she had been of both young men, she had not been able to conceive of herself married to them for a lifetime. Although divorce had become so commonplace within their set that it was almost fashionable, Julia still believed in the sanctity of the marriage vows.

Julia's broken engagements had enhanced her social standing, for as curious as it was to her, the assumption seemed to prevail that because she was "hard to win," she was worthy of greater regard and more ardent pursuit. She knew she was considered a charmer and a flirt. And flirt she did, for this appreciated social behavior was ironically the easiest for her. Her banter pleased, yet allowed her to keep her private thoughts comfortably hidden. Only through her painting could she express her inner self. Julia knew that her mother had never fathomed her decisions to end her engagements, but then to Mamma, she knew she was something of an enigma.

"I was thinking about my wedding colors again," Daphne said, her brown eyes bright with excitement. "I'm not sure if I want blue after all. What do you think of yellow? The color of daffodils?" Daphne whispered, for her engagement to Harold, while presumed, was not yet formally announced.

"I think yellow sounds fine, but blue would be pretty as well. It's your decision." Daphne's eyes assumed that dreamy look that had become her most common expression of late. Then Daphne's eyes cleared and she smiled broadly. She covered her mouth to repress a giggle. "What did I say that tickled you?" Julia asked.

3

"You said that whatever I chose was fine." Daphne leaned closer. "But we both know that the colors will be whatever Mamma decides," Daphne answered, and again tried to repress her giggles. "I was only thirteen when Louise was married, but I still remember how Mamma won at each turn."

Julia fought to keep from laughing at the memory of the war that had lasted for months. "I remember the battle of the flowers as well. But I've forgotten just what they settled on—"

"Orchids," Daphne answered quickly. "The conservatory was festooned with orchids—Mamma's favorites. . . . It was lovely actually, wasn't it?"

"Yes, I guess it was," Julia agreed with her sweet nineteen-year-old sister. "I think it was Mamma's prodding that led Auntie Gertrude to choose orchids for Clarice's reception too."

Daphne nodded. "Well, they aren't my favorite flower, but lucky for me I don't mind them, as they shall probably fill the conservatory in Lenox for my wedding as well."

"Lucky for Mamma that it is your wedding and not mine. For—"

Again Daphne grinned and said in a whisper: "Mamma will be *so* thrilled when you actually decide to marry, that I'm sure she'll consent to whatever flowers you wish. Whatever kind of wedding you wish—as long as it's socially acceptable—when you marry—"

"*If* I marry," Julia said, half-seriously.

"Oh, nonsense," Daphne retorted. "Of course you shall marry. And it wouldn't surprise me if the gentleman's initials turned out to be P.M.!"

4

"P.M.? Now who might that be?" Julia sallied.

"Dearest . . ." Henrietta Miles Davenport said to Daphne, her gloved hand tapping Daphne's shoulder. Daphne turned her attention to her mother providing Julia with a moment to reflect upon Daphne's teasing about Percy Martin.

Julia wondered if Percy, who was presently courting her, might be the unfocused man in her fantasy after all. He had proposed a dozen times during the past year. Always with just the proper air of lighthearted jocularity that freed her from answering and still preserved his pride, friendship and hopes. Percy made her laugh more than any young man she'd ever known and she enjoyed his company and easy conversation. She believed that despite his casual air he truly loved her. But did she love him? She fancied him, but that was not necessarily the same as love. Mamma would be thrilled by the match, but that alone was not a good reason to get married. Yet, despite their frequent verbal dueling, Julia loved her mother dearly and would be happier than she cared to admit to finally please Mamma.

Julia glanced a few rows behind to where Percy sat with his parents and sisters. His boyishly attractive face, with eyes almost as blue as her own, immediately caught her stare. He gave her a smile and a playful wink. Julia felt her cheeks redden and wondered if Percy had read her thoughts. She smiled in return and pretended that she was scanning the pews and had just happened upon him. She played the role expertly, then turned away.

A glance in Mamma's direction showed that her eagle-eyed mother had not seen her momentary loss of composure. Mamma's elegantly coiffed head, beneath her ribboned and plumed hat, was cocked in the direction of Louise, Julia's twenty-six-year-old sister, and Louise's children, Gwendowlyn and Thomas Junior. Beyond them, Julia's brother-in-law, Thom, engaged in conversation with Papa. Julia caught her father's eye and smiled affectionately. With his reddish-blond mustache, thick silver-blond hair and blazing blue eyes, he looked handsome enough to be a bridegroom himself, Julia thought.

Julia saw that the last of the wedding party had disappeared behind the arched doorway. Soon they and the other members of the Appleton and Courtney families would begin their slow procession. Julia needed to stretch, but decorum forced her to wait until those in the first three pews filed past her.

To entertain herself, she studied the family members already standing. Sally Courtney, dressed in a pink brocade gown and flowered hat, appeared like a vision of spring on this frigid December evening. Julia supposed her own gown, a Worth design of buttercream satin with printed faille ribbons in an English flowered appliqué of rose and earth green, evoked a similar effect. Julia didn't usually give the serious concern to fashion that Mamma, her sisters and friends did. Visits to their dressmaker were more a matter of unwanted obligation than joy.

Stretching her legs beneath her gown, Julia returned her gaze to her family. A man was crouching in the side aisle, speaking with her father. She could not see his face beneath his dark hair, but even bent in his

6

somewhat awkward position, he remained an imposing figure: his shoulders broad, his legs solid and long beneath his finely tailored tuxedo. Something about him intrigued her but she could not place him. With aroused curiosity, she watched, waiting for him to rise. As she stared, she mentally filed through the names on the guest list, to which she'd paid scant attention. He must be an out-of-town guest, she decided. The name Mr. Coster from Boston came to mind because Mamma had made a point of what a fine catch he was. It had been at that juncture that Julia's attention had wandered. Little had she expected that she would be regretting so now.

Julia had no idea how long it had taken her to realize that the man was staring directly into her eyes as she was into his. She quickly looked away to her gloved hands that were twisting the chain of her gold purse. Yet she paid scant attention to her nervous fingers as she continued to see his face in her mind's eye, as acutely as if their eyes had remained locked.

His face was so beautifully sculptured that it brought to mind the magnificent Greek statues. Julia imagined the pale marble statue of David enlivened into a blaze of harmonious tints. The man's ebony-colored hair was just a shade darker than his strong brow and large eyes, made all the more striking by their contrast to his fair complexion, which even from her distance suggested a clean-shaven yet manly beard. His straight nose and finely curved lips balanced the power of his cleft chin and strong jaw. His mouth broadened into a brief but polite smile. It had been the glint in his eyes that had

7

sent a chill up the back of her neck. His black eyes had looked *through* her, piercing her as they belied his smile.

Although the chill had subsided, her heart continued to pound. Suddenly the church seemed unbearably stuffy. Her racing heart and the constriction in her throat made her want to run into the cold night air. Run until she was too exhausted to feel the fear, the joy, the instant and ineffable recognition. For this man, at whom she dared not look again until she regained possession of herself, was *the* man whose face had eluded her in her wedding fantasy but moments before.

Ian Woods was grateful when Mr. Davenport, seemingly unaware of the preceding moment, resumed their conversation. From the corner of his eye Ian absorbed the girl's extraordinary profile as he recalled the vision of her full faced.

Never had he glimpsed a greater beauty. Her perfect high-cheeked oval face and alabaster skin were tinted with a pinkness that grew as their eyes held. Her eyes were so very large and round, their delft-blue color brilliant and yet almost translucent as she stared at him so openly and artlessly for a moment. Just before she looked away, down to her slender hands that played with the chain of her purse, he detected the pink tint rising up her high forehead to the edge of her upswept, glossy wheat-colored hair. He stole another look at her slender form in her cream-colored, flowered gown that graced her elegance as subtly as did the strands of pearls adorning her neck and the rose-colored garland crowning her hair.

GILDED HEARTS

The tautness in his jaw and the surge in his groin warned him. It had been a time since he had been so dangerously moved by the vision of a girl. He would let it take him no further, for he would never again allow himself to be tossed into the tumultuous sea that others called love. He had been steadfastly single-minded for the past five years and would remain so. His heart would rise in awe *only* for the building he would design. Buildings that would soar through the skies of the city. In less than two years, the twentieth century would burst through the gilded, antiquated nineteen-hundreds. He, Ian Woods, would be one of its foremost architects. Architects of skyscrapers, architects of progress—

". . . Mr. Woods?" Charles Davenport said, after having risen during the moments that Ian had helplessly drifted away.

"Yes, sir? I apologize," Ian replied. There was no use trying to cover his bad manners, although he silently chastised himself for them. Charles Davenport's face broke into a smile and his eyes twinkled, not unkindly.

"She's quite a beauty, isn't she!" Charles answered with a knowing smile. His eyes led Ian's to the blond beauty, her back to them now, as she gracefully stood in the aisle. "And I suppose it's my right, however immodest, to say so, since she's my daughter."

Ian abruptly turned his perusal to Charles's face. His daughter . . . Why, of course! It was obvious. The girl had his eyes, his coloring. "I didn't realize, sir. Yes, she is quite lovely. And the other two young women? Are they also your daughters?" Ian inquired, remembering the other two attractive females, who paled in contrast to the blonde's radiance.

"Yes, they're all my brood," Charles said with a proud smile. "Julia, the one you were staring at," he said evenly, his eyes direct but warm, "is my middle daughter. The one leading the two children up the aisle is Louise, the eldest. Thom, the gentleman I introduced you to, is her husband. The lovely lady in mauve, walking between the two girls, is my dear wife, Henrietta. And the pretty, pert little one on her left is my youngest, Daphne. I have to fork over the cash for one of these big matrimonial events myself in a couple of months," Charles added, gesturing at the church with a disgruntled expression that fooled neither man. "Dang it. I guess that's what the money's for! Keeping the gals happy! And Daphne is a sweet girl . . . But don't mention her marriage, 'cause the engagement announcement isn't going to be made until the end of the week. Henrietta would make my life *miserable* if it got out before, and she learned I was the culprit."

Ian laughed along with Charles, suspecting that his own mother and Mrs. Davenport were cut from the same cloth. But then, weren't all of society's women the true powerbrokers, while they allowed their men to hold the illusion of being kings? In the world of business and finance, kings they were, tyrants even— but at home and in society their power was titular and limited mostly to writing checks. Only in their offices and clubs could men still be men. "I won't speak a word," Ian assured Charles.

"Good," Charles replied, and patted him on the

10

shoulder. "What would the public at large think if they knew their 'evil' corporate giants quivered at the mere *thought* of the wrath of their wives?"

Ian laughed again. He liked this man more than he'd ever expected he would, which was a bonus, since he intended to make Mr. Davenport a business proposition by the end of the week. But Ian didn't wish to impose further at the moment. "I ought to let you get back to your family, Mr. Davenport."

"Please call me Charles, and I shall call you Ian. I suspect that despite the fact that I'm old enough to be your father, you and I may turn out to be great friends, should you decide to settle into New York after all."

Ian offered his hand to Charles. "I just may at that, Mr. . . . Charles," Ian answered with a heartfelt smile. "I sincerely hope we will become friends, although I must insist that it's difficult for me to think of you as old enough to be my father," Ian continued sincerely. Once again he appraised the handsome, robust man who appeared to be in the prime of his life. Ian's own father had died when he was still a boy. "I hope I'll have the pleasure of your company tonight after dinner."

"Better yet, I shall cajole my sister, Gertrude, into disrupting her table plans and into moving you across from me at the dinner table," Charles promised, to Ian's delight. He knew that with Charles for company, dinner would not be dull. "We'll put you next to Julia," Charles added, then stared at him with a puzzled expression before he broke into a gentle grin. "Julia's my blond daughter."

Ian had momentarily forgotten, so taken had he

11

become with Charles. From the manner in which Charles's grin widened, Ian realized he'd given himself away again. Ian preferred to think of himself as inscrutable, but somehow he didn't mind that this unpretentious man was able to read him so quickly. They shook hands and Charles started across the pew. Ian had taken a few strides up the side aisle when he heard Charles call his name. He turned back to the steel magnate. "Sir?"

"Julia's not married. She's been engaged twice but broke them off, which I thought was a smart move, between you and me. She's being courted by a nice fellow from a family so old-society and filthy rich that it makes ours look like we just got off the boat. He's a decent chap, Percy is, but he doesn't seem to have much direction," Charles continued as softly as he'd begun. "I don't think he's going to catch her either. But don't ever tell Henrietta I said that. Now, that's *two* life-endangering secrets I've told you. See you later."

Ian watched Charles hurry across the pew and up the center aisle. With a shake of his head, Ian broke into a hearty laugh. God help him, he thought, if the beautiful Julia had half the character of her fine father! . . . The fact that he thought of the girl at all sobered him. She was Charles's daughter, nothing more to him. He would treat her with the courtesy he would be expected to offer to any young woman under the circumstances. Ian had a feeling that Charles was exactly the kind of gentleman who would be interested in the future, and therefore interested in a business proposition that would help to create the firm that he and Ned Barrington, a fellow architect and his best friend, were about to open: Woods & Barrington. Architects for the future! He would make himself remember that, if tonight he did find himself seated next to the alluring Julia. He would not allow her beauty to cause him to forget the purpose of his life, not even for a moment.

Chapter Two

"I SIMPLY ADORE WEDDINGS!" HENRIETTA EFFUSED TO Julia and Daphne as they accompanied her up the church aisle.

Mamma's remark, so obviously pointed that it tickled Julia, forced her from her turbulent thoughts about the man who'd been speaking with Papa. Julia recognized that it was she who most vexed her mother's otherwise efficiently planned and expertly executed life. For her broken engagements and unwillingness to give her hand in marriage to Percy prevented her mother from successfully completing her life's destiny—marrying her daughters off to suitable husbands. Even the imminent excitement of planning for Daphne's spring wedding did not seem to appease Mamma sufficiently. "Is that so, Mamma?" Julia asked with such feigned surprise that it was only Mamma's steely character that allowed her to suppress a public frown, while Julia less successfully suppressed her own grin. Mamma regarded her silently, then turned and smiled at Mrs. Ferguson, seated to their right. Julia tried to hide her impatience as they stopped before Mrs. Ferguson so that Mamma and she could exchange pleasantries. They'd been part of the procession now for at least twenty minutes and were still but three-quarters of the way up the aisle.

Lily Ferguson smiled and touched Henrietta's hand. Henrietta noted that Lily's outdated green velvet gown did little for her pallid complexion and untinted, graying hair. Lily had been such a vibrant, fashionable girl in their youth, during the War Between the States. Even Archibald's untimely death a decade ago was no excuse for Lily to have let herself go. For Archie had at least died with his fortune intact, which was more than could be said for many other widows.

Henrietta's thoughts returned to Julia's arch comment and mocking grin that she'd managed to transform into a perfectly lovely smile that only a mother could read for its true intent. Even as a child, Julia had been the most provoking. Louise had been the perfect little lady, as had Daphne. But Julia had been as recalcitrant in conforming to the proper display of social graces as she had been clever at anything that pleased her, like riding and especially her dabblings in drawing and paints.

Henrietta always suspected that Julia possessed a strong streak of her father's nature. Charles had been a bit of a headstrong rake—and a dashing captain in the War—when they'd met. Through Henrietta's firm handling he'd grown into the perfect husband. Though she'd not yet seen Julia to the altar, Henrietta knew that her same firm hand had reined Julia as well. For

15

since Julia's debut five years ago, she'd remained the most beautiful and socially admired girl. Still, Henrietta found it difficult to apprehend why Julia remained so casually indifferent to the power she wielded. For while Julia's quick wit and playful nature allowed her to enjoy her center-stage role at any social event, Henrietta knew that, at heart, her daughter never took it seriously.

Henrietta glanced at Julia, waving at her best friend, Betsy Livingston, seated to their left. "Daphne, dear," Henrietta whispered to her younger daughter just loud enough to be heard above the whishing sounds of their satin evening gowns, "even the plainest girl always glows as a bride, don't you agree?" Pleased with Daphne's affable smile, she subtly drew Daphne closer. "I do think Clarice looked almost pretty, and *far* younger than her years. And that Monsieur Worth! Such an artful designer he is. Clarice appeared almost slender. I can hardly wait until we see the sketches he will do for your wedding gown!"

Julia smiled benevolently at her mother. She knew Mamma must be counting the hours until Daphne's engagement announcement to Harold Ogden Baldwin appeared in the leading newspapers and the society columnists began plaguing her with telephone calls for further details. Harold's family, like Percy's, was among the most prominent and oldest in New York society—the society her mother held in such high esteem. Just as, after almost thirty years of marriage, Mamma still seemed somewhat awed by the Davenport family. One would think that Mamma had come from an impoverished background, but the Miles family seemed no different from any other in society to Julia, although she supposed that their fortune was later made and possibly smaller. Still, nothing thrilled Mamma more than the amalgamation of gold and family trees.

Obliquely Julia's eyes scanned the church but she caught no glimpse of the man whose face had made her tremble. By the time she'd dared to glance about, he was no longer at Papa's side. Julia was grateful as they finally picked up momentum, and he hoped Mamma would not slow down again before they reached the church doors. The crowd that had been bundled before them had passed beyond the doors into the antechamber. Julia was anxious for fresh air and a possible view of the man, although he was probably long gone. However, she had no doubt that if he had been to the church he would also be at the ball after the family dinner. Unconsciously Julia had taken her mother's elbow and quickened their steps.

"Julia, Daphne, look! There's Mrs. Woods. I must stop and say hello," Mamma insisted.

Julia didn't see Mrs. Woods. She wasn't even sure she would recognize the woman, who was not a member of Mamma's intimate set. "Where is she?" Julia asked, trying to disguise her impatience. Mrs. Woods was a dowager into whose select circle Mamma aspired. Julia didn't understand why, since the woman was neither richer nor more interesting than any of Mamma's considerable number of friends. Julia remembered seeing one or two of Mrs. Woods's oil paintings at a ladies' charity exhibition. She'd found them singularly lacking the slightest hint of latent talent.

17

"I wish . . ." Julia whispered to Mamma, but the rest of the words stuck in her throat. For seated between Mrs. Woods and her daughter, Florence, a former schoolmate, was *that* man and he was staring directly at her with what seemed to be amusement in his eyes.

His expression put her on her mettle this time. She had caught his glance so unexpectedly that she pretended not to have seen him at all. She forced herself to appear indifferent as she approached the Woodses with Mamma and Daphne. Julia forced her eyes to remain politely directed at Mrs. Woods, but she could only pretend to listen to the ensuing conversation.

". . . lovely to see you, as well, Mrs. Davenport. I must tell you, though, that you and your girls look like absolute visions," Mrs. Woods said. She peered from behind her lorgnette. "As I watched Louise and her husband and children pass, and then yourself and your other daughters, I simply could not decide which of your gowns was my favorite. Of course I wouldn't have revealed my conclusion even if I'd come to it," she concluded with a royal chuckle.

Henrietta was taken aback. For Mrs. Woods, an acquaintance more than friend, was not one to effuse and she was most certainly in the know about fashion. Her own gold *crepe de chine* gown was as charming as it was expensive. "How very nice of you to say, Mrs. Woods. I'd just been commenting to my daughters about how elegant you looked, as always. Was I not, Daphne?"

"Yes, Mamma, you were," Daphne agreed, with a sweet smile to Mrs. Woods, knowing that she was the woman whose friendship had always eluded Mamma, much to her consternation.

"How very sweet of you," replied the long-faced matron, properly flattered. "Let me see . . ." she continued warmly as she looked from Daphne to Julia. "You are Julia? . . ."

"Yes, Mrs. Woods," Julia responded with a pretty smile.

"And of course, then you are Daphne," she concluded, then returned her gaze to Mamma. "It has been my pleasure to know Louise since we served on the same hospital charity fund-raiser last spring, I believe."

"Yes. Louise mentioned to me then what a pleasure it was to serve under your guidance," Henrietta replied. In truth she had made Louise tell her every detail of her encounters with Mrs. Woods.

"It was my pleasure," Mrs. Woods demurred. "Now, I'm sure you have met—but just in case, allow me to introduce you to my daughter, Florence."

"Hello, again," twittered the thin, birdlike dark Florence. "It is nice to see you again, Julia. Julia and I were schoolmates, Mother," she explained.

As the introductions continued, Julia steeled herself for the moment when she would have to meet the man's eyes again. She could not remember Florence having a brother and it overwhelmed her to think that this man of her dreams might in reality be Florence's beau. Instantly Julia was sorry for her lack of charity. Flo had always been a shy, unattractive and unpopular girl in school. Julia could not remember having seen her at any of the dances in years. But for all she knew, Flo

19

might have been in attendance. It was the girl's unfortunate fate to be one of those persons whose presence went perpetually unnoticed.

". . . and Julia," Mrs. Woods said. The sound of her name brought Julia to attention. "I don't believe you've met my son either, then. Miss Julia Davenport, please meet Mr. Ian Woods."

"My pleasure," Ian said. He smiled with a practiced distance.

"Very nice to make your acquaintance," Julia replied as her eyes met his black eyes again. The glint she'd received before was absent. Julia wasn't certain if she were relieved or disappointed. She was too nervous to think or feel.

"As I said," Mrs. Woods continued—Julia was relieved to be able to affix her eyes on his mother—"Ian has just graced us with a visit from Chicago, after a long stay in Paris. I do so hope that I may successfully entreat him to remain in New York. I have told him that if he is to design commercial buildings, he may do that just as well in New York and still be among civilization!"

"I understand exactly how you must feel," Henrietta said. "I am sure that once Ian has reacquainted himself with society it will be difficult for him to drag himself away. And it must be such a comfort to you to have him home again," she added with true sympathy.

"Yes . . . yes, it is. We must definitely have tea sometime soon, Mrs. Davenport," Mrs. Woods said, pleased with Henrietta's comments that apparently mirrored her own sentiments.

Julia saw the joy fill Mamma's face. Should she? Did

she dare risk possible transparency that neither Mrs. Woods nor Mamma would detect but which Ian might see? Allowing herself no more indecision, she plunged. "Mrs. Woods. I saw your painting in the ladies' exhibit at the charity auction a few months ago. I thought it was wonderful. I can still recall the vividness of your wine grapes against the gold goblet."

Mrs. Woods's face lit. "Why, *thank* you, Julia. I've heard that you are a fine painter yourself. From Miss Manzella, who apparently tutored you for a time as well."

Julia smiled. Poor Miss Manzella. She was such a talented colorist but had to earn a living that too often meant wasting her talents on those with none of their own. "Thank *you,* Mrs. Woods, but I merely play at my painting and such."

"I suspect that you are being unduly modest, my dear. In any case, you must all come to tea. This week coming if possible, Mrs. Davenport," Mrs. Woods said with insistence. She turned to Julia. "I have some really fine paintings that hang in my picture gallery that I should love you to see. Many of the great masters' works. Would you like that?"

"I think it would be most exciting and I would love to come! Don't you agree, Mamma?" Julia found it difficult to keep from laughing as she gazed at her mother. She had to give Mamma credit. For although Mamma was probably ecstatic, her demeanor remained calm and socially impeccable.

"I think it would be lovely. I will have to check my calendar and that of the girls and then send you word of our availability, Mrs. Woods," Henrietta answered

21

with a pleasant smile. "May I send word on Monday morning?"

"Oh, that would be just fine, Mrs. Davenport. It was lovely chatting with all of you. I look forward to tea!"

Julia realized that Florence had remained as much a shadow as usual. "Florence, of course that will give us a chance to visit as well?" Julia inquired thoughtfully. She felt pleased and a little guilty when the girl's sharp, thin face lit up in response.

"Of course. We can reminisce about our delightful school days!" Florence answered with glee.

Julia returned Flo's warm smile and allowed her eyes to slip to Ian's face. Although a polite smile played on his face, his eyes told her that her performance that the others so readily believed had not fooled him. Julia quickly turned to Mrs. Woods as good-byes were warmly exchanged. Following her mother and sister to the antechamber of the church, she realized that her escape had not come a moment too soon! For she could not have remained neutral under the light of his amused scorn for much longer. Julia's heart continued to beat rapidly and she had to work hard at maintaining her composure as the frigid night air hit her flushed face. She wanted to cry. For Ian was the first man she'd ever truly desired to know, and although she'd won Mamma's most fervent gratitude, she'd engendered Ian's disdain.

"I've never spoken with Mrs. Davenport at length." Ian listened to his mother and sister babble on. "I've always suspected she was something of a sycophant, but I believe I was wrong. And Daphne seems so very sweet, doesn't she? I hear that she's to be engaged to Harold Ogden Baldwin. But that Julia, not only is she a real beauty but seems to be equally cultured and talented, don't you think?"

Ian helped his mother into the horse-drawn carriage. "Yes, Mother. One could safely call her a real charmer." Neither his mother nor his sister saw the sardonic grin that played freely now on his face, which turned toward the darkened street, as the carriage headed for the Appleton mansion.

So, Julia was as quick as her father, but she used her cleverness with a woman's wiles. He would have to be most alert with that blond beguiler. One false move and he could find himself tangled in her web and unable to extricate himself. The pressure he felt in his heated groin when he conjured her face impressed upon him in a most graphic manner the need for vigilance.

Chapter Three

JULIA COULD NOT REMEMBER HAVING SPENT A MORE disconcerting dinner. Could it only have been hours ago that her heart had jumped with pleasure when Papa announced that Ian Woods would be seated at their table and would be taking her in to dinner? When Ian took her arm and led her from the reception room to the dining room, she'd seen no sign of lingering scorn in his eyes. He led her in with skillful conversation that she managed to match, although her mind was hazy with excitement. As Ian helped her into her chair, his arm brushed her shoulder—by accident or intent, she did not know. But the mere brush of his hand against her bare skin sent a sensation so strange and yet so exciting through her. Their eyes met and for the second time she experienced the intensity of his gaze. So he too had been jolted by the electricity that had coursed between them. It had not been her imagination.

For the first time, Julia was less than casual about her comeliness. She gave Ian her most dazzling smile, the

24

same smile she'd been told so often couldn't help but break a man's heart. In response, Ian seemed to study her for a moment, but no expression registered on his face. He gave her a polite half-smile and turned his attention to Louise, seated to his right. For the rest of the seemingly endless dinner, Ian divided his attention between Louise and Papa, who sat across from them. Julia's mortification, saved only by cousin Bart Appleton's jovial chatter as he sat between her and Daphne, threw Julia into quiet self-consciousness. The few sentences Ian addressed to her as their lobster thermidor was being served were markedly desultory, making them worse than no words at all.

Julia forced down what particles of food she could manage. How could she have been so wrong? her heart cried out. This man hadn't the slightest interest in her. He'd made it painfully obvious in the politest of manners! Julia wished to plead a splitting headache and have their driver take her home. But her pride would not allow her to give Ian the satisfaction. For she had no doubts that when their eyes first locked in the church her feelings had been perfectly obvious to this man, who didn't seem to miss a nuance of expression.

By dessert Julia had stilled her churning stomach with the reminder that the ball would soon start, hundreds of guests would arrive, and among them would be Percy Martin. She could hardly wait to see Percy's smiling blue eyes as they gazed at her with all the warmth and admiration that Ian's coal-black eyes lacked. Ian was speaking briefly of his love of Chicago, which surprised most at the table. Then he mentioned his mentor, an architect, Louis Sullivan, with a passion she found disconcerting. Let him go back to Chicago, then, to his precious Mr. Sullivan! She, for one, did not give two straws if she ever saw this cold, arrogantly handsome Ian Woods again!

"Julia, there you are!" Daphne and Betsy rushed upon her as she stood in a corner of the Appleton conservatory, where the ball was soon to begin. She pretended to be studying the *Venus de Milo* statue that stood amid the ferns and orchids festooning the enormous Corinthian-columned marble-floored room. "We've been looking for you everywhere! Come with us to see the bride's jewels in the drawing room beyond the library," Betsy insisted as she tugged Julia's arm.

"Yes, come," bright-eyed Daphne seconded. "Mamma said that they are exquisite. Especially a ruby bracelet she mentioned, and a diamond pendant. Hurry, before it gets too crowded for a long look!"

"No . . . you two go on. My head aches a bit," she replied truthfully, "and I can use the cool air while most of the people remain in the dining and drawing rooms." Julia's eye caught an ornately carved marble love seat next to the verdant profusion of ferns, fronds and orchids. She pointed. "I think I will rest there awhile."

"Shall I get Mamma? You do look rather pale," Daphne said with alarm.

"We'll stay with you until you're feeling better," Betsy offered. "We can see the jewels later."

Their concern warmed her. "No, please, go on! I'm fine. Really. I'm sure that by the time the guests begin to arrive for the dance, I shall feel fit as a fiddle again!"

"Are you sure?" Daphne asked, unconvinced.

"Yes, really."

Betsy grinned. "I'm certain that when Percy Martin arrives Julia's headache will have disappeared so that they can dance through the night."

Julia's blush made her sister and best friend giggle. Julia smiled despite herself. Thus assured, the two girls ran off, leaving Julia to her solitude. Again she found her thoughts of Percy to be a perfect tonic for her rejection by Mr. Woods. As she sat on the cool marble love seat, Julia realized that her other comfort was that she could discard the fake smile that had numbed her face by the time they rose from dinner. She had heard talk of the pangs of love, the pain of a plummeting heart. But never before had she felt such, and if she never did again, she would be the happier for it. . . . Ian's face, his broad shoulders, his large, gracefully masculine hands, his chiseled features and large dark eyes, fringed with thick lashes, filled her mind's eye. Stop it! She exerted her strongest discipline to banish these thoughts and images from her mind. "I don't give two straws about him!"

"Two straws about whom?" the voice asked, first startling, then shaming her. What was wrong with her? She had spoken aloud without realizing it! She'd believed she'd been alone in the conservatory, and yet the very object of her misery stood before her. She dared not look at his face. For she feared that if she saw the mocking expression she guessed to be in his eyes, she might lose herself and burst into tears.

She felt him sit beside her and caught a glimpse of his long solid thighs that seemed to overpower the small stone seat. Still, she could not look up. "Are you feeling ill, Julia?" he asked with such genuine concern that good manners, at the very least, forced her to raise her head.

She did not try to dazzle him with a smile this time. For what was the use? He probably had a girl in Chicago, for all she knew. Or worse yet, he *just* didn't find her appealing. "I have just a bit of a headache, Mr. Woods. Thank you for asking."

Ian knew that he should rise, make his excuses and flee to another room. He had done his utmost to convince her that he lacked any particular attraction to her during dinner. The food he'd eaten with such apparent heartiness now lay heavy in his stomach. From the moment his hand had accidentally touched her shoulder—he could still remember the cool satiny feel of her alabaster skin—he knew that he wanted her. He should leave the lovely Julia to her solitude. As soon as her beau arrived, he was sure that her broken-hearted countenance would lighten. Beautiful girls were so fickle and so easily repaired by the showering of adoration that they'd grown to believe was their due. "Would it bother you if I lighted my pipe, then, Miss Davenport?" he asked, knowing he was defying his best instincts.

His request confused her. Did he feel obliged to sit with her? Was he feeling sorry for her? Worse yet, had he realized it was about him that she'd stupidly spoken aloud? Well, she didn't need his concern or his pity! "If you like," she answered with as indifferent an air as she could convey.

"Then my tobacco will not make your headache worse?" he asked. Perhaps he'd misread her attitude, for her blue eyes proclaimed little interest in his continued presence.

"No. I just needed a bit of air. I am already feeling better," she answered casually and smiled. But her smile was not reflected in her eyes. She said no more as he lit his elegantly carved pipe. The tobacco's sweet scent pleased her, but she chose not to acknowledge this fact.

Ian began to feel himself an unwanted intrusion. Perhaps her unhappy expression had been about her beau and not himself at all, Ian thought, feeling embarrassingly confused. He'd been so sure that he had this beautiful girl figured out, but she continued to stare at the ugly ornate statue across the room, seemingly oblivious of his gaze. The mingling of her light perfume with his tobacco pleased him almost as much as her sculptured profile and the tender palette of colors of her hair and complexion. Suddenly he wanted to get a glimmer of the girl beneath her exquisite exterior. "So, Miss Davenport, I take it that you find my mother a talented painter?" he asked with a desultory air meant to veil the implicit challenge of his question.

She did not turn to him at first. So that's why he'd lingered, she thought. To rub in the fact that she'd been transparent to him in her flattery of his mother! When she met his eyes, she found them as neutral in expression as his tone had been in asking the question. Still, she knew that he meant to embarrass her. Well, she would not be as easy a target as he might expect, she vowed. She smiled pleasantly. "I wouldn't have said so had I not thought it," she answered, her tone modeled after his own. "Of course I am not an authority on great art. I am sure that as an architect with all the formal training you must have had—at the Ecole des Beaux Arts in Paris I presume?"

He nodded, surprised that she would have known where the finest American architects were trained, though he did not say so.

"What do you think of your mother's painting?" she asked innocently.

Touché, he thought, fighting his grin, as he realized that she had artfully thrown his question back into his face. "I think that Mother's artistic inclinations keep her happy and contribute to worthy charities."

Julia repressed her smile at his trenchant humor. "Well, you would know better than I about such things," she repeated, punctuated this time by a bright smile.

"And what keeps you busy, Miss Davenport? Besides your own 'dabblings' in the arts, as I believe you expressed it earlier tonight."

His expression indicated that he was genuinely curious, but she hesitated in letting down her guard. Although she was the last to make any claims to the quality of her painting and drawing and was the one who had referred to her work as "dabbling," she nevertheless felt herself bristle at his easy acceptance of her as just another girl who did little more than play at life. If that was how he wished to view her, so be it. "Oh, I would say that my life would sound terribly mundane to you!" she began, falling into her routine of easy social discourse. "Except for the hours in which I teach Sunday school and volunteer at the settlement house established for children of unfortunate circumstances, I do what every girl in our set does. I go to the opera and theater, skate and take sleigh rides in the park during the winter. And of course visits to family out in Long Island, Tuxedo and the Adirondacks."

"And in spring you and your mother and sisters tour Europe I suppose?" he asked, his smile broadening.

"Yes, of course. And most of the summer we spend at our home in Lenox. I especially love it there, for I far prefer the openness of the country to the stone and iron of the city," she continued with spontaneity. "What I love most is to ride my horse through the mountains and feel the wind and crisp air of the Berkshires against my face."

So he had been correct. She lived the life of privilege just like all the girls he'd ever met in New York. Yet, there was something about the sparkle in her eye when she spoke of the country and riding. The information he'd sought, to confirm his opinion of this girl, was oddly pleasing him, despite his disdain for the frivolity and indulgence that it reflected. "Newport, yachting trips, dances, all of that too, I suppose?" he asked with seeming approval, leading her down the road to where he wanted her, as he checked off the life he refused to allow himself to be ensnared by.

"Yes, all of that. I told you that my life was perfectly ordinary, Mr. Woods. I'm sure you find it rather wasteful, but I enjoy my lot in life. I had nothing to do with the fate that bore me into a comfortable family and society, but I don't feel the need to apologize for my life either."

"I wasn't implying—" he began, unexpectedly on the defensive.

"Nor was I suggesting that you were. But please . . . From fragments of conversation at dinner, I gathered that you have already led a far more exciting and stimulating life, first in Paris and then in Chicago. Please tell me about it, for I was at the Exposition in Chicago a few years back and much enjoyed my brief stay in that city. And do tell me more about this Louis Sullivan. I, of course, know Mr. Hunt, the famous architect, who is a friend of my parents. I've heard the term 'skyscraper,' but I'm not certain I'm terribly informed about the concept of buildings reaching into the clouds."

Ian marveled at her skillful manipulation of the conversation, the turn about so it was now he who was on demand to reveal himself. He had no intention of doing so, yet he admired her adroitness. He knew that if he were a callow youth rather than a self-possessed, world-experienced, indeed world-weary man of thirty, he would have been drawn into the gilded net she so gracefully and quickly wove. "Oh, I think that my ambitions and views of Chicago and Louis Sullivan would bore a lovely, vivacious girl like yourself to tears. I much prefer listening to your conversation," he added with a proper smile.

So, he thought her too silly to speak about serious topics! Julia felt her face flush in anger. She glanced away just as the orchestra's first notes filled the large conservatory. With relief she noticed that many guests had begun to enter the room, among them Percy Martin. Percy strode toward her, much to her pleasure, for she'd had all she could stand of this contradictory, infuriatingly superior Ian Woods. She turned to Ian with a disarming smile. "If I continued to chatter I'm certain that I should soon make you weary, for idle conversation doesn't appear to be something that appeals to someone as serious as yourself," she said archly, but smiled brightly as she watched the surprise register in his eyes.

What a baffling girl! "I did not mean to appear rude or bored," he answered, attempting to hide his fluster. "Perhaps you would like to dance, if—"

"Julia!" a happy male voice interrupted him. Ian glanced up and saw a young man smiling excitedly at Julia.

"Hello, Percy!" Julia replied in kind. "Let me introduce you to Mr. Ian Woods. Mr. Woods, Mr. Percy Martin," Julia continued as the men shook hands.

"Nice to meet you," Percy said warmly. "Are you the architect I've heard so much about lately?"

"I am the same, though I don't dare to ask what it is you've heard," Ian bantered, but Percy's hearty laugh told him that his reputation for being something of an iconoclast had apparently already become grist for the gossip mill.

"Are you planning to stay in New York, Mr. Woods?" Percy continued.

"Ian. Please call me Ian."

"Ian, then, and I am Percy, of course."

Ian found that he couldn't help liking this young man

who seemed as happy and easy within the fabric of his life as Ian had felt himself constrained at the same age. "I may, but I have to see to some business possibilities before I can say for sure."

"Well, I hope you do stay. It gets to be rather boring, the same old faces at the dances and dinners . . . Ian, that reminds me. I'm having a sleighing party week after next. I'd love you to come if you're still in town."

"If I am, you can be assured that I would be happy to. It's been years since I've been to a sleighing party. Sounds like fun."

"Oh, we usually have a jolly time! My mother and Mrs. Bruce will chaperone, but they're good old gals. I hope you can make it. Now, if you don't mind, I'd like to steal *this* gal away for a whirl around the dance floor."

Ian rose as Percy took Julia by the hand and waltzed her across the ferned and flowered room. Then he sat again and relit his pipe. What infernal foolishness had possessed him, he wondered, as he felt the disappointment flood through him until rationality once again took hold. She was ravishing and bright. But beyond that, she was no different from the rest. He thought of Betty Cornell, the only girl who had ever captured his heart and then proceeded to rip it to shreds with practiced skill. It had been years since he'd allowed himself to think of her at all. Eight years ago . . . Actually, he had Betty to thank for causing him to flee to Europe, which had eventually led him to escape the overseeing of his father's fortune. In Paris at the Ecole des Beaux Arts, his broken heart had been mended by the discovery of a truer passion. A commitment that was not contingent upon the whimsy of a woman. This week he was sure he would see all his hard work and ambition come to fruition. But that would be due to Charles Davenport, not his enchanting daughter.

He would stay in New York, though he would miss Louis Sullivan and pretty Tanya, the daughter of the proprietors of a small restaurant he frequented in Chicago. He liked to believe that she'd never expected more than their shared lovemaking and kindness, but he knew that he'd been something of a cad with her. Nor was she the first. Tanya believed that he wouldn't marry her because she was from the working class. Never did she believe that her character far surpassed that of the girls of his own class, no matter how often he tried to reassure her. He would miss Tanya, her wide and guileless brown eyes, her succulent body. He wished her well.

Ian looked around the room at all the pretty girls who looked as if they'd stepped from the pages of a fashion magazine. He supposed he ought to ask someone to dance and walked toward a voluptuous red-head.

"He seems like a nice chap, that Ian," Percy said as he waltzed Julia around the room in their third dance.

"He's all right, I guess," Julia answered. "But he seems like a bit of a snob to me."

"Well, I'm glad of that," Percy answered with a laugh. He danced her to a corner of the conservatory.

"What do you mean?" Julia asked with a puzzled smile.

"Oh, I don't mind telling you that it made me jealous

to see you sitting next to a handsome older man. So I'm glad he's not your type."

"He's not an *older* man, Percy," Julia chided. "He's probably just thirty or about that."

"Well, you know what I mean," he replied with such a warm smile that Julia wondered why she'd been arch with him. Percy was so devoted to her. They stopped dancing and Percy walked her to a group of chairs beside a potted palm tree.

"Julia. I guess that seeing you with that man and . . . well, that's not it, but I guess I really want to talk to you . . ."

"Then let's sit down and talk," Julia said, taking Percy's arm. She guessed what he was going to ask her. But this time he seemed more nervous, less up to casual banter. He was going to ask if he might approach Papa and request her hand in marriage. Sweet, dear Percy. Wouldn't he be most surprised by her answer! For she had decided that she would marry him. Julia turned her eyes to Percy's kind, fair face. She resisted the temptation to give him a big bear hug but instead squeezed his hand. "I'm glad you want to talk to me, Perce," she said, calling him by her affectionate nickname for him. "I—"

"Excuse me," the voice interrupted. Julia was shocked to find Ian beside her. "May I have your permission to ask Miss Davenport for this dance?" he asked Percy in a most courtly manner.

Say no, Julia silently pleaded, but she knew that Percy, always the gentleman, would accede with grace.

"Only if you promise to bring the lady right back to me," Percy allowed with characteristic good humor.

Ian offered his arm and there was nothing she could do but accept. He walked her toward the center of the dance floor. Julia gave him a slight curtsy, as much to lighten the tension between them as to still her anxiety. Ian took her in his arms. She felt a jolt course through her, just as she'd felt the first moment their eyes had met. Wordlessly they danced. Expertly he whirled her around the floor. Julia did her best to resist the frightening impulses flooding through her. When the orchestra struck up another number, they continued to dance as if they'd been dancing together all their lives. As the music flowed around them, Julia's head almost rested against Ian's shoulder. She wanted to move against him, her body curving against his strong edges. Her head began to lighten, leaving her dizzy in a feverish way. Did she dare to gaze into the face of this man who was making her body dance within itself in a sweet painful surge of feeling?

Julia remembered phrases from romantic novels she'd read, phrases that only suggested pieces of a puzzle of an intimate nature she was not to know before she was wed. She'd learned the facts of life from Louise years before Mamma had valiantly broached the subject, but it had interested her in a way that felt oddly removed from the reality of love and feeling. She'd not risked asking how this set of facts related to matters of sympathy and mutual understanding. For Julia had known from the earliest of ages that she seemed to think too much about things that others found silly or overly contemplative for a girl. Many a night, as she lay alone in her bed, she'd tried to dream of passion, but she hadn't enough clues for it to make any sense. She understood passion for riding and sunsets and spiraling mountain roads. When she painted, she felt as if it were another part of herself, an unknown part that transcended everyday Julia, that possessed her mind and her hands. So often the colors seemed to mix themselves.

Whirling in Ian's arms, she felt as if she'd never danced before, certainly never in this way. A wave of dizziness almost overcame her as she lost herself in his large black eyes that mirrored her sweet yet terrifying sensations.

Ian felt the surge that seemed to course through Julia's body, making her blanch. "Are you all right, Julia?" he asked, his voice slightly hoarse.

"I'm feeling a bit dizzy," she answered, her eyes conveying more complex feelings than her words.

Quickly he led her to a far corner of the conservatory, to a marble seat secluded by vegetation near a window that was slightly ajar. Julia sank onto the seat and he rested beside her. She studied her hands, but Ian was relieved to see the color returning to her ivory cheeks. Ian filled his pipe with tobacco and found his hands less than steady. He didn't want to continue to gaze at the flushed girl who elicited a passion in him that was as intense as it was dangerous. He suspected that she was baffled and frightened by what had passed between them.

Society girls were sexual innocents until their wedding nights. The exception only gave greater validity to the rule. Sex and passion were subjects beyond the girls' pale. The most that could be hoped for from these girls were kisses or chaste caresses. The men spent their passion with ladies abroad or those pretty, if hardened demimondaines, those women on the fringes of respectable society who were supported by wealthy lovers. But one did not take a carriage ride through Central Park on a Sunday with such a woman. Ian suspected that many of the gentlemen he knew actually preferred to exhaust their passions on Wall Street, or in a hunting party, polo, a high-stakes card game or drink. Even after their conjugal rights entitled them to more.

To Ian's thinking, lovemaking was an art, and like any other, had to be practiced. Even then, it was only with the ineffable magic of love that one could transcend one's separateness and soar to the heights of passionate fusion. . . . Ah, how few, but precious those moments. . . . But they were not to be known with this blond goddess beside him. She would marry Percy, or some other fine but bloodless chap. He wanted her. He had from the moment their eyes had first met. But he would not have her. He could not have her. Nor must he allow the deep spring he'd tapped within her, still a mysterious stream to her, to well again. He must deliver her to the tepid arms of dependable Percy Martin.

So, this is love, Julia thought as her erratic breathing subsided. She felt as if she'd climbed to the highest peak, where the air had been more intoxicating than the finest fragrance, but too thin to support her, and—

"It's snowing again," Ian said softly.

Julia gazed up at him. "The angels are at work." She laughed self-consciously. Her laughter died when she saw that he seemed to ignore her remark. He appeared bored with her. But how? . . .

"I think it has been rather rude of me to keep you from Percy for so long, don't you? If you are feeling better, let me escort you back to him." This time Ian knew that his face was sufficiently inscrutable. Her cheeks flushed with confusion at his seeming disinterest.

"I'm feeling fine, thank you, Mr. Woods. Why don't you remain here and finish your smoke," she said, rising quickly. She gracefully smoothed some unseen wrinkle in her gown. "Thank you for the dance," she said with a smile that did not extend to her blue eyes that shone brighter as she suppressed the glimmer of tears.

This was so difficult! He did not wish to hurt her, yet . . . "Wait, Julia . . ." he called softly, falling naturally to her Christian name.

"Ah, *there* you two are! I was beginning to worry that you'd stolen my gal away from me," Percy said good-naturedly, unaware of the ensuing tension. Neither gave the other away, although Julia's flush grew a deeper tint.

"I'm sorry," Ian stated evenly. "But Miss Davenport felt a bit faint for a moment, so I had her rest here."

Percy studied Julia's rosy face. "You do look a little flushed. Do you think you have a fever?" he asked and casually placed his hand to her forehead. "You feel a little warm . . ."

"I feel wonderful! I just needed some air. Now, what I'd *adore* is another waltz with you, Perce."

"Let's have a go at it, then!" Percy answered with a toothy smile. "Excuse us, Ian," he said. Julia pulled him toward the dance floor.

As they danced, Julia turned her face close to his ear. "I am certainly glad you rescued me, Perce," she told him with a bright smile.

"Rescued you? Was Ian rude to you? He doesn't seem like a bore."

"I just don't like him," Julia replied petulantly. "He's so conceited that he makes me as cross as two sticks!" Percy's confused expression made her stop.

"Does that mean that you like me better?" Percy teased in his usual relaxed manner.

"I like you much better!"

Percy gleamed in response, but Julia knew that her feelings about Ian were far more complex than she'd led Percy to believe. How she wished they were simple. She intended to have as little to do with Ian during his visit in New York as she could. More likely than not, she wouldn't have to see him again. Against her will, she glanced to where she and Ian had sat and fought the sinking feeling in her stomach when she spotted him dancing with red-headed Mary Hoffman. She returned her attention to Percy.

As Percy waltzed her around the room, a high, tinkling laugh grabbed her attention. It was Mary Hoffman, giggling in response to Ian's equally merry laughter as they danced past. Ian didn't seem to notice her, so enraptured did he seem with Mary.

"Percy," Julia said with an attempted lightness, "I really am tired. Perhaps I'm coming down with a silly cold after all."

"I told you that you felt feverish," he responded a bit paternalistically. "Let me see you to your mother. I bet she'll rush you right home and to bed."

"Oh, I hate to end the evening so soon!" she lied. She wanted Percy to remain oblivious to the humiliating hurt she'd suffered. In bed, resting against the satin pillows, tucked beneath her warm white quilt, was where she wished to be. In privacy she could think. Maybe she could figure out what had happened to her tonight.

Chapter Four

Late Wednesday morning Kathleen, Julia's personal maid, bounded into Julia's bedroom. "Miss Julia," she said, her green eyes alight. "Miss Livingston is waiting in the reception room. Should I have Peggy show her into the drawing room?"

"No, Kathleen. If you can please help me fasten my dress, I'll be ready in a minute. You were right to urge me out of bed this morning. I do feel so much better. Even my sniffles seem lighter."

"What did I tell you?" Kathleen bantered to her mistress, who had a genuine smile on her face for the first time since she'd arrived at home Saturday night from the wedding dance unexpectedly early. Kathleen's nimble fingers fastened the hooks of Julia's green cashmere afternoon dress, starting with its high black velvet collar. This dress, with its matching velvet ribbons in crossed panels that formed a lovely design down to the pointed cuff at Julia's wrists, was one of the

43

dozen of Julia's new winter gowns, and one of Kathleen's favorites. When she finished, Kathleen stepped back to view Julia, who was only five years younger than herself, but so much taller and more slender. And beautiful. "I think this dress is so pretty," Kathleen said with pride.

Julia turned to the mirror above the vanity. "You were right, as usual, Kathleen," Julia stated as she seated herself. "This dress is warm and rather smart-looking, too. Now, let's get my hair up and start on our Christmas shopping! You and Ellen must *disappear* for a while when we are in the ladies' section of the store, for Betsy and I have long ago decided what we are going to get for each of you. And of course I didn't write it on my list, so it won't do you any good to try to take a peek at it!" Julia teased, as Kathleen began at her hair.

"Miss Julia, you don't have to—" Kathleen began to protest. Julia was more than generous to her throughout the year, but her Christmas presents were always so lovely and extravagant. Like the silk-and-lace blouse that Julia had given her last year, which she treasured.

"Nonsense. Of course I don't *have* to. But you and I are friends, aren't we? And I know how much you enjoy pretty things. It gives me great pleasure to see your eyes glow so happily, Kathleen. Not to mention the challenge to hide your gift successfully."

"I do not snoop," Kathleen protested in vain. She placed the last of the pins in Julia's upswept hair, then giggled. "All right, but it certainly devils me the way you manage to hide it every year, when I think I know every one of your hiding spots!"

Julia laughed in response. Again Kathleen thought how nice it was to see Miss Julia back to her bright self. She suspected it was more than a cold that had made her so quiet and blue. Miss Julia had not only accepted her confinement without her usual fuss and restlessness, but Kathleen had had to cajole her into rising on this fair and temperate Wednesday morning. Even her Christmas-shopping excursion with Miss Betsy hadn't seemed to spark her. Yet Miss Julia's color was back and her cold mostly gone.

For herself, Kathleen was glad to finally be getting out of the stuffy house. Her life with Miss Julia was usually *so* busy and hectic, filled with visits in town and to great houses and country homes, walks in the park during good weather and what-not, that Kathleen usually fell asleep in her small bedroom upstairs as soon as her head hit the pillow.

Not only was she pleased about the outing, for Kathleen loved to see the brightly decorated shops and all the items of luxury that filled their display cases, but she was always happiest when Miss Julia spent the day with Betsy Livingston. The two young ladies had been friends forever, and through them, Kathleen had found a friend in Ellen Donahue, Miss Betsy's maid. The young ladies were so kind that it often felt as if all four were friends rather than mistresses and maids, yet she and Ellen made sure never to forget their places. Although both she and Ellen were but a few years older than their mistresses, they were obliged to remember that they were in part chaperones, for no unmarried ladies of society went out into the city unaccompanied. In the country, the young ladies were permitted to take afternoon rides and picnics unchaperoned, even with their beaux or male friends. But the city could be a dangerous place, as Kathleen herself knew too well, when she'd lived on Hester Street with her mother and brothers. It was through Margaret, her older sister, who had been Miss Louise's maid until her marriage, that Kathleen had come into the employ of the Davenports.

Each time Kathleen thought of her sister, who had married a handsome liveryman, Johnny, and moved to Philadelphia after Louise's wedding, her heart saddened. For Margaret was the only family she had left, except for one brother whose whereabouts she hadn't known for years. Kathleen took solace in the fact that it had been her good fortune to become Miss Julia's maid, for she remembered how Margaret had to stifle her quick temper when she was endlessly at the mercy of Miss Louise's whims and flashes of anger. Of course, Daphne was a sweet young lady, although Kathleen had little use for Justine, Daphne's maid. Justine was French. Most of the household staff were Irish like herself, except for James, Mr. Davenport's butler, who was a proper English gentleman. Justine didn't speak English very well, or pretended not to, for that Justine was one to put on airs. She liked to pretend she was a lady of the house rather than a servant like the rest of them.

No, Kathleen thought, she had no reason to be resentful of her lot in life. She knew that today, for instance, as both of their mistresses strolled through the grand shops on Fifth Avenue, going about their business with laughter and chatter, she and Ellen Donahue would hang behind, close enough to be of assistance, but having the luxury of a quiet chat. Ellen was seeing a man who worked in a dry-goods store downtown, and Kathleen was anxious to hear of the developments. If Ellen were to marry, despite Kathleen's own loss, she would be more than happy for her friend. For herself, Kathleen doubted that she would marry, although the postman, Tommy O'Hara, had certainly been giving her the eye of late. Tommy seemed like a nice fellow and was born in the same county from where her mother had come. But at twenty-eight, Kathleen feared that her rosy bloom had already faded. She was content with her life, and the rest was the Lord's will.

". . . Kathleen?" Julia said. Kathleen stood quietly behind her, seemingly lost in some thought. Julia loved Kathleen, who was as sensitive a soul as she was bright and cheery in demeanor. Many a night they sat and talked. Julia was fascinated by the tales of Kathleen's life. So often Julia wondered if the world she herself lived in had much to do with the "real" world. Kathleen smiled at her. "Sorry I've been so bad-tempered these last few days," Julia apologized sincerely.

"Oh, think nothing of it. You've been sick. You know how I get when I've got a cold or fever . . . I can hardly remember my own name, let alone anything else! Now, let's get your cape on," Kathleen said as she walked to Julia's bed, where the fur-trimmed brown cape lay upon the hand-embroidered bedspread.

"Yes," Julia answered, allowing Kathleen to help her on with her cape. "I think I've memorized every object in this room the past few days. It will be good to see some new scenery!"

47

Julia started from the room but Kathleen lingered for a moment. Even after all these years in the fine Davenport mansion, the richness of this large bedroom, decorated in a sweet feminine manner, still thrilled Kathleen. She glanced at the Gainsborough portrait—Miss Julia had taught her a little bit about art—that hung above the mantel, two other portraits, in delicate oval frames, on each side of it. Beneath was the lace skirt on the mantelshelf that matched the lace skirt of the bed. The mantelshelf above the fireplace held delicate Dresden figures and an ornate miniature piano—rococo was what Miss Julia called it. Her eyes took in the draperies of rich creams and pastels overlaid with a string of beads. They hung over the dresser, behind the bed and above the glass curtains. The large room was filled with looking glasses and mirrors, in which the delicate lace and rich draperies were reflected from above the kidney-shaped vanity, the mahogany dresser and long, gilt-framed mirror on the overmantel. The blue Persian rug with its borders of gold and rose and darker blue flowered design was Kathleen's favorite of the dozens of rugs in the house.

Kathleen was always surprised that Miss Julia often seemed to enjoy the relatively bare surroundings of her small painting studio on the third floor more than the warmth and beauty of this room. But Miss Julia's painting was a special thing that Kathleen appreciated even if she only sensed its meaning to her talented mistress, who kept this part of herself private. Kathleen believed that it was the hidden parts of each being that were God's gift, and most fascinating for that reason alone.

Proceeding down the long, winding staircase to the first floor, Julia was beginning to feel like her old self again, after three days of brooding melancholy. The fact that she'd come down with a cold had given her an excuse to withdraw without arousing the family's suspicions, although Julia suspected that Kathleen had been aware that more was troubling her than her illness. Julia had almost confided in Kathleen, for so often they talked about emotions and the meaning of life and love. Kathleen, a devout Catholic, had her church's teachings and rituals, which offered her solace. Although Julia went to church and believed in God, her religion seemed to place more emphasis on free will and thereby the responsibility of a person to make her own decisions within the framework of the church's doctrine.

Julia had been tempted to ask Kathleen about love, specifically in relationships to men. She suspected that Kathleen might have more information on that subject. But to do so meant acknowledging that Ian had produced a most disturbing effect within herself. Instead, Julia had decided to banish all thoughts of Ian from her mind. Tomorrow night she was to go to the opera with Percy and his parents. If Percy later proposed, Julia had decided that she would accept. As she approached the landing of the first floor, Julia felt herself to be frowning again. She consciously set her face in a smile. When she saw Betsy sitting in the reception room, her smile became genuine.

"My goodness!" Henrietta said. Seated at her desk in the family drawing room, she watched Julia and Betsy gaily fall into the room with boxes piled up to their chins. Their maids followed behind, also overloaded with more bags and boxes. "Should I ask if you girls completed your shopping?"

"Not quite, Mamma," Julia said laughingly. "But we got a great deal of it done, as you can see." Julia placed her bundles in a corner of the room and the others followed suit. "And we had a wonderful luncheon at Delmonico's!"

"Not there, don't place them in here," Henrietta directed. "Miss Pendleton," she said to her austere but efficient secretary, "would you get the downstairs butler to help Kathleen get those boxes upstairs?"

"Certainly, Mrs. Davenport," Miss Pendleton said, going about her task at once.

"Hello, Betsy," Henrietta said. "Forgive my manners but I'm in an absolute tizzy! You know that Daphne's announcement will appear tomorrow and we've been trying to get out all the personal announcements today. And this morning we saw Monsieur Worth—it was so hard to choose one bridal design over another, since they are all so magnificent! It wore Daphne out and we're *still* not decided. In fact, Daphne went to her room and Justine informed me that she's fast asleep, so I don't think I'll wake her to join us for tea. . . . But you will take tea with us, won't you, Betsy?"

"Oh, I'll be glad to. It's gotten quite frosty out and tea sounds lovely."

"Good, dear, then do let the girls take your wraps and sit down and make yourself comfortable. I'll just clear up the last of this clutter on my desk and join you two, and you can tell me all about your day!" Henrietta thought again what a dear girl Betsy was and how curious it was that while she was quite pretty and was always attractively dressed, she had so few beaux. But she had seen how Betsy withdrew into shyness at social functions. When she did engage in conversations she frequently chose subjects too serious to hold a young man's interest.

"I think we'll freshen up first, Mamma," Julia said. "We'll be right down."

With that, the girls flew up the stairs before Henrietta could tell Julia about the flowers. When she was their age, young ladies walked rather than ran like children. How times had changed! "Julia!" she called, too late. Henrietta looked up from her desk to the bouquet of roses that Percy had brought to Julia. Henrietta had restrained herself from opening the accompanying card, but she was most anxious to see what it said. She knew that Percy was the perfect match for Julia and hoped that Julia realized so before it was too late. Gossip had informed her, through Louise, that Penelope Osborne was said to have a terrific crush on Percy. While Penelope, of course, was no serious challenge to Julia's beauty and charm, Penelope was quite an attractive and vivacious young lady—younger in fact than Julia. A young man would continue to court only so long, without proper encouragement.

The telephone rang and Miss Pendleton arrived in time to answer it. Henrietta still thought of the telephone as a nuisance. Julia and Betsy reappeared. "Julia, I assume you didn't hear me call to you. Look at the flowers on the rosewood table!"

Julia saw the roses. "They're very pretty, Mamma," she answered with little enthusiasm.

"They're for you. They came earlier, from Mr. Percy Martin. He delivered them himself, thinking you were still ill. Do open the card, dear!"

Julia opened the envelope and read Percy's note. She smiled. He really was sweet.

"Well?" Henrietta demanded, standing at her side.

"Well, what?" Julia teased, knowing how her mother hated to be left in suspense.

"What did he say?"

"He said that he hoped I was feeling well enough to attend the opera tomorrow evening with his parents and him. Here, perhaps you'd like to read it for yourself." She handed the card to her mother with a grin.

The telephone rang again as Henrietta skimmed the note. Percy had signed it "With deep affection." That was what Henrietta wanted to see. She remembered how excited she'd been to receive flowers when she was being courted, but Julia seemed less than—

"Mrs. Davenport," Miss Pendleton called. Henrietta turned to see Miss Pendleton standing with her hand over the mouthpiece of the telephone. "It's the reporter from the *Tribune*. He has a question about the announcement. I think you should take the call yourself." Now, *what* problem could there be? Hadn't she hired Miss Pendleton to handle such matters? And here she was—"He says that he shan't be able to guarantee placement in the upper-right column—"

"What! He most specifically *promised* me . . ." She fluttered. "Tell him to kindly wait one moment. I shall take the call in the library." Henrietta lifted her skirt and hurried out of the room.

Julia and Betsy watched as Miss Pendleton held the phone, her perpetual frown crossing her brow. Julia didn't like the stuffy, humorless woman at all. Besides, she knew Miss Pendleton to be a first-class eavesdropper. With the woman remaining in the room, neither she nor Betsy would be able to enjoy the tea and biscuits that the parlor maid had just brought in on the shining silver tea service. Miss Pendleton returned the telephone to its cradle after listening to Mamma's voice, which even Julia could hear from across the room.

"Excuse me, ladies," Miss Pendleton said in her usual affected voice. "But I believe that I shall attend to some business in Mrs. Davenport's absence."

"Please feel free to attend to whatever you like, Miss Pendleton," Julia replied, subtly mimicking the woman, who was closing the double wood doors behind her. A glance at Betsy, her hand clasped over her mouth to cover her giggles, made Julia burst into laughter when the woman was gone.

Betsy reached for a biscuit as Julia poured their tea. "You don't like her at all, do you?" Betsy asked rhetorically. "I don't either. She's so officious. Just like my mother's secretary. I wonder if they go to some school to learn to act like prigs." Betsy began to giggle. "I had so much fun today, didn't you?"

Julia smiled fondly. "Oh, I did! And I'm not even weary after three days of being in bed. But we always have a good time together, don't we?"

"Certainly do. It was sweet of Percy to bring you

flowers. He's so devoted to you, Julia. And I think he's so personable and handsome! You'd be crazy not to marry him!"

"Do you really think so, Betsy?" Julia asked seriously.

Betsy noted that Julia's blue eyes clouded again, as they had when they'd discussed Percy at luncheon earlier. Something was disturbing Julia. She'd thought so when she'd called each day after Julia left the dance early. If she were Julia, she'd be ecstatic to have a man like Percy courting her. But then, she'd be ecstatic if she were Julia, period. But it was more than just Julia's ambivalence about Percy. Usually Julia would have confided in her, but despite their bustling day filled with chatter and laughter, Julia had seemed to drift off into some private thought from time to time. Betsy knew better than to probe. Julia would not talk until she was ready.

"I wish that someone like Percy wanted to marry me," Betsy said with a sad sigh. "We both know that the rare times I do get courted, it's by some dullard who couldn't possibly hope for attention from someone like you. Or some jolly fellow who's ugly as sin!"

"Oh, Betsy!" Julia reacted angrily. "There you go selling yourself short again. It's simply that you are *so* special that it's going to take an equally special young man to recognize you. I get by because some find me pretty and I banter easily. I say what they want to hear, but you—"

"I don't because I can't seem to. I'm no good at small talk! I watch you, Julia, and I try to learn, but before you know it I find myself talking about books, or even worse, science. Then the attractive men run. I know that I'm fair-enough-looking so that at least they approach me. But even Saturday night, at Clarice's wedding, I was talking with this very nice Mr. Coster, from Boston. Before I knew it, I was talking about stocks and bonds. It wasn't long after that that he was dancing with red-headed—bubble-headed, if you'll forgive me—Mary Hoffman for the rest of the eve—"

"Mary Hoffman? Are you certain?" Julia interrupted, confused as the memory made her heart beat more rapidly. She placed her teacup on the table between them and leaned toward Betsy.

"Well of course I'm certain," Betsy answered with a puzzled expression. "He even escorted her to her carriage. I was leaving with Mamma and saw him do so. I overheard him ask if he might call on her. She giggled the way she does and said of course she would welcome his visit. Why does that surprise you?"

"It doesn't surprise me. I mean, I don't doubt you—of course I don't—but . . . Never mind, it's not important." Should she tell Betsy about Ian? She'd started to at lunch but had stopped herself.

"Then why does Mary Hoffman interest you suddenly? You don't like her either," Betsy persisted.

"Mary Hoffman doesn't interest me. It's just that I'd assumed . . . Oh, never mind."

"Julia Davenport, don't do that! You know how I hate it when you start to share a secret and then stop mid-sentence!"

Julia was torn. Mamma would probably return to the drawing room any moment, or worse yet, Miss Pendleton. Moreover, she didn't know if she wanted to discuss Ian. She'd been so sure that *he'd* been the one who would have seen Mary to her family's carriage, and yet—

"Julia!" Betsy demanded, a frown on her thin small face.

A hearty knock, followed by the sliding open of the drawing room doors, halted their discussion.

"Good afternoon, sweetie! Hello there, Betsy!" Papa boomed as he entered the room in the company of two gentlemen. One Julia did not know, but the other was none other than Ian Woods! "I thought your mother was in here," he said. "Well, allow me to make the introductions, then. Julia, I don't believe you've had the pleasure yet of meeting Mr. Ned Barrington. Ned, this is my middle daughter, Julia. And the lovely lady beside her is her friend Miss Betsy Livingston."

Both girls acknowledged the introduction as Ned Barrington, a short brown-haired man with a walrus mustache, soft brown eyes and a winning, warm smile shook their hands. Julia glanced at Betsy and immediately knew from Betsy's sweet smile that she was taken with Ned.

"And of course, Julia, you've met Mr. Ian Woods at the wedding, but allow me to introduce you, Ian, to Betsy as well," Papa said in his comfortably amiable way.

As Betsy and Ian exchanged a few words, Julia tried to still her hands and maintain a calm, casual air. Ian, in his business suit with its starched round white collar, appeared even more handsome than she'd remembered all those days she'd lain in bed thinking of him.

"I heard that you've been in bed with a cold," Ian

said to her in an even, friendly manner. "I'm glad to see you've recovered without any ill effect."

"Thank you, Mr. Woods. I am feeling quite well again," she answered, trying to pretend that she was speaking with just anyone.

"Is there any tea left in there?" Papa asked. "Sit down, gentlemen. How about a cup of tea? I'd suggest something stronger but perhaps we should wait for that until after our meeting. Julia, dear? Will you do the honors?"

"Of course, Papa," Julia said. She rose and poured the cups of tea. Betsy brought around the plate of biscuits and when the parlor maid appeared, she was sent to the kitchen to bring more refreshments.

Julia did her best to pretend to engage in polite conversation, but she spoke as little as possible. When Papa innocently commented on her uncharacteristic quiet, she pleaded lingering fatigue from her cold. Luckily Betsy and Ned hit it off at once and carried the conversation with an ease and style that Papa heartily enjoyed. Ian was almost as silent as Julia. Never had she been so relieved to see her mother enter. The older woman quickly forgot her harried manner when she saw the two young men in the room. Julia found it easy to see how her mother had been the belle of the ball in her day. For within moments she had charmed both Ian and Ned. Julia noticed that when he laughed, Ian had deep dimples that matched the cleft of his chin. His laugh had a deep, relaxed quality, much like Papa's. . . . So he hadn't spent the rest of the evening captivated by Mary Hoffman. Surely that had been his choice; she knew Mary too well to doubt it.

After what felt like an eternity, but was really no more than twenty minutes, Papa suggested that the gentlemen retire to his study. Ned asked if Betsy would be there when he returned, but Betsy, in a lovely manner expressed her regrets that she was expected at home. Ned asked if her home were close by and she informed him that she lived but two blocks down the Avenue. Even in her agitated state, Julia was happy to see that Ned seemed as interested in seeing Betsy again as she guessed Betsy was. She wished there was some way that she could arrange a future invitation, but with Ian in the room she couldn't unless she included him. That she could not do.

After the men left for Papa's study, Mamma, free to behave harried again, announced that there was a crisis at hand and that she was too upset even to repeat it. She excused herself to the library, taking Miss Pendleton with her. Finally Julia and Betsy were alone.

Neither said a word at first. Julia was afraid that Betsy, having put two and two together, was about to quiz her. She didn't think she could deal with interrogation right now and regarded her best friend with caution.

"He's terrific! Don't you think?" Betsy whispered, as high color tinted her pale complexion. "Tell me, honestly, Julia. No flattery. Do you think he seemed interested in me . . . I mean, did he seem to like me—you know . . . ?" Betsy flustered.

So worried with her own concerns, Julia had forgotten for a moment. "I say this with total sincerity. I think he is *quite* taken with you. Why, he almost risked embarrassing himself, what with Mamma and Papa in the room, inquiring where you lived and all of that! I have no doubts that you shall be hearing from Mr. Ned Barrington. Does that please you?" Julia asked, knowing the answer.

Betsy's grin and gleaming eyes answered. "Oh, you know it does! Why, when I forgot myself, as usual, and began talking about the little I know about architecture—"

"Little? Betsy, you are the smartest girl I know. You know more than a *little* about so many subjects, it dazzles me! I, unfortunately, know very little about the subject. I mean, we learned to speak French and Italian and received a smattering of history. Of course in all those visits to Europe one couldn't help but learn to identify the finest of palaces and masterpieces of art.But I know nothing of science or architecture or a million other subjects. Sometimes I feel so ignorant!"

"Ignorant? How can you even suggest that? Besides, you're an artist. A very talented one, even if you don't feel free to see yourself as such. . . . So you think he really liked me?"

"I see a man in your future who is a charming young architect . . ." Julia said, mimicking a fortune-teller.

"Oh, Julia, I hope so. And your performance reminds me! Sally Compton told me that she and Carole Butler and their maids made a secret trip cross town to Eighth Avenue, to a Madame something-or-other. She's a *real* fortune-teller," Betsy whispered. "She read tea leaves and then their palms. Oh, Julia, let's have an adventure. I'm sure Kathleen and Ellen will keep our secrets. We can take a hansom cab there and the girls can have their fortunes told too. Oh, can we? Please? I can call Sally and find out the address. Then we can go in a day or two. What do you say?''

Julia knew that they would be risking reprobation should their mothers get wind of their adventure. But it *did* sound exciting and they'd spoken about fortune-telling before. "I think it sounds thrilling," she whispered back. "Let's do it!"

The ringing of the grandfather's clock caused Betsy to rise at once. "Oh dear! I should have been home by now. I'll fetch Ellen and dash out. I'll telephone you tonight!" Betsy gave her a big hug and kiss.

Julia followed her across the room. Betsy turned, her eyes alert. "In all my excitement, don't think that I didn't realize that there's something about Mr. Woods that makes you blush," she whispered. "See, just the mention of his name is doing it again. I'm onto you, Julia!"

Julia felt the heat in her cheeks as Betsy turned down the hall to find Ellen. "I don't know *what* you're talking about!" she called after Betsy in vain.

Chapter Five

SOON AFTER BETSY'S DEPARTURE, JULIA ESCAPED TO HER studio. The studio had originally housed one of the live-in staff like all the other rooms on the third floor. With Papa's help, the small corner room had been converted into a simple but comfortable painting studio. Julia's easel was set at an angle to the windows through which the sunlight flooded. In the other corner of her room, beneath the high bookshelves, rested a large drawing table and chair. Above the mantel, Julia had hung two of her own oils. One was of the verdantly shaded Berkshires, painted from a drawing she'd rendered on the veranda of their summer home in Lenox. Next to this was a seascape showing an angry ocean under storm-darkened clouds, an image she'd captured from her aunt's terrace in Newport. In a corner nook of the room, above the old brocade love seat, hung her one attempt at self-portraiture. This painting had displeased Mamma, for she said that Julia had made herself appear plain and unconscionably sad. Julia rather liked the painting, not for its modeling, which was lacking, but because of the expression, an elusive expression, in the girl's eyes. She always thought of the painting as "the girl."

Julia worked at laying down a wash for a new landscape. A sketch she had done of a scene from her Uncle Walter's Long Island estate was her starting point. Julia allowed her imagination to alter her subjects in composition and color. Often her finished paintings, filled with light and shadow, captured a mood that was simply to her own liking. Daphne felt her work lonely. Kathleen said her paintings spoke of an inner spirit; Louise complained that landscapes bored her—each looked just like the other; Mama wanted to know why there were never any people about. Papa didn't offer a critique, but had asked to have one of her seascapes. Weeks later she'd discovered it framed and hanging above his desk in his office. Betsy insisted that Julia displayed great talent and should be studying with a fine teacher.

For herself, Julia merely loved to paint, even if she was not eventually pleased with the final product. She enjoyed being lost within the work, lost from herself and yet with herself. Sometimes she would hum tunes that fell into her mind as she painted. When she stopped, she would often stare from the window that offered a view of Central Park. Sometimes when she was at a loss for inspiration she would sketch the rolling tree-filled grounds of the park.

But her work for the past hour had not freed her

mind from her encounter with Ian and the questions it aroused. Why were he and his partner, Ned Barrington, meeting with Papa? And why at home? With her spirit too earth-bound to properly begin this new painting, Julia removed the fresh canvas and placed it in its drying rack. She replaced it with another Berkshire scene, this one taken from a mountain summit: a panorama of the valley and clusters of villages and lakes below. She'd not worked on it for a few weeks and now viewed it with a fresh, critical eye. What she'd failed to convey were the distances and patches of sunlit tints that darkened into an almost moss green in the shadows. She stepped back a half-dozen steps and squinted, which she'd discovered helped her to see how the light and shadow should fall. Walking back to the easel, she picked the proper brush from its container but then stepped back again, and lost herself in the darks and lights, her teeth unconsciously chewing at her thumbnail.

"Julia, may we come in?" Papa asked as he knocked at the closed door. Julia jumped. She'd been more engrossed than she'd known.

"Of course," she called out, pulling her finger from her mouth. Only after Papa entered did she realize that he had said "we," for there stood Ian. Julia felt her body tense. She'd assumed that Ian and Ned had left long ago. Why had father brought him into her study? She wanted to cry out childishly: *go away!*—but couldn't, of course. Nor could she manage more than a slight smile.

Ian, unlike herself, seemed relaxed if apologetic.

"We've interrupted you in your work, I'm afraid," he offered.

"Yes . . ." Julia responded, but as Papa frowned she forced a smile. "No . . . I mean, I was just surprised . . . Please, won't you come in," she continued. Papa's smile told her she'd redeemed herself. Julia walked around from the easel, for she did not want Ian to see her work. He seemed to sense her thought, for as he entered the room he lingered at the fireplace and then wandered to her bookshelves filled with volumes of art picture books. He scanned the titles but had the manners not to remove a book.

"I'd told Ian how we'd set up this modest studio for you a few years ago. I knew you wouldn't mind me including it during our grand tour of the house. Nothing like taking an architect through a house, I'll say," Papa continued easily. "Asked me questions about this and that. None of which I could answer. I should have had Richard Hunt here. I told Ian he did our place right before he became real prominent with that château of Mrs. Vanderbilt's. Got him at bargain prices for what he charges these days, I'm told, but that was nearly twenty years ago, anyway. Before that we had a smaller house down the Avenue on the corner of Eleventh Street. I kind of liked it when society allowed us to live closer to downtown. But with the park across the street and all, this place has made Henrietta and the girls happy, hasn't it, dear?"

"Yes, Papa," Julia answered, and smiled softly. Making Mamma and his daughters happy seemed to bring Papa so much pleasure.

"Excuse me, Mr. Davenport," James's cultured English voice resonated from the doorway. "There is a call from your office. Your secretary advised me that it is most important, sir."

"Dang it," Charles complained. "If you'll excuse me, I'll see what the crisis is this time. In the meanwhile I'll leave Ian to your company, Julia. If that's all right with the two of you, that is?"

"Of course, Papa," Julia answered lightly, to please her father.

"It's fine with me, Charles," Ian answered. "If Miss Davenport is sure that I won't be an unneeded intrusion."

"Well of course you won't," Charles replied as he stood at the door. "And you have my permission to call her Julia, just as all her friends do. Right, sweetheart?"

"Yes, of course, Papa," she replied, but he was already bounding down the staircase.

"Mr. Woods, please make—" Julia began.

"Ian, please." His eyes were soft, yet he stood as if he were unsure how to proceed.

"Ian, then. Please make yourself comfortable." She placed her paintbrush back into its container and started for the chair beside the love seat.

"Oh, no," he insisted earnestly. "Please don't stop your work on my account."

Julia found it difficult to look at him. Her hands were clammy, yet her face felt flushed and her stomach had begun to churn. "I couldn't be that rude," she stated honestly.

"I'd feel like less of an imposition if you'd go back to

your work. I'll content myself by leafing through some of your art books, if I may? You have one of my favorites on Rembrandt."

Of course, as an architect, he would have a genuine interest in art, Julia realized. Betsy had been the only visitor to her studio who had earnestly studied any of her treasured books. "That will be fine then." Julia suddenly realized that he had not asked to see her canvas that was facing the last of the winter day's light. She doubted that she could give her work any concentration with him in the room, but even an attempt would offer her the safety of being hidden from his view and provide her tremulous hands with an activity. Quickly she began to mix her colors on the wood palette.

Ian pretended to study the masterpieces that he knew by heart. From the corner of his eye he watched her, dressed in a muted green dress with velvet trimmings over which she wore a blue painting smock. Her loveliness, the bright tint of her upswept wheat-colored hair, shimmering in the backlight of the late-afternoon sun, the delicate curve of her brow, the pink of her high cheeks, all worked on him. He almost didn't dare to gaze at her willowy graceful figure. He wanted to see her canvas, wanted to walk about the small studio and study the various aspects of this enchanting girl. He turned another page instead. He should have left with Ned after they'd concluded the purpose of their meeting with Charles. Julia disappeared behind her easel and he breathed a silent sigh of relief. At least his eyes could freely roam the room now. His glance caught the landscapes above the fireplace. From his chair he didn't have a good view, but he was struck by a sense of strong light and composition. He wanted to see better. "Hope you don't mind if I stretch a bit," he said, as he rose and sauntered casually across the room, careful to maintain the effect of the screen between them.

"Of course not," Julia answered as calmly as she could. Her shield of easel and silence worked in reverse, increasing her sense of his presence to alarming acuity. Each of his steps, muffled by the thick rug, brought him closer. She could feel his presence in the ensuing silence. She wondered what he was studying; he struck her as a man who was not content to glance.

"Did you paint the landscapes above the mantel?" His voice brought her unexpected relief. Then she worried. For his tone had given her no indication of his evaluation.

"Yes."

"They're very good. Really. I'm not just saying that to be polite," he said, as his voice drew closer with each word. Then he stood facing her. "May I glance at the canvas you're working on?" She looked up at his handsome chiseled face and saw what she took to be a new attitude in his eyes, one she could not decipher. Was he mocking her? She did not want him to evaluate her painting before her own eyes, for she knew that she would watch him closely as he studied the almost completed pastoral scene. She did not want his opinion to matter, yet she feared a possible dismissal of her efforts. Her painting, unlike her social demeanor, revealed her private self. Ian had already found her

67

social appeal less than captivating. She feared that he would consider her work in the same class with his mother's paintings: dabblings that kept her busy and contributed to charity auctions. Until this moment Julia had never had such a profound sense of the importance of her painting to herself.

Her blue eyes darkened with hesitation and her full, lovely mouth tightened. Ian sensed that she wished him not to view her work as she stood before him, her shoulders drawn straight, her arms wrapped around her. Her smile did not alter his perception nor her desultory tone as she said: "If you wish. But it is not finished and I merely amuse myself by—"

The valley scene was even better than the two landscapes above the mantel. This girl had talent. "You're quite good," he interrupted. He hadn't expected to discover that she was talented as well as beautiful. The combination was far too threatening. His eyes were pulled from her painting by her laughter.

"Oh, I do think you're saying so to be polite! But thank you anyway. As I said, I enjoy playing with paints but certainly don't take it seriously. In fact, if it weren't winter, I'd probably be racing my horse up Riverside Drive right now." She flashed him a pretty smile and laughed again as his serious, confounded expression grew neutral. Even as she laughed she wondered why she'd chosen to devalue her artistic efforts. But then she knew. She would not offer up for his derision such an important aspect of herself.

"I see." Ian ended his musing and laughed. Why had it entered his mind that this girl, blessed not only with breathtaking beauty but also with a strong artistic propensity, should even think to appreciate or develop her latent abilities beyond the arena of "dabbling"? Girls like her were schooled in fancy girls' academies. They were toted about Europe by their mothers in spring and fall, where they visited museums and palaces and received a tour guide's summary of art and history. Then they returned with a steamer trunk of the latest Paris fashions meant to entice the finest American catch—a suitable husband. He'd mistaken once again an inherited quickness in her eyes for artistic sensibilities. At least she was honest enough to put him straight. "Well, you have a good eye."

Ian's dismissive smile made her turn back to her canvas. He wandered across the room beyond her view. Julia wished Papa would return and take Ian away. His condescension, which she knew she had helped to elicit, depressed and wearied her. His footsteps halted.

Ian stopped before the portrait. Damn this girl! Could she actually be oblivious of the power she possessed? he wondered. Or was she merely pretending? In this self-portrait he saw the same expression he'd seen when their eyes had first met. Passion, all the more startling because of its guilelessness, poured from the eyes of the girl in the portrait. Not a simple sexual passion, but a depth of seeing beyond that which most saw or wanted to see, and the ultimate vulnerability that this second sight always evoked. It was all there. Where was Charles? Ian wanted to turn away from the portrait, but it held him. Suddenly he was overwhelmed by the desire to break through Julia's facade, to unfold this hidden aspect of her as he held her in his arms, brought her lips to his own, felt her breasts pressing against his chest.

What was he doing? Julia wondered. Unable to stand the suspense any longer, she laid down her brush and stepped from behind her canvas as she wiped her fingers with a damp rag. Ian was staring at her self-portrait. Oh, how she wished it wasn't hanging on the wall! The intensity of his expression as he stared at the portrait made her feel nakedly exposed. "Do you like it?" she asked quietly, when she stood beside him. His slight start indicated that he hadn't heard her approach.

"I think it's wonderful," he answered softly. He gazed deeply into her eyes, which made her want to turn away, but she couldn't. "When did you paint it?" The intensity in his eyes belied his casual tone. How she wanted this man to know her, yet she feared these feelings that welled inside and quickened the pounding of her heart.

"I didn't paint it," she lied. "A friend did." Her eyes dared him to defy her.

"A close friend, I take it?" he asked. Why did he feel this jealousy that someone had viewed this hidden secret in the Dresden doll of a girl before him?

"Yes. A close friend. A very imaginative one. For I don't think it reflects me at all, but I hung it because it rather amuses me."

"What amuses you about it?"

"I think it is a little romantic—something along that line. A figment of his imagination?"

So, it was a he, as Ian had surmised! "I think it's far better than that."

"In what way?" Although he searched her face, Julia was determined to give nothing away.

"Passion," he answered so softly she wasn't certain she'd heard him.

"I beg your pardon?" Julia asked. Could he have said "passion?" For such words weren't bandied about in polite company. She saw a muscle flex in the hollow of his cheek. Her eyes were drawn to his full lips and she felt a heat rise within her just as she'd experienced in the church. She wondered if she were suffering from a relapse of the cold—perhaps she'd overdone it today, for she felt feverish and weak. Her eyes linked with his own in a most direct manner that somehow she knew was dangerous. Her knees weakened and she knew that she had to sit down, had to move away from the magnetic force that pulled her closer to him.

"Passion," he repeated. "Passion of the soul. It's rare and always in the eyes . . ." He had no doubt that Julia was a virgin. He doubted whether she'd even experienced a passionate kiss. But here she stood before him, her face flushed, her eyes wide and dewy, almost transparently blue in the fading afternoon light. The scent of her perfume mingled with the odor of paints and the turpentine on the rag she twisted in her hand. Her face tilted upward toward his own. He had only to extend his hand to her shoulder and draw her to him. "It's always in the eyes," he whispered. Her lips parted slightly and her beautifully formed pearly teeth glistened.

He is going to kiss me, Julia thought. How she wanted him to!

"If it isn't one bundle of problems, it's another!"

71

Charles's voice boomed. Instantly they stepped apart and turned to him. He had stopped at the threshold and was turning on the gaslight that had been converted to electric just a few years before. "Getting dark up here."

Julia immediately followed suit, switching on an electric light near the nook where she and Ian had stood. When she turned, she saw that Ian had crossed the room to where her father stood.

"I always have to remind this girl to turn on the lights. Otherwise she'll ruin her eyes. Julia still prefers to read by gaslight or candle. Not that I can blame her. I'm not sure I'll ever quite adjust to the glare of the incandescent bulb. Anyway, I apologize for keeping you, my boy! I just had to hang on until my secretary hunted down the proper papers. But the crisis was solved, I'm happy to say."

The way Papa nonchalantly chattered assured Julia that he'd not suspected what had almost occurred between herself and Ian.

"I assume that Julia kept you properly entertained?" Charles asked. He took out his pipe and by gesture invited Ian to do the same.

"She certainly did. Julia's a fine artist," Ian offered, as Charles stretched his frame onto the love seat and Ian followed by sitting in the brocade tasseled chair.

"That she is. What do you think of her self-portrait?" Charles asked conversationally. "Unusual, and not a likeness in the common sense, but interesting, I'd say."

Julia quickly turned away from Papa and Ian before Ian could catch her embarrassed flush. She walked toward her easel with the pretext of placing her rag with the others behind it.

She should have known better than to lie. She was never one, even as a child, to get away with it. She stayed hidden behind her easel as she listened.

"I told Julia that I found the expression in the girl's eyes quite interesting . . . reminiscent of the Mona Lisa's smile. What intrigued me is that one can't tell exactly what she's thinking, and that she's not one to let you know easily."

"Yes, yes," Papa answered vaguely. Julia knew that this kind of discussion didn't intrigue Papa. "If Julia were a man I think she might have become an artist. It's just as well, from my point of view, that she's a girl, on that score. It just doesn't seem manly to me, although that shows my lack of culture, I guess. Of course, what you've done with your talents is quite different, Ian. What are you fiddling with back there, Julia? Come join us—there's something I have to tell you."

Julia did her best to maintain her composure as she crossed the room and sat beside her father. Papa patted her on the shoulder. "You two have a lot in common, because Ian can draw rather well, also. You must see some of his sketches of the tallest buildings . . . sorry"—he looked at Ian and laughed—"skyscrapers is the new name, that he and Ned have designed. Should I tell her?" he asked, glancing at Ian, but continued before Ian could answer.

Papa had that grin on his face that always made him look as if he were the cat who'd swallowed the canary and enjoyed every morsel. "Tell me what, Papa?" Julia

73

asked. She was in no mood for further surprises. Her head ached badly. All she wanted was to escape to her room and go to bed. She had no appetite for dinner.

"I'll tell you, as long as you can pretend to be surprised when I make the announcement at dinner tonight. Louise and Thom are coming, and the Pells, I believe. I've tried to get Ian to join us but he has a prior engagement, apparently. Do you promise to look surprised?"

"Yes, I promise I'll do my best."

"Well, that's good enough for me. Julia can be darn poker-faced when she wants to be," Papa added.

"Oh, can she?" Ian responded amiably, but Julia saw the sardonic twist to his smile that Papa seemed to miss.

"The news is, Julia, that your dear old Papa had been getting bored. I'm too young to spend the rest of my working life bored. But ever since I had the pleasure of meeting with Ian and Ned last week, I've been excited. See, they're young men who are anxious to get on with the future. I'm all for that. I'm sick of hearing all the talk at dinners about the good old days. We're going to begin the twentieth century in less than two years. We're just at the horizon of a changing world, and since I intend to stick around long enough to see a good deal of it, I want to help it along if I can. That's why I've decided to become the silent partner in the visionary, exciting new architectural firm of Woods and Barrington! But I won't ramble on. Once you've seen some of the work they've already done with Mr. Louis Sullivan, and the terrific, bold plans they've got for New York commercial buildings, you'll know exactly why I'm so excited. I feel like a young man just starting out again myself!

"So, you can expect to be seeing a lot of Ian and Ned around the house, especially until we get the office picked out for them. Until then we're going to meet in my study. So what do you think, my girl?" Papa asked expectantly.

"I think it sounds wonderful, Papa!" Julia answered, caught up in her father's enthusiasm. She turned to Ian. "Congratulations to you and Mr. Barrington," she offered. Although she held her smile, the jolt of realization hit her. Then Ian wouldn't be returning to Chicago! He was to be a frequent guest at the house. More than a guest, for Julia sensed that Papa was feeling toward Ian as he might a son. Julia felt a bit jealous suddenly. She knew that Thom Travers was too timid and too humorless to ever gain Papa's affection beyond that given to a proper son-in-law.

"I hate to be rude, but I must be going," Ian said, and rose. "I will be late for my dinner engagement if I don't leave at once." He offered Papa his hand and then the men clapped shoulders.

"We'll walk you down. I'm surprised Henrietta hasn't sent one of the parlor maids to find us by now. You and Ned must come to dinner later in the week. But do have a pleasant evening at the Hoffmans'. John Hoffman is a stuffed shirt, but his daughter Mary is certainly a pert little redhead, so you should be properly entertained. Don't you agree, Julia?" Papa said, then winked at Ian.

Neither seemed aware that Julia didn't answer. So he

was courting Mary Hoffman after all! All she'd succeeded in doing was making a fool of herself this afternoon. He had caught her in another lie, and worse yet, she had almost thrown herself at him! If Papa hadn't entered the room, she might have . . . She didn't even want to think of it! How Ian must be laughing at her beneath his polite smile. She'd show him a thing or two!

"Ian, again, congratulations," she said, as she offered her hand in a firm shake. "And do send my regards to Mary and her parents. She's a very sweet girl. Perhaps Percy Martin, my beau, will come to dinner one evening and you can bring Mary. And if Ned would like the company of Betsy, we could have a regular little party afterward! I'm sure Percy would love to see you again! You can tell him all about your skyscrapers, which I'm afraid will probably go right above my head—no pun intended." She laughed and smiled brightly.

"That would be my pleasure, Julia"—he smiled in kind—"although I believe that with a little study you would easily comprehend architecture. I suspect you are a quick student," he said cordially. Papa, already turned toward the door, did not see Ian's audacious grin, nor the blazing look she gave him in return.

"You two go ahead. I want to put my paints away and freshen up for dinner. Please tell Mamma I'll be down in a bit, for I am quite hungry. Good evening, Ian. Please, do send Mary my best!"

Ian caught the toss of her head before she disappeared behind the easel. "I certainly will. And I will hold you to that dinner invitation, for I think Ned would be most happy to see Betsy again. Do send Percy my regards . . . and thanks for allowing me to see your dabblings."

Julia could hear the sardonic jab in his voice, although she was certain that it had bypassed Papa. Her hand clutched the paintbrush container so tightly that her knuckles whitened. She wanted more than anything to toss the pewter container at him as he followed Papa out of the studio.

Chapter Six

CHARLES SAW IAN TO THE FRONT DOOR. A MOMENT LATER he burst into hearty laughter.

Henrietta appeared with a puzzled look on her face. "What is so funny? And where is Julia? Cook is holding dinner. Louise and Thom arrived, and George and Martha Pell as well. They're in the parlor. Daphne is entertaining them while I slipped out."

"Julia is washing up. She'll be right down," Charles answered. He chuckled again.

"Why are you laughing? I am miffed with you already, as I will explain later," Henrietta whispered with an accompanying frown.

"Oh, it's just a joke I heard at the office. Nothing for your delicate ears, my dear Henrietta," he answered, and patted her on her fanny.

"Charles! What has gotten into you?" Henrietta marched in a huff toward the drawing room. "Aren't you coming?"

"In a minute, my dearest. I want to wash up first." As he started up the staircase he allowed his smile to

broaden again. He'd been right. There was definitely
an attraction between Julia and Ian. His phone call had
taken only two or three minutes but he'd intentionally
left them alone to their own devices. They had been
gazing at one another so intensely when he reappeared
that they hadn't realized he'd stood at the door watching them before he'd tiptoed back down the stair and
up again, announcing his presence. If Henrietta even
suspected what he was up to . . . But he was a good
judge of character. Ian was a gentleman and could be
trusted to behave with honor. Attraction. Sympathy is
what some called it. Percy Martin was a nice enough
chap, but he was basically a weakling with no goals, no
direction other than to live off his family fortune and
look in on its accrued interests now and then.

Julia had always been his favorite. She was spunky
and talented. She was special. He wanted for her what
he'd lost because he hadn't the strength to defy his
family. He wanted her to know love and passion, as
he'd known it once and let it slip right out of his hands.
Not that he hadn't grown to love Henrietta—deeply in
fact—the way one does from sharing a life for almost
thirty years.

But there was a spark in Julia that he recognized in
Ian. He only hoped that he wasn't inadvertently going
to create a roaring forest fire when he was only trying
to let nature take its course. No. He was a man of instincts and his gut told him he was right. He began to
laugh again as he remembered the spark of jealousy
he'd seen in Julia's china-blue eyes when he'd mentioned the Hoffman girl. He didn't know if Ian
had caught it, but he had noticed that Ian hadn't

bothered to mention that he found Mary Hoffman a silly young woman or that he was forced to attend this dinner to please his mother, as Ian had told him when Ned left earlier.

"It's a lovely landscape," Louise commented to Julia. But her eyes merely grazed the canvas on Julia's easel. "I don't know why you always refuse to donate your work for exhibition in the annual ladies' charity show," Louise scolded. Julia was struck again how much like Mamma her older sister was. Julia waited for Louise to get to the point. For she knew that Louise's desire to view her latest work was nothing but a ploy for a private conversation. Private conversations with Louise always took the form of a lecture. Julia had never felt especially close to her older sister. Although she loved Louise, she guessed that were they not related they would never have been friends. It was with Daphne, so sweet and gentle in temperament, that Julia felt a friendship beyond sisterly love.

"I understand that Papa left Ian Woods in your company for a time after tea today," Louise stated neutrally. She wandered to the corner nook and reclined gracefully onto the love seat. "Come, sit down beside me." Julia complied. "We haven't had a girl talk in so long a time," Louise continued. "You're such a private person. Mamma and I chat about this and that every day, and sometimes Daphne joins in, but you never were one for that. . . . So, I guess I'm forced to prod you, as usual!" Louise laughed.

"I'm happy to tell you anything you'd like to know," Julia answered. At least Louise was not one to beat about the bush in the obvious manner Mamma sometimes attempted.

"Mamma tells me she expects you will soon allow Percy to ask Father for your hand." Louise leaned toward her with anticipation. "Tell your big sister *first!* Is that so?"

Julia smiled with relief. When Louise had first made mention of Ian, Julia's chest had tightened and she'd felt unexplainably nervous. But Percy . . . So that's what she wanted to know. Julia smiled with genuine affection. "I've been thinking seriously. I'm to attend the opera with Percy and his parents tomorrow evening."

Louise nodded in acknowledgment, the expression on her plump face so like Mamma's as she brushed at her mop of dark curly hair.

"I've pretty well decided that should Percy ask again, I will say yes."

Louise pulled her to her ample bosom, hugging her. "That's absolutely divine! Just wonderful! Exactly what I wanted to hear! Percy's a perfect catch. He's handsome, charming and from such a fine family. I told Mamma she had nothing to worry about and that she'd just imagined that you'd taken a fancy to that Ian Woods!"

Julia pulled back in genuine astonishment. "Why would Mamma have thought such a thing."

"Oh, you know Mamma tends to jump to conclusions that are based more on impulse than logic. She is absolutely *furious* at Father! First for leaving you unchaperoned up here with Ian, and worse yet, announcing at dinner this silly business alliance with Mr.

Woods and Mr. Barrington. Although Mamma says that Ned Barrington does seem like a nice chap and even seemed to be taken with Betsy. But Ian is another story. And I *know* more than Mamma even *suspects!*" Louise's voice lowered to a hush although they were quite alone in the studio. "Should I even begin to tell you? . . ."

Julia waited quietly, knowing that her sister would be unable to hold back whatever gossip was about to burst forth, any more than a roar of thunder could help following a lightning bolt.

"I've known about Ian for years. Betty Cornell and I were schoolmates. We were presented to society at the same ball. Do you know who she is?"

The name struck a chord of recognition. Julia remembered that Betty Cornell was a beautiful dark-haired woman who was married to John Hollis. Rumor had it that their marriage was not as happy as one would like. Julia had heard implications that Betty took lovers on her trips to Paris and London. But Julia didn't abide by most gossip, and since this woman was not within her own circle, the stories had held little interest other than that of the mystery of infidelity. "Yes, I remember her."

"Well, her wedding to John Hollis was executed rather more quickly than fashion would dictate. There were stories at the time that she was 'in the family way.' Well, she did have their son prematurely, as they say. But I happen to know, through a very close friend of mine, whose name I won't disclose since she swore me to secrecy years ago, that Betty Cornell, as she was still then, had confided in my friend, who was her closest friend, that she'd allowed a certain young man certain unmentionable liberties. And that man was Ian Woods! Even my friend was never certain of the details. Only that Mrs. Cornell was dead set against any engagement, for even then, Ian was a rebel."

Julia's heart beat rapidly. She was as afraid to hear what Louise was going to say as she was desperately curious to know. "What do you mean a rebel? I hadn't thought much about him one way or the other, but obviously Papa thinks he's a reputable gentleman. Papa would never embark on a business venture with someone of less than sterling character."

"Papa may have made a real mistake this time. For Ian has become stranger since his return from Paris and his two years in Chicago. We dined with the Hunts the other night, and Mr. Hunt told us exactly what he and all the other fine architects think of Mr. Louis Sullivan. They think his ideas are ridiculous and Ian carries them even further. But that's another issue, which I'll put aside for the moment. It's really a shame, too, for Ian's mother is such a lovely lady. I've worked with her on some charity committees, as you know. And certainly Florence, while perhaps a bit . . . colorless, shall we say, is a perfect lady. I suppose that Ian took after his father."

"Anyway. What I was telling you, is that Mrs. Cornell apparently threatened to disown Betty if she had anything further to do with Ian. The story I got from my friend was that Betty was terribly lucky that a milksop like John Hollis was so taken with her. I'm told that to this day he has never suspected that their eldest son is really Ian's child! Of course, as soon as the engagement was announced, Ian fled to Paris and stayed there all those years. When he came back, trained in architecture, he immediately fled to Chicago. Not for the lofty reasons he so boorishly expounded at Clarice's wedding dinner, but just not to be near Betty. I'm told that the boy is the spitting image of Ian, as a matter a fact."

Julia was stunned into silence, but Louise, so excited in her telling, didn't seem to notice.

"And there's more. Again, I can't say the source, but I happen to know that not only did he take up with many disreputable women *openly* in Paris, which I must admit is shocking but seems to be almost common among bachelors of our class these days, but also he *blatantly* took up with some *common* shop girl in Chicago and supported her in a small flat where he lived more than in his own. A Tanya something-or-other. He even had the audacity to have her to dinner when some of Thom's friends visited with him a year ago while on business! They said the girl was little more than a common tart and could barely speak proper English!"

Louise had said her piece and now waited for Julia's reaction. Actually, Julia had barely been able to absorb all she'd heard. "Well . . . that is certainly interesting gossip. It sounds like one of those novels Mamma always hated for us to read. But what does all of this have to do with me?"

"Well, nothing, I'm happy to say. It's just that, as I said, Mamma, not even knowing half of the *truth*, but knowing enough to be concerned about his obvious interest in you, since the man is such a bounder—"

"Interest in me?" Julia began to laugh. "I think that Mamma is terribly mistaken. Her alarm should be for Mary Hoffman, for it seems that Ian is courting her."

"Is he? I didn't know that. But Mamma said she didn't like the way he looked at you. And she said that since you met him you've been acting quite moody. Of course you were ill with that dreadful cold, so Mamma was probably upset for no reason. But even I must admit that although he's a cad, to put it politely, he is even more handsome than he was as a younger man and docs have an air of charm about him. But obviously Mamma has nothing to fear. I'm sure that after she speaks with Father tonight, he will see the foolhardiness of his plans to participate in Ian's architectural venture. Father can be such a child at times, albeit a dear child, but have you ever known Mamma not to make him see her more sensible viewpoint?"

"No, I haven't." She hated when Louise and Mamma spoke of Papa as if he were a child to be manipulated. To Julia, Papa was a strong, wise, wonderful man. She doubted that Papa had impetuously entered into this new venture with Ian and Ned.

The knock on the door by the parlor maid sent by Mamma to call them back downstairs was a blessed relief to Julia. The maid was sent back with the assurance that they would be promptly returning. As they walked to the door, Louise kissed her on her cheek.

"I'm so glad to know that everything is fine with you! I will most certainly be *thrilled* to have Percy as a brother-in-law. We must have these girl talks more often, Julia. I feel that you and I have never been as close as I would have hoped. But I'm sure, once you too become a married lady, that our relationship will change. And in just a few months my baby sister will be a bride!" Louise glowed. "Oh, we are such a fortunate family. I give thanks daily for all the Lord has bestowed onto us." Louise whispered as they started down the steps, "Leave it to me to assure Mamma that she can devote full attention to Daphne's wedding plans."

Julia gave her sister a bright smile. "Well, of course, for Mamma needn't bother herself with manufactured worries. And thank you for confiding in me." Julia hoped that Louise and Thom and the Pells would leave soon so that she could retreat to her room and sort through all the troubling feelings and information about this man who had descended upon her life like a pack of locusts.

It had taken Julia long into the night to fall asleep, for her body, as weary as it was, would not relax. She'd felt like bounding from her bed and running until the nervous energy within her subsided. She'd read until her eyes would not stay open, but once she had turned out the light, she envisioned Ian's face. She tried to banish all thoughts of him. She wanted to be horrified by Louise's stories. Yet all she'd heard intrigued her more than horrified her. Suddenly she was jealous of all those men and women, many younger than herself, who knew the secrets and intimacies of carnal love. Of passion. Passion—that was the word Ian had used. Julia felt vaguely sinful. She knelt, the moonlight a halo around her bed, and said her evening prayers again.

In her dream, she was in a strange bed. She had just

awoken and it seemed to be the middle of the night. The only light came from the bright full moon. She looked up and there was a man standing above her, but instead of crying out, she seemed to know who he was and that he was supposed to be there. "Ian," she said to the shadowy, broad-shouldered form in a voice that was her own yet different. He didn't answer.

She heard the bed groan and felt the weight of his lean, hard frame as he sat beside her. The quickening of her heart and constriction of her breath made her close her eyes as his hand gently stroked her cheek and then the nape of her neck. She could feel his breath brushing her eyes and then her mouth like a delicate breeze. As she sighed in response her breath was caught by his gentle warm lips. She reached around his neck and brought his chest to rest upon her as he nibbled at her lips in a manner that made her begin to shake deep inside. He lay upon her now, kissing her eyes, the hollow of her cheek, then her lips again as she clung to him. She drew him closer, her fingers running through his thick black hair as his hand fell to her breast, making her jump as her nipple hardened. Suddenly she began to push him away as she cried, "No! You mustn't! Stop!"

Julia awoke with a start and bolted upright. It had been a dream, her mind told her as her breath continued to come fast and hard. . . . A dream, not a nightmare, but more frightening than any nightmare she'd ever had. For as she wrapped her arms around herself she knew that she could deny it to herself no longer. She loved Ian. Worse yet, she wanted to know him as she had in the dream. She wanted more. Shame flushed her cheeks and made her sweat, although the room was winter cold. How could she think such thoughts—especially after all Louise had told her this evening! She was mortified that she had conjured thoughts of these intimacies that she had never known. But her dream had felt so real! So real that a strange heat lingered in the most intimate parts of her body.

She lay back upon her pillow, on her stomach, closing her eyes, and gradually her breathing returned to normal. As she was falling back into the lull of the twilight before sleep, she found her own hand caressing her cheek, her fingers touching her lips, and suddenly the flame that had heated her in the dream flared again. She pulled her hand from her face and tucked it beneath her pillow. Just before she drifted off, Ian's black-eyed, chiseled-featured face filled her mind.

Ian sat at the desk that had once been his father's, studying the blueprints of Louis Sullivan's office building being constructed in lower New York. Sullivan's precept of "form following function" in these steel structures that could reach to unheard-of heights was just a starting point in Ian's visions. The trick was to get the support to demonstrate what he and Ned Barrington could do if given the commissions they sought. They could have no better supporter than Charles Davenport, for even greater than his initial financial backing was his reputation and influence in the corporate world that had grabbed the Industrial Revolution and wrestled it into fortunes and empires. The accumulation of money in New York was not an end but a means toward an end. Possessing the wealth of kings, too many of these men had demanded that the most prominent architects build them castles that badly imitated the palazzos of Italy, the ornate châteaux of France. Even the surge of office buildings were designed to disguise their commercial function, to hide the age of steel instead of herald it. There had been no architect who had gone on record by refusing to create the gilded palaces for the royalty of industry and Wall Street. Ian knew that the revolutionary concepts of Louis Sullivan were laughed at by those New Yorkers who considered Chicago to be little more than a provincial crossroad of the railroads.

Ian rose and poured himself another Scotch. He'd come home from dinner at the Hoffmans' with a pounding headache. Charles's characterization of John Hoffman as a stuffed shirt had been an understatement. Mrs. Hoffman was a quiet, graying matron who faded into the setting, reminding him of his sister, Flo. Mary was pretty and entertaining in an inconsequential way. It was only her physical attributes, especially her creamy breasts and shoulders, that she wisely showed to their best advantage, that pleased his palate. But like many sweets, she left a cloying, sickly effect upon him. He didn't know how much longer he could continue to pretend to court her. It was his certitude that she cared little more for him than he did for her that made it easier. He sensed that he was little more than a decoration, another accessory like her fan or ruby choker or sapphire bracelet. She was a superficial, silly flirt, whose expressions were tried out for their effect rather than as a reflection of true emotion or thought. But he would use her to keep himself and Julia apart.

GILDED HEARTS

The mere thought of her name filled him with a knowing sadness. Each time he saw her he realized how much he wanted her. He had seen his own desire reflected unknowingly in her eyes. He, who had vowed never again to fall in love, was dangerously near the edge of a deep chasm into which he dared not slip, for his heart and all his romantic illusions had been battered eight years before. Not until a few weeks ago had he even known of its only remains: a son, Timothy, whom he'd seen, unobserved, just once, two weeks ago. To have had a son all these years and not been told! Anger softened his lingering ardor for Julia and hardened his heart. He went back to his work.

Chapter Seven

"Miss Julia! You're still not dressed!" Kathleen admonished. "Why, Mr. Percy and the others will be coming round for you in less than half an hour. Shame on you." Kathleen looked from Julia, curled up on the corner of her bed in her petticoat and lace blouse, to the Persian-lamb-trimmed gray wool skirt and matching Persian-lamb jacket and muff hanging from the wardrobe. "And I thought you loved skating!"

"Oh, I do. I guess I was just daydreaming," Julia explained as she rose.

"You've certainly been doing enough of *that* lately. But I suppose that's what happens when a girl gets engaged?" Kathleen teased.

"I don't think that's funny, Kathleen," Julia snapped. "I'm always punctual and I'll be ready on time tonight as usual."

"I'm sorry, Miss Julia," Kathleen flustered. "I was only—"

"I'm the one who's sorry," Julia interrupted her. She

didn't even know why she had snapped at Kathleen. She just wasn't herself lately and she was so tired right now. Still, that was no excuse. "I've been insufferable lately, haven't I?" Julia walked to Kathleen, who held her skirt and gave her a quick kiss on the cheek. "Forgive me, will you?"

Kathleen smiled in return. "Of course, though there's nothing to forgive. I think that you need some rest. Since last week you've been on such a whirl that *I* fall asleep the minute my head touches the pillow. But I can tell from the way you've been yawning so in the morning that you have hardly got a wink yourself. What with accepting Percy's proposal, then off to your Uncle Walter's home until this morning, and helping your mother and Miss Daphne with the engagement-party details for Saturday night. And now this skating party tonight, and with Christmas Eve coming Sunday —excuse me for saying it, but this whole house has been in an uproar, and it's only beginning!"

Julia grinned. "Wasn't it clever of me to make our escape to Uncle Walter and Aunt Beatrice? I'll tell you a secret. I wish that we could leave tomorrow for Lenox and come back on Saturday well-rested in time for Daphne's party. Mama is in the worst tizzy. I don't remember it being quite this bothersome when Louise was married. . . . But you weren't here then, I almost forgot. I feel as if you've been with me all my life, Kathleen. And it must seem like that to you these days, unfortunately, when I've been in such bad humor."

"Oh, don't say that, because it isn't so and you know it. . . . There," Kathleen stated as she finished fastening Julia's skirt. As always, Julia looked lovely. Only up close would anyone see the slight rings of tiredness around her bright blue eyes. "Now I'll go downstairs and get your skates."

Julia sat before the dressing mirror, fixing her hair, and thought about the past week and a half. Kathleen was right, her life had been such a flurry of activity that she again found herself wishing that she could curl herself upon her bed and go to sleep. Julia knew that once she was skating, she would find a second wind. While Daphne had expressed her disappointment that the lack of snowfall had changed Percy's party from sleighing to skating, Julia was pleased. She was actually excited, for Betsy, whom she hadn't seen in nearly a week, was coming and Julia was thrilled that Ned Barrington was to be her escort. Betsy had seen Ned three or four times since their meeting in the parlor.

Julia couldn't help it if her thoughts momentarily fell to Ian, for he was Ned's partner and Papa's business associate. Betsy had innocently confirmed that Ian would be attending the skating party tonight with . . . who else but Mary Hoffman. Julia had not set eyes on him since that late afternoon in her studio. It had taken all of her willpower to banish all daydreams about him. Still, she awoke in the deep of each night from her dreams of lying in his arms. She'd thought that the dreams would stop once she'd accepted Percy's marriage proposal.

Just as she'd expected, last Wednesday evening, after the opera, Percy had escorted her for a walk into his parents' conservatory. There, after telling her a few jokes, he'd suddenly become nervously serious. He'd proposed and Julia remembered now, with a smile, that he'd appeared actually shocked when she'd accepted. In those few unchaperoned moments, he had kissed and held her. Julia had been kissed before but never quite as intimately. She'd found herself more disappointed than intimidated by Percy's lingering wet kisses. Although it was not exactly unpleasant, certainly it was nothing like the dream she'd had about Ian the night before and all the nights since.

Julia recalled that her embarrassed guilt must have heightened her color, for Percy quickly apologized for taking greater liberty than he should have. He assured her that as she became less afraid, she would grow to like "that aspect" of married life—that was how he put it. Julia had smiled but remained silent, allowing Percy's hand to linger for a few minutes around her bare shoulder. But inside she was chastising herself for thinking of Ian as she sat intimately close to her husband-to-be. Perhaps there was something dreadfully wrong in having such an overactive imagination. Percy's kisses, his arm around her, did not make her tremble inside as her dreams had. She must have read too many of those novels that Mamma called vulgar. Obviously the passion these books hinted at, these French ladies who fell into a "swoon" when their men merely touched their hands, were nothing more than flights of fancy. Yet, hadn't she felt something like that when her eyes had locked with Ian's?

Percy had understood that their engagement would not be formally announced for at least two weeks—for it was Daphne's moment to shine. They decided to tell their immediate families that evening, for Julia knew after her conversation the night before with Louise that it would set Mamma's mind to rest. Then on Christmas Eve, the night after Daphne's engagement party they would announce their engagement. The society columns would carry the news of their impending marriage the first week of January, after the holiday flourish had ended. Percy urged a wedding in June, but Julia suggested that they should wait until at least the end of July, to give Mamma a chance to recoup from Daphne's June wedding. Percy, as good-natured as always, accepted her decision.

Julia had lain awake long into the night, wondering if she'd made the right decision. She believed that she did love Percy, if friendship, empathy and sympathy were such components. In time she would learn to love him with all her soul and passion. What she *thought* she felt for Ian could be no more than fancy. She simply had a crush on him. But she was twenty-three and too old to allow such a crush to affect her life. It was after two in the morning when Julia heard Papa's footsteps climbing down the stairs. A few minutes later she rose and threw her robe over her flannel gown.

When she entered Papa's study, she found him sitting in his leather chair, smoking his pipe. Perhaps it was merely the angle of the light thrown from the old gaslamp, but for the first time, Julia noticed deep lines and crags in his handsome face. Yet, when he looked up and smiled at her, his blue eyes were as bright as ever. She sat on the hassock before him.

"And what are you doing up? Are visions of wedding dresses dancing through your head?" he asked.

"Not exactly. I just couldn't sleep. I guess I am excited. But why are you up so late, Papa? Are all these engagements getting to be too much? Or are you calculating the cost of two summer weddings in your head?" she teased back.

"You know nothing pleases me more than pleasing my gals," he answered, then chuckled. "And it certainly pleases your Mamma." His smile faded and he puffed on his pipe. "Julia," he began, "I want to know if you feel as though your mother is pressuring you. I mean, we both know how important it is for her to see the last of you two well-married, and of course I want you to be happily married too, but I don't want . . . I mean, I don't want you to feel forced into it."

Julia was not only touched, but relieved that she could answer truthfully. "I don't feel forced. Mamma carries on and all, but as you said, I've always been spunky and had a mind of my own. Vexing, I think is how Mamma usually puts it." They laughed and suddenly Julia wished that by magic she could be a little girl again and spend many more years basking in the warmth and protection of her father's love. "Percy has asked me to marry him many times, Papa. He's a wonderful young man and I believe he loves me deeply." Julia felt herself blushing. She'd talked with Papa about a million subjects, but never love. "I think I'll have a happy life with him."

Papa shifted about for a moment, looked away and then at her again. "Perhaps this is a subject that should be left to your mother and sisters, but I've got to ask. Do you . . . I mean, are you in love with Percy? I mean, are you certain that this is the man you want to spend the rest of your life with?''

To hesitate was to give herself away, and it was too late for that. She had made her decision. "Yes, Papa."

"Well, then, if you're happy, I'm happy." He leaned forward and kissed her on the forehead. "I guess I better start saving the cash all of this is going to cost me! Which means that I'd better be extra bright and alert at the office tomorrow."

Julia laughed at his teasing, but sensed that his heartiness was strained. "Papa?" she asked as he rose. "Do you object to my marrying Percy?"

"Of course not, Julia," Papa answered. He stared at her for a moment and it seemed to her that he was debating whether to speak further. "I think Percy Martin is a fine young man. He comes from a good family. And I have no doubts that he is very much in love with you. I don't think he's harboring any doubts about his proposal, but then, why would any man be less than jubilant in catching a prize like my Julia?" His eyes sparkled with pleasure. "Come," he said with a smile as he walked her toward the study door. "It's time we both got some shut-eye. . . . But, Julia, remember, the 'I do' isn't done until the minister says so," he said cryptically. "Going for tea at Mrs. Woods's tomorrow, so I hear?" he said, so abruptly changing the subject that he took her by surprise.

"Yes. . . . Are you still as excited about your new business venture with Mr. Woods and Mr. Barrington?" she couldn't help but ask as they stood in the drawing room.

"If that's a polite way of asking me if I believe any of that infernal gossip about Ian that your mother told me last night, I can tell you I don't. I like Ned, but it's Ian who really excites me. He's the one with the vision. You had a chat with him. What did you think?" Papa asked so casually that Julia felt contrite for her first reaction that the question had held any hidden intent.

Julia forced her face to remain neutral. "We didn't speak about very much. He does seem as if he's very passion—I mean, very committed to his work, which I know very little about. I'm sure if you think so highly of him then he deserves your esteem, Papa."

"I agree with you. I'm sorry you didn't get better acquainted. But then, he'll be around a lot, I suspect—for business—so you'll probably have a chance to get to know him quite well. I invited him and Ned to Christmas Eve dinner and of course they'll be at Daphne's engagement party the night before. I think Ned has a thing for Betsy."

"Oh, I think so too. And she's quite taken with him. Betsy's the smartest girl I know, Papa, and I don't say that because she's my best friend. But men seem frightened by her intelligence and knowledge, even though she's quite pretty, don't you think?"

"I do, and I agree with you. Most of the young men today are little more than jellyfish—not like in my day, when they were fighting a war to save this nation. I think any man who's put off by Betsy is just a damn fool!"

Had Papa inadvertently given his true feeling away? Did he think Percy was a "jellyfish"?

"Why the sudden frown, Julie? You didn't think I was including your Percy in my usual exaggerated opinion, did you? I certainly wouldn't want you to think I felt that way."

Julia smiled with relief. "I was beginning to wonder. It's important for me to know that you approve of Percy. I *know* you're taken with Mr. Woods. Perhaps because he's as outspoken as yourself?"

Papa laughed. "I hadn't looked at it that way, but I guess in my day I was a bit of a rebel too—until your mother tamed me, that is. But you've heard all those stories, about me being this handsome rake of a captain, since you sat at your mother's knee, haven't you?"

Julia hugged and kissed him. "I love you, Papa!" she said. "Perhaps I won't marry at all and live with you forever!"

"And have your mother distressed for the rest of my life? It's appealing—not your mother's nagging, but the idea of keeping you here—but not *that* appealing! Now, off with you," Papa said and tugged at her long braid as he used to do when she was a little girl.

Julia started up the stairs.

"Julia?" Papa called out softly, so as to not wake anyone.

"Yes?"

"Remember, I'm always here if you need an ear. Besides, I like talking to you, you know?"

Julia turned and smiled. Again she thought Papa looked worried—no, almost sad. "Me too. I'll remember. Papa . . ." she began, but instantly stopped herself. As desperately as she wanted to tell him of her turmoil since she'd met Ian, she just couldn't. "Never mind. Sleep well."

"Julia?" Daphne called, and knocked on her door, then swung it open. "Are you ready? Harold and Percy are already waiting downstairs. They've got our skates."

"I'm ready," Julia answered, and rose, happy to flee from her thoughts.

Julia found the crisp early-evening air invigorating. It was a perfect night. In the cloudless sky the moon shone bright yellow, lighting even the center of the lake, as their skates cut into the ice. They'd had a jolly carriage ride with Percy and Mrs. Martin, Daphne and Harold, and Betsy and Ned. Jokes had flown from one edge of Mrs. Martin's carriage to the other. Julia liked her future mother-in-law, whom she had known most of her life. Mrs. Martin was younger than Mamma and at times seemed like a girl herself, laughing easily and keeping up with all the light-hearted conversation that coursed through the richly decorated carriage that was replete with winter furs for additional warmth.

Percy was a steady skater, though not as agile as Julia, but he seemed to adore it when she would glide to the innermost circle of the lake and cut a graceful figure eight, which she would end with a long twirl, her arms free of her muff, which Percy held, enabling Julia to twirl for what felt like forever. Percy and a few friends surprised her with a quick round of loud applause when she finished. Her cheeks and nose were already reddened from the cold and the flush of exertion, and her color heightened further as she blushed and laughed at the attention.

Julia skated to Percy's side and retrieved her Persian-lamb muff. Percy linked his arm with hers and they began a turn around the outer edge of the lake, which was romantically lit by the kerosene lamps set up by the concessionaire, who also provided the refreshments in the pavilion.

"Are you having a good time, Julia?" Percy asked as they skated arm in arm.

"A wonderful time! And you?" she asked, knowing already that he was. Percy loved any kind of a party, although Julia suspected that this turn around was more to please her than himself, for he would have been happy to rejoin most of the crowd of twenty who were already resting in the pavilion.

"I'm having a swell time, although it is getting a little chilly. I'm glad to see you so happy. You seem like your old self again!" he said with a grin.

Julia knew he meant this as a compliment, yet she felt herself bristle. She had not seen Percy since the night before she'd left for Uncle Walter's, almost a week before. She'd never thought that Percy noticed the subtleties of her moods, but instead of being pleased to discover this discernment on his part, she was annoyed. "What do you mean, like my old self? Have I behaved badly?"

"Oh, I didn't mean that, Julia," he answered easily. "What I meant was that since Clarice's wedding, when you came down with that cold, you've seemed tired and a little strained. Especially on the night I proposed," he said, with what Julia thought was a pride in his assumed perspicacity.

Relieved, Julia rewarded him with a big smile. "I didn't realize that you were so keenly attuned to my moods. And of course you are absolutely right. I'm afraid the effects of that cold lingered on. But I feel perfectly wonderful and revived right now."

"Oh, I know you backward and forward, my dear wife-to-be," Percy said with a grin. "And I can't wait until I can know you even better, if you know what I mean," he whispered, although they were quite alone.

Julia blushed at the intention of his remark, which seemed to please Percy enormously. He laughed good-naturedly and kissed her on her cheek.

"How about heading toward the pavilion?"

"Oh, one more round, please!" Julia asked, for suddenly she felt a rush of nervous energy again. Percy nodded and they continued past the pavilion and around the lake. Skating toward them were Betsy and Ned. As they stopped to chat, Julia saw that Betsy glowed with happiness. As the four exchanged greetings, Julia noticed that Ned continued to keep his arm linked with Betsy's and turned to her after each comment he made. How wonderful to see two people so obviously in love, Julia thought. Suddenly she felt terribly saddened. She knew she didn't feel the joy registered in Betsy's and Ned's eyes, and here she was engaged to Percy. She had told Betsy of their engagement, and from the way Ned smiled at her and Percy, she assumed Betsy had told him. She couldn't help but wonder if Ned had informed Ian. It was then that she realized she hadn't seen Ian or Mary Hoffman.

"Want to skate another round with us?" Percy asked Ned.

"We'd love to, but I think Betsy and I should return to the pavilion. Ian had a late meeting, but he said he and Mary would be here by eight. So I think we'd better check and see if they've arrived, if you don't mind."

"Hi there!" Paul Ellis called out as he skated past them with Sandra Bruce on his arm.

"No, of course not. In fact, I'm sure Julia and I will join you soon. Save a hot toddy for me, will you!"

With that, Daphne and Harold glided over to them. "Julia, Mrs. Martin asked us to bring you two in for a rest. She promised Mamma she would watch that you didn't overexert yourself. Harold and I had some of the wonderful food the Martins brought. We'll have another round and meet you back at the pavilion."

"Oh, please, Ian. Let's hurry and have a skate," Mary demanded. Her smile turned into a pout when he didn't move to rise from his chair where he sat drinking a hot toddy. "Everyone's been skating for *hours* already," Mary continued in her usual hyperbole.

"In a moment, Mary," Ian said with a forced smile. How he wished he'd followed his instincts and called Mary to cancel with some excuse. He was in a vile mood and more than a little drunk, although Mary clearly had no idea. He suspected that Mary's desire to skate had more to do with its being an excuse to snuggle up to him than because she desired the physical exertion. Mary's interest in sports seemed merely another social display.

Ironically he had always loved to skate and was quite expert at it. Good enough that he supposed he could take a few spins in his semi-inebriated condition with little difficulty. But he wanted to stall. For since he'd seen neither Julia nor Percy since he'd arrived, he assumed they were on the ice. He would be able to get through this evening only by seeing Julia as little as possible. He'd heard Mrs. Martin send Daphne to fetch them. When they returned, he would take Mary for a skate—a long skate. The plan of the evening was that they would skate until nine, then all return for a party at Percy's. Ian intended to make his excuses despite Mary's inevitable anger, ask Ned to have Mary accompany him and Betsy to Percy's and see her home. Then he would have a drink in the solitude of his father's study and think out this whole mess. His meeting with Betty Cornell Hollis, after Ned and their secretary had left the office, had been even more upsetting than he'd steeled himself for. It had also been startling. He had worried that once he saw her again all the old feelings and hurts would seep through the portion of his heart he had long ago sealed. How shocked he had been to discover that he felt nothing. What he had not expected, however, was her seemingly unending wrath at his—

"Ian! You're not even listening to me!" Mary complained. She tugged at his hand. Too weary for another battle with a woman, he rose. Still she pouted, so he grabbed her around her waist and with a few steps pulled her onto the ice, as she giggled loudly all the way.

Ian linked his arm with hers, but as he'd expected,

Mary turned her body in such a manner that her breast pressed against his upper arm. She was a less-than-adequate skater. Lucky for her that she had her pretty features and coloring, an enticing bosom and her father's huge fortune, which she would some day inherit, Ian thought, as he grinned at her. For in reality, she was an irritating, silly girl. Ian saw four skaters halfway across the lake. Two of them had to be Julia and Percy. How he wished it was Julia who was on his arm.

"Ian, are you mad at me?" Mary asked in what sounded like a genuinely concerned voice.

He felt himself softening. He would have to stop seeing Mary, for as shallow as she was, she had feelings like everyone else. Part of her must sense his lack of affection. "No, of course not," he assured her, then smiled. "What makes you ask?"

"You've just seemed terribly distant all evening. I know you're a moody man, but you've been almost cold the past few days."

"I've just been working rather hard and it's catching up with me. In fact, I must admit, I'm quite exhausted tonight," he added, seeing the perfect opening for his later excuse. "I'm sorry if I've been less than attentive."

"Oh, that's all right! Truly! As long as you're not miffed, but it was silly of me to think that anyway." She gave him a hug, then stumbled on her skates, but he caught her before she fell. "Oh, look, here comes Julia Davenport and Percy Martin! I *suspect* that they will soon be engaged. She's quite pretty, and Percy is a charming man, don't you think?"

So their engagement was being kept a family secret, more or less, as Ned had told him the other day. For Mary was the first to learn the latest gossip. When Ned had told him the news in confidence, Ian had displayed little more than polite interest. Yet inexplicably, he had been shocked. Hadn't he known all along that Julia was Percy's girl? Still, Ian couldn't help believing that Julia's acceptance of Percy's proposal the evening after their own encounter in her studio was more than coincidence. He knew he hadn't imagined what had passed between them. Well, Julia was a smart girl and he wished her the best with Percy. For himself, he intended to stay out of her life as much as possible. . . .

"Ian, you're doing it again. You haven't heard a word I've said!" Mary pouted again and pulled a subtle distance away. Then she brightened. "Hello!" she trilled to the approaching skaters. "Is that you, Julia?"

Mary was doing exactly what Ian didn't want her to do, but he had no power to stop her.

"Let's skate on," Julia whispered, at the recognition of Mary Hoffman's voice. "I can't stand that girl!"

"Oh, we can't do that. It would be too rude. Mary's not half-bad once you get to know her. We have to say hello."

Julia smiled quickly at Ian as greetings were exchanged, but then kept her eyes on Mary's face. Mary chattered on about nothing, as usual. Glancing at Percy, Julia realized that he seemed to find Mary quite entertaining.

"Percy, dear," Mary bubbled, "it has been *years* since we have had a skate. Let's do change partners for one whirl around! You wouldn't mind, Ian, dearest, would you? Percy and I have been friends since we were children in Newport."

Ian glanced furtively at Julia, but he couldn't read her expression. He smiled gallantly. "Well, of course not, unless Miss Davenport would mind," he replied with a quick smile that he tried to keep from growing into a grin. He had thrown it in her lap.

"Why so formal, Ian?" Mary asked. "I understand that Julia's father is a partner in your new firm, is he not?"

"Silent partner, yes. And friend," Ian answered quickly.

"Yes, of course. Please call me Julia," Julia answered with no suggestion that he ever had.

"Well, then, let's change partners," Mary bubbled. She took Percy's arm and skated off, leaving Ian and Julia glancing awkwardly at one another.

"May I?" Ian asked. Arm in arm, they began to skate slowly, and just as they had danced together so perfectly, so they skated, which did not surprise Ian at all. He knew that they could glide off more quickly, but he kept their speed slow, wanting to create a distance between themselves and Percy and Mary.

Julia didn't speak and looked straight ahead. They were halfway around the edge of the lake, at the furthest point from the pavilion, when Ian spoke, startling her.

"You're as proficient a skater as you are a painter," he said softly.

"Thank you. You're quite good yourself," she answered automatically, looking at him.

"Yes, I am," he said, and grinned.

Julia laughed at his honest answer and Ian chuckled as well. Their eyes met and held just as they skated beneath a hanging lantern. Julia felt a shiver creep down her spine and her knees started to weaken as they glided, their eyes unable to do anything but search each other's faces. In her mind's eye, the image from her dream of lying in Ian's arms as he kissed her played back with a will of its own, making her blush and search in vain for conversation to break the dangerous spell.

It wasn't until after she fell that Julia realized she had stumbled on a twig. Ian scooped her up without losing his balance. The pain was so intense that she wasn't sure at first from where it issued.

Ian saw the grimace of pain in her face, although she bit her lip, apparently to keep from crying out again. "Julia, what's wrong?" he demanded. "Where does it hurt?" he asked, alarmed. As he held her tightly around her narrow waist, he saw her hand reach down below her skirt. She began to rub her leg as she leaned against him for balance. "It's your ankle, isn't it? Can you step down on your skate?"

"I don't know," she said. "But I'll try." The grimace of pain that shot across her beautiful face gave him his answer.

"There's a bench over there." He swooped her into his arms, noting that despite her heavy clothing she was feather-light, and skated the few yards to the bench, where he carefully set her down. He sat beside her and lifted her leg onto his lap. "Let me check it," he said, as he quickly unlaced her skate to her ankle.

Even the touch of his gloved hands caused her to cry

out in pain. "It's just a sprain," she offered bravely as she watched Ian remove his gloves and begin to massage her ankle. Despite the cold and her heavy black wool stockings, she jumped. But this time it was not from the pain, but from the touch of his hands. He pulled her onto his lap and she bent her leg at the knee as he gently massaged her ankle. Already she saw that it had begun to swell.

"It's got to be wrapped, the sooner the better," Ian said. He removed the ivory cashmere scarf from around his neck and began wrapping it around her ankle.

As gentle as his touch was, her ankle was throbbing so that Julia let herself rest against him, her face pressed against the fur collar of his frock coat as he worked. Her hands were cold and she realized that she must have dropped her muff in her fall. She began to rub her hands together.

Satisfied with his emergency bandage, Ian leaned back against the bench, careful not to shift, for her closeness was more than he could resist. He saw her rubbing her hands and took them at once into his own ungloved hands. "You're freezing," he said softly as he began to warm them. "Did you drop your muff?" She nodded in response. "Do you want me to skate over and get it right now?" She shook her head, then lifted her face from his chest and looked up at him. There was more than physical pain in her eyes.

"Please, don't move," she whispered, shocked by her own words. He didn't smile and she saw the muscle in his jaw pulsate. As if she were in a dream, Julia gently pulled her hand free and touched his cheek.

Then she drew his face closer to hers, until she could feel his breath. She stretched and pulled his mouth onto hers. As he kissed her, she wanted to laugh and cry at the same time. Even his first kiss was not foreign to her. She had kissed him so many times just like this in her dream.

Ian knew he should stop this at once, but he couldn't. From the moment his lips touched hers, no thought beyond desire was possible. He stroked her cheek, which was hot and cold at the same time. Then he kissed her again, his senses luxuriating in the softness of her mouth. He nibbled at her lips and felt her draw him tighter to her. He caressed her hair and let his tongue explore the sweetness of her lips. She gasped and opened her mouth to him, and he felt her shiver with desire as his tongue began to learn the secrets of the silken recesses of her mouth.

Julia tried to make herself stop, but she couldn't. His tongue in her mouth shot a wave of tremors through her and she was shocked to hear the sigh that came from deep within her. As they had danced that first night, she found herself intuitively following him. Their lips and tongues danced together.

Ian felt his groin heat and his manhood come to life. He doubted Julia could tell, what with his heavy coat and hers between them, but as he kissed her again he knew that he had to resist himself and her. He pulled himself from her with all the willpower he could muster.

Julia was mortified. She sat upright, then slid down off his lap onto the bench. Even the pain that shot from her ankle as she shifted didn't hurt as much as her embarrassment. She wanted to say something, but there was nothing to say. She had thrown herself at him and had loved every second of it. Passion, yes, that's what it was. She could no longer deny it. But she was engaged to Percy! Julia thought of Percy's kisses in his parents' conservatory and then the next night in her own hallway. It was a surprise that both could be called kissing. She realized that never again in her life would she experience what had just passed between herself and Ian, and she began to cry. She couldn't help it, as much as it mortified her further. "It hurts!" she cried out, giving in to the spasming pain from her ankle, which at this moment was both solace and penance.

He saw the two figures skating by. "Percy! Mary! Come here at once!" Ian shouted through cupped hands. He called again. Percy started across the lake in a fast skate, with Mary following awkwardly behind.

"What's happened?" Percy asked as he tried to catch his breath.

"It's Julia's ankle. She tripped on a twig. I've wrapped it, but she can't put any weight on it, and it hurts her terribly."

"Oh, my poor Julia," Percy said. He plopped down on the bench beside her and threw his arm around her shoulder. "We'd better get her back to the pavilion right away."

Julia dared not look at either of them; instead she studied her hands. "My muff," she managed to say.

"She must have dropped it during her fall. Stay with her and I'll skate over and get it." Ian looked behind him, through the skeletal grouping of trees. "Just as I remembered. The road goes right through here behind

111

us. I'll bring the muff and then skate to the pavilion and have them bring a carriage around. We can carry Julia to it through those trees," he said, pointing.

"Oh, don't be silly. I'm sure if I just stand up . . ." Julia, desperate to be out of this situation, rose, but the sharp pain in her ankle sent her toppling backward. It was Ian who caught her. As soon as he sat her down, she pulled away.

Ian revealed no reaction. "I'll be right back," he said.

"Good." Percy put his arm around Julia's shoulder, snuggling her. "Before you know it, Julia, you'll be safe and sound in your bed—"

"No! You're all making too much out of this. It's just a little twist," Julia protested.

"We'll let the doctor decide that," Percy countered. "But I'd guess that in bed is just where you belong. Don't you agree, Ian?"

"I couldn't agree more," Ian replied, unable to resist the childish *double entendre* as he stared into Julia's pained eyes, which registered his remark before they lowered. He forced a smile and skated to retrieve her muff.

Not only had Julia understood his remark, but she'd caught a glimpse of his sardonic expression as he skated away, which served to intensify her mortification.

Ian was angry at his cheap remark, but seeing Percy's arm around Julia had made him seethe inside, like a jealous schoolboy.

"Whatever has happened?" a huffing Mary asked as she collapsed on the bench beside Julia. "Ian passed me as if he didn't even see me, and he had the angriest look on his face."

"Julia hurt her ankle," Percy said. "It looks like a bad sprain. I'm sure Ian was just intent on getting help, right Julia?"

Julia stared ahead at the silhouette of Ian's figure already skating back toward them. "What? Oh, yes, that's right."

"It must hurt a lot," Mary said, and patted her arm. "I don't think I've ever seen you cry."

Julia hadn't realized that a stream of tears was rolling down her cheeks. She brushed them away. "Yes, it hurts. It hurts very badly," Julia said, knowing that Percy and Mary naturally assumed she was speaking about her throbbing ankle.

Chapter Eight

"ARE YOU CERTAIN IT'S JUST A SPRAIN, DR. CLARKE?" Mamma asked in a worried tone.

"Absolutely," he answered as he finished tapping her ankle. "There," he said and gently patted her knee. "If you promise to stay off that foot—completely off it, young lady, for a week—I promise you it will be as good as ever."

"A week! That's impossible!" Julia cried out. "Daphne's engagement party is in three days and then Christmas Eve and then the new play opening at the theater . . ." Julia beseeched Dr. Clarke.

"I'm not saying you have to stay locked away in your bedroom. You may be at all those functions, as long as you're carried to and fro and remain *seated.*"

Julia was about to protest again, but Dr. Clarke, who had brought her into the world, looked at her so sternly that she knew it would be in vain, especially when she glanced at the gallery of other equally serious faces in her bedroom: Mamma, her mouth pursed; Papa, his eyes darkened with concern; Kathleen, attempting a weak smile; and Ian, somber and looking about her room.

Dr. Clarke removed a bottle from his leather bag. "I want you to take a tablespoon of this elixir now. It should take the pain away and make you drowsy. Have you eaten dinner?"

Julia shook her head.

"Henrietta, I want her to have a light meal before she takes this, so it won't be hard on her stomach." He turned to Julia. "This will make certain that you get a good night's sleep, young lady. One tablespoon after you've had some broth and bread."

"I'll make sure she takes it, Doctor," Kathleen said and took the brown bottle from him.

"Well, that's it. Otherwise, I think the patient will live," Dr. Clarke said with a laugh. He patted Julia on her cheek.

"I'll see you downstairs, Herman," Papa said.

Dr. Clarke turned to Ian. "By the way, young man," he said, "you did a good job of bandaging her ankle with your scarf. Smart thinking."

"I—" Ian started.

"You've got a clever beau, Julia. And it's not all that bad, for he'll get to carry you about for the next week, won't he?" Dr. Clarke chuckled.

"He's not my beau, Dr. Clarke. Percy Martin is," Julia quickly explained and hoped that for once she didn't blush. She dared not look at Ian.

Dr. Clarke laughed unembarrassedly. "Percy? Fine

young man. I delivered him as well, or didn't you know? Fine young man. Going to invite me to the wedding? You'd better!"

Charles glanced at Ian as Herman continued to chatter and saw that the younger man's face was unreadable. Charles was still curious about what had happened. First, Julia was such a good skater and so agile that it was unlike her—still, anyone could have an accident. But from the moment Ian had entered the house with Julia in his arms, tears streaming from her reddened eyes, Charles had a sense that there was more than met the eye to this. Julia wasn't much of a crier like Louise was—that one could cry like a faucet at a moment's notice. Ian had seemed upset about something more than a sprain, even a severe one. After Ian had gently lowered Julia on her bed, Charles had the sense that Ian wanted to do nothing more than flee. Good manners had held him, Charles figured, but he noticed Ian avoided looking at Julia.

"Herman. This is Ian Woods. I apologize for my bad manners. Ian is a friend of the family's and a business associate of mine. He's a brilliant new architect in partnership with another fine young man, Ned Barrington."

"Sorry for the mix-up," Dr. Clarke said as he shook hands with Ian. "Was your father the late John Woods?"

"Yes, sir."

"He was a fine man, your father. We belonged to the same club. So you didn't follow in his footsteps and take up banking, I take it."

"No, I didn't, Dr. Clarke."

"Architecture . . . Interesting field. Now that I think of it, I believe I heard your name mentioned in conversation just a few weeks ago. Weren't you in Chicago?"

"Yes, I was. But my partner and I have opened a firm here just this past week."

"That's fine, wonderful. Send my regards to your mother, won't you."

"I certainly will."

Charles was glad that Herman was such a talker, for it gave him time to think of an idea. "Henrietta," he said. "Julia must be starving! Why don't you and Kathleen go down to the kitchen and have Cook prepare her some dinner. I'll see Herman downstairs myself and then come back up. Ian, why don't you sit and chat with Julia for a few moments until I return? I don't want my girl to get lonely, and it was just like Julia to insist that Daphne and Harold continue on with Percy to his party. She hates to spoil anyone's good time."

"But, Papa . . ." Julia began. Papa looked at her with such innocent eyes that she didn't know what she could say that wouldn't appear rude or alarming.

"Charles . . ." Henrietta began, her eyes narrowing.

"Oh, dang it, Henrietta. I think we can leave the two of them alone for *two minutes* without any worry, don't you?" he asked, knowingly forcing Henrietta to disguise her distrust of Ian.

"Why, of course, I wasn't even thinking of that. Hurry, Kathleen," Henrietta said, pulling Kathleen toward the door. "Julia must be frightfully hungry and I want her to be able to take her medicine as quickly as possible. Thank you for arriving so quickly, Herman. Perhaps you'll stay for a cup of tea?" Henrietta added, remembering her manners.

"I'd love to," stout, gray-haired Dr. Clarke said. "Since Nancy passed on, the house is pretty lonely. And I haven't had my dinner either—"

"You haven't?" Charles jumped in. "Well, then, you must have a bite to eat here, since we obviously pulled you from your table. Right, Henrietta?"

"Of course, Charles. I'll have one of the girls set the table."

"And, Ian, I'm certain you haven't eaten either. You will join us too. Right, Henrietta?"

"Why, yes, certainly," Henrietta answered, unsure of what Charles was up to. But it was something, and she didn't like it! No more than she liked leaving Ian in the room with Julia. It was *unseemly*. But there was little she could do about it now. Henrietta smiled, then pulled Kathleen out the door with her.

"How about a drink before dinner, Herman?" Charles offered as he ushered Dr. Clarke out. At the door he turned to Julia. "I'll be back up in a couple of minutes, sweetheart. You don't mind, Ian, do you?" Charles kept a straight face as he watched them both fluster yet think they were cleverly hiding their nervousness.

"Of course not, Charles. Except that I don't think I'll be able to stay for dinner—"

"Nonsense, my boy. You were to have had dinner at Percy's, weren't you? . . . Oh, I get it. You left your gal there alone . . . you're anxious to get back to that pretty Mary Hoffman—"

"No. I'm . . ." Ian blurted, then quickly caught himself. "Actually, mother isn't feeling well, so I intended to see Mary to the party and make my apologies."

"Oh, I see. I'm sorry to hear that. Send her my best. I'll be back in a jiffy, then."

As soon as he and Julia were alone, Ian began to pace nervously. Julia couldn't help but watch him. He looked like a trapped animal who couldn't make his escape. And it was all because he wanted to be rid of her as soon as possible! Julia couldn't stand the silence.

Ian knew that he had to explain to Julia why he had rebuffed her. But how? He had only a few moments that he might never get alone with her again. "Julia, I—"

"Ian, I—"

Despite their nervousness, they laughed, having spoken at once. Ian stopped pacing and walked to the side of her bed. He took a deep breath. "I'm sorry, Julia. I really owe you an apology. An explanation—"

"It is I who owe you an apology," Julia interrupted in a trembling voice. "I behaved in such a—a manner that I can't believe—"

"No, you didn't—"

"I behaved so impetuously," she whispered. Her face flamed and her eyes looked away from his dark eyes, from his face that she had felt against her own. The memory further shamed her. "I'm engaged to Percy Martin—"

"I know, but—"

"You know? You mean you *knew?* Then you must think me no better than the most common—"

119

"No, of course not! It was *just* a moment that we both lost control. It means *nothing* more than that."

So, in trying to be polite, he had allowed the truth to slip. From what Louise had told her, Ian was more than used to "loose" girls. In his eyes she was just another one. Of course it had meant *nothing* to him, while to her it had meant her heart and soul! Better that he think her a tart than know how much she loved him. That would be the ultimate humiliation. By tomorrow he would not even remember their intimacies. For all she knew, he would indeed go back to Percy's party. She hadn't believed his story about his mother being sick. As much as she ordinarily hated gossip, she didn't doubt that the rumors about Mary Hoffman being quite "affectionate" were true.

"You're right," she said, forcing a smile. "It meant nothing. But I do hope you will keep our secret and allow me to maintain my reputation. You are not one to 'kiss and tell,' then, are you?" Julia forced herself to giggle in an imitation of the coy manner of Mary Hoffman, wondering how she'd even come up with that expression. Instantaneously she realized it was from a novel. She thought of the French character who'd become a fallen woman. "One must sometimes give in to one's passion, mustn't one?" Julia mimicked in a tone she imagined that the character, Rosette, must have used, the very line that had so shocked her when she'd read it. Ian's face hardened. Then he threw his head back in a hearty laugh.

"You are far more 'sophisticated' than I'd thought." He walked to her and took her hand. "Yes, one must give in to one's passion from time to time. It will remain our little secret." His sardonic smile cut through her. "By the way, I don't think I've offered my best wishes on your soon-to-be-announced engagement."

To look away from his cold, gleaming eyes would be to give herself away. How she wanted to blurt the truth. She felt the tears well behind her eyes and the knot tighten in her throat. "Thank you," she managed to reply. "And don't forget your scarf," she said to change the subject. Her eyes looked to the scarf draped across the brocade chair.

Ian studied her face, for he still could not believe how thoroughly he had misjudged her. Her countenance remained cool, except for the knit of her brows, which he attributed to her pained leg. And to think that he had been about to tell her that despite his best intentions he was falling in love with her! To think that he had believed her kisses and sighs had come from deep within her soul, only to find that she was playing a game with him. "Keep it," he answered evenly. "As a reminder of our brief 'moment of passion.' Perhaps you'll feel the urge to indulge again, and it would be hard for me to resist, for you are *such* a pretty girl, as you well know. But I must ask you to keep my secret as well," he said, then glanced at his pocket watch. "Mother is feeling quite well. I am most anxious to get back to my lady and of course I do want to protect Mary's reputation as well as your own. Society is so full of gossips and snoops that one can never be careful enough, isn't that so?"

His smile chilled her. She nodded. Ian turned away

from the bed, then walked back to her. He glanced at the door. His hard eyes frightened her. "Now I know why you lied to me about your self-portrait. For you weren't ready to reveal your secret passionate nature to me at that time, were you, my Dresden doll?" He stroked her cheek and she turned her head away, feeling as if her heart had shattered so that it would never be repaired. "Oh, I see," he said. "Your passion has dissipated from the pain of your ankle no doubt. Although it didn't seem to adversely affect it earlier, did it?"

Had it been his imagination or had he just seen a glimpse of fear in her eyes? Why, of course! She was afraid that her father or someone else would enter and that she would be exposed for what she really was.

"Please leave. Right now." There were tears in her eyes when she turned to him. He felt stricken, for she looked so miserable and pained as the tears rolled down her alabaster cheeks. "My ankle is hurting terribly. I want my medicine and don't want to cry in front of a stranger."

A stranger, she called him. After the way they had kissed and touched. "I can't do that because it would arouse suspicion, and I promised your father. I'm certain he will be right up." He walked to the chair, lifted his scarf, then tossed it at her. It landed against the pillows beside her. "Your souvenir."

"I don't want your silly scarf!" She couldn't stand this any longer. "I'll just throw it away," she said as she grabbed it and threw it off the bed.

"Do what you like with it. I don't care—" Ian heard

Charles's footsteps on the stairs. He quickly walked to the door. "Charles," he said. "I was just coming down to get you or Mrs. Davenport. I'm afraid Julia's ankle is paining her quite badly. She's tried to be brave, but the pain must be so acute that she can't help but cry. Perhaps she should have her medicine as soon as possible."

Charles strode into the room. Julia's eyes were red and tears streamed down her face. He wondered if something else had happened. Perhaps his plan had backfired . . .

Julia saw the concern wrought across Papa's face. Why did she sense that he knew something was upsetting her other than her ankle, which was truly throbbing now. She forced a smile through her tears. "I'm sorry, Papa. I tried to be a good soldier. But it does hurt so. Worse yet, I've embarrassed Ian. For he wanted to comfort me but didn't know how. And that's because only the medicine will take the pain away. And I've put Ian through enough of an ordeal for one evening, don't you think, Papa?"

"I'm certain Ian didn't mind at all. After all, you didn't do it intentionally, now did you? An accident's just an accident. Right, Ian? Sometimes things just happen by chance with no reason at all. Don't you agree, Ian?"

"Most definitely. I was trying to convince Julia of exactly that, but I'm not certain that I succeeded."

For Papa's sake, Julia forced another smile and said in a sweet voice: "Oh, but you most definitely did, Ian. Most definitely." She turned back to Papa. "I do think

123

we must let Ian leave. I've imposed on him more than enough for one night. And he was telling me how he was concerned about Mrs. Woods."

"Why, of course. Please, don't let us hold you. And thank you, Ian, for taking such good care of my girl."

Charles clasped him on the shoulder. Ian cringed inside, feeling as if he had badly betrayed Charles's trust. He vowed that he would never do so again. "It was nothing, Charles, really." He was as furious at Julia as he was at himself. He turned to her at the door. "I certainly hope you feel much better very soon," he said politely.

"Thank you. And thank you for all you did tonight." As soon as the words were out of her mouth, Julia regretted their double meaning.

"Don't bother yourself about it. It was nothing. Nothing at all! Good night, Julia. And sweet dreams."

"I'll walk Ian down and be back up in a minute, dear," Papa said.

Julia held her rage until she heard them well down the first flight of stairs. "God, I hate him!" she whispered through clenched teeth and hit her fists upon her pillow. Too late, as the pain shot through her, she realized that she had kicked her feet as well. I hate him! she thought, as she burst into tears.

"Julia! Oh dear, I told Cook to hurry!" Mamma said as she rushed to her side and took her into her arms. Kathleen followed Mamma in with a tray of food. "Now, now. Crying won't help. Kathleen, hand me the soup, please. As soon as you eat something, we'll give you your medicine and you'll feel so much better, now won't you, dear?"

Julia nodded, but she knew that the pain she was feeling couldn't be taken away with any medicine.

Ian decided to take a walk through the park before heading home, for of course he had no intention of rejoining the group at Percy's. A light snow was beginning to fall and it danced gracefully around the lighted lampposts and caused the soles of his shoes to make a crunching sound as he walked down the path. He decided to walk across the park and up to the Dakota building on Central Park West, for its eclectic design of mansards and gabled windows appealed to him. He remembered that when he was just a boy, the building on Seventy-second Street loomed singularly above the lake on which they'd skated tonight. For in the early eighties, between the Dakota apartment building and the newly constructed Museum of Natural History on Seventy-ninth, there remained untracted soil and shacks inhabited by squatters. Ian remembered seeing shabbily dressed women feeding their chickens. Now, of course, buildings belied the existence of what had still been patches of shantytowns in Manhattan little more than fifteen years ago.

The full moon shone brightly on the empty, frozen lake silhouetted by wintered trees now wearing a light layer of freshly fallen snow. Ian sat on a bench, the beauty of the scene calming his senses. Perhaps now he could think more clearly.

He began to recall Betty's visit to his office earlier this evening. After he had telephoned her, he was still not assured that she would honor his request for a private discussion. She had entered with her maid at the appointed hour and had left her maid in the outer office. Dressed in a velvet-and-fur ensemble, her long black hair swept up beneath a small plumed hat, Betty had grown from the beautiful girl he'd remembered into a stylishly attractive matron. She was as beautiful as ever at thirty, yet he detected a hardening of her finely sculptured features and in her large amber eyes. Even her initial smile extended no further than the corners of her lips. In that smile, he recalled her mother's countenance, and once again he remembered that haughty woman who had succeeded in driving them apart.

Ian had tried to be cordial and delicate. For despite all that had happened, he had once deeply loved this woman when she was just a girl. But she allowed not a glimmer that they had ever known one another more than socially, let alone been desperately in love. The purpose of his request for her appearance had been to discuss the boy she had borne, whom Ian had never known was his child. At first Ian had refused to believe it, although he knew of no reason Samuel Walters, an old friend since their schooldays, would have had to fabricate such a story. Yet, from the moment Ian had surreptitiously set eyes upon the seven-and-a-half-year-old boy, he knew that Timothy could be no one else's child. For the boy had the same coal-black eyes, the same straight dark brow. And as the boy laughed and talked to his nurse, Ian thought that even Timothy's smile was exactly like his own.

No more than the mention of her son had inflamed Betty's rancor, as if she were a torch that had been ignited. She rose instantly, her back rigid, her chin high, her eyes as fiery as her words, as she told him that just because they had once been "sweethearts" was no reason for him to expect her to discuss the intimacies of her life with him. Any doubt that may have lingered vanished, for Ian had merely mentioned having passed Timothy in the street, had commented on what a fine-looking boy he was and had asked his age. Betty's attack had virtually stunned him into silence. By the time he could speak, she already stood at his office door, her hand on the brass handle.

"Betty, wait," he'd called out and with a few strides was upon her. "I warn you. If you will not sit down and tell me the truth, I will discover it one way or the other. If Timothy is my son, as I believe he is, I will not be deterred by your rages or ruses. You can make it easier on both of us by just speaking the truth. For I am no longer the soft, starry-eyed boy whom you wrapped around your finger eight years ago."

For a moment her face seemed to soften, her eyes widen in response. In that moment he saw the Betty he had fallen in love with when they were both just seventeen. He reached out and touched her hand. "That boy was conceived in love. I have a right to know."

She swallowed hard. Her eyes narrowed and her face became rigid once again as she glared at him. "You have become even stranger than they say, Ian. I will not even dignify your statement with a response. Go on with your life and leave me, my husband and children to ours. You speak of love but you know nothing about it! I warn you, let it be, unless you are so filled with spite that you can't accept the fact that we were little

127

more than children who shared nothing more than a childish crush."

His hand tightened on her own. "Children seldom share the intimacies we did in that patch of woods in the mountains."

She wrenched free. "Is it money you want? Have you depleted your inheritance so that you would lower yourself to blackmailing me for my girlish indiscretions? I see now that Mother was always right about you! And you knew so too, which is why you ran like a scared rabbit! I only regret that I ever set eyes on you, Ian Woods! Go back to Paris or Chicago or wherever! My husband is a powerful attorney. I warn you that it is you who will rue the day, should you try to contact me again or bother my children!"

Ian stood silently as she stormed into the outer office, fetched her maid and slammed the office door behind her. Hell has no fury like a woman scorned, he thought. But wait! He had not rejected her! It had been Betty who insisted that she never wanted to see him again, that she had never loved him and that she was going to marry John Hollis. Yet tonight she had raged at him as if he had been the one to break her heart.

Despite her ranting, if the boy was his, he would find out. From there he was not sure how he would proceed. First things first. Ian rose from the bench and brushed the snow away that had accumulated on his overcoat. Women! They were far more trouble than they were worth! Either that, or he had a most definite propensity for falling in love with the most devious of their species.

Julia . . . How she confused him! But it was his own fault. Had he followed his decision to keep his distance and continue to devote all his emotions and energies to his work alone, then he wouldn't now be trying to figure out what had happened tonight. He had left her Fifth Avenue mansion with the absolute conviction that she had merely been toying with him. That the kisses and touch he had believed to be so heartfelt and overwhelming that neither she nor he could prevent them, had turned out to be nothing more than a bold flirtation, admitted by her very own words. But as he walked through the park, he'd come to suspect that perhaps he was wrong. For there had been something in her eyes that belied her words, although he was too hurt and angry to comprehend it at the time. He had pulled away from her kisses to protect her. Perhaps she had not understood that. But surely a girl as beautiful as Julia must be aware that no man would *willingly* choose to withdraw from her lips and that sigh that had warmed him to the core despite the chill of the night air. At twenty-three, despite her sheltered and pro-tected upbringing, surely she had to know. Or did she?

Ian kicked a small stone, coated with snow, down the path in lieu of kicking himself. How insensitively stupid he had been! For he had sensed, as Julia so tentatively kissed him at first but soon passionately responded to his probing lips and tongue, that she was responding from instinct rather than experience. Then he had pulled away without explanation and assumed that her tears flowed from her pained ankle just as they had during their confrontation in her bedroom. She had tried to tell him. But when he had tried to reassure her, his words had instead convinced her that her kisses had meant nothing to him. He had been too blind to see that she reacted from pride and cleverness. Even her silly comment about one giving in to one's passion had struck a false note at the moment, but his wounded pride had prevented him from thinking clearly.

He had intended to tell Julia during their few un-chaperoned moments in her bedroom that he was falling in love with her but that he could not declare himself in order to protect her. First, she was engaged to Percy, although he knew that engagements were often broken without creating terrible scandal. Hadn't Julia broken two herself, according to what Charles had told him? But what he dared not expose her to was the possibility of a scandal if Timothy proved to be his son and he decided to act upon that information. Even if this did not happen, Ian knew that he was not good husband material. He was well aware that he was an object of ridicule and scorn to many members of the society into which he'd been born. He was considered a rebel and malcontent. If he and Ned were to maintain their integrity, the kind of commissions they sought would be difficult to come by. While his father had left him a substantial trust fund, Ian was unwilling to live from it as so many of his generation did. He was a man and would earn his own way in the world. It would be years, if ever, before he could offer a girl like Julia the kind of affluence to which she was accustomed. To expect her to accept substantially less was to believe in fairy stories, as Betty had proved to him eight years ago.

As Ian wended his way toward his mother's home on Madison Avenue, he decided that he must write a letter tonight and have one of the maids deliver it to Julia in the morning. In writing he could clearly explain himself and their misunderstanding. He would offer his friendship to her and Percy.

Two hours later, he tore up his fourth attempt and turned out the gaslamp on his father's desk. He would have to find a way to talk with her alone. Then, when he could watch her lovely face, he would be assured that she truly understood.

Before turning in for the night, Kathleen tiptoed into Julia's room to check that she was sleeping comfortably. Kathleen was distressed to see that despite the medicine Julia had taken, she was uncharacteristically tossing about in her sleep. The small light by her bed was still turned on and Kathleen saw that Julia's face appeared pained. Even in her sleep her ankle must be distressing her, Kathleen thought. She walked to the side of the bed, intending to turn out the light. Julia's cry in her sleep so startled her that Kathleen nearly knocked over the small glass lamp. She wondered if she should wake Julia.

"Ian . . . Ian! . . . Don't say that . . ." Julia whispered, her voice anguished.

It took Kathleen a moment to realize that Julia was still asleep and obviously having a nightmare. But why was she repeating Mr. Woods's name? Ah . . . suddenly it all became clear to her. From that night of Clarice's wedding, when Julia returned home early with that devil of a cold, she hadn't been herself. Kathleen had suspected then, but since Miss Julia's engagement she had assumed that she had been mistaken. Well, she had been right all along. It wasn't Mr. Percy Martin

131

Julia was in love with—Kathleen had never thought so.

But she was in love, most definitely, and it was with that handsome, mysterious Mr. Ian Woods. Kathleen didn't know whether she should wake Julia, and she began to feel as if she were most wrongfully eavesdropping on the most private thoughts of her mistress.

"Ian, it isn't true . . ." Julia pleaded with him, but he wouldn't listen. His black eyes were hard and unyielding. He wouldn't believe her, no matter how many times she told him how much she loved him. No matter how many times she told him how she had never loved Percy or any other man, never kissed or touched any other man as she had him.

"There are names for girls like you, Julia," he said ominously. Then he began to laugh at her, his head thrown back in derisive mirth, even as her tears began to fall. "Ah, the tears now, too," he said, mocking her, and laughed harder. He stopped as suddenly as he had started. He walked to her bed and loomed over her. He stared so hard into her that she felt herself paralyzed. Then he sat at the edge of her bed and pulled her into his arms. She wanted to struggle away but she couldn't move. His voice was dark and heavy. "We both know what you want, don't we, princess?" She could only manage to shake her head but then he swept her into his arms and his kiss took her breath away as he laid her back down upon the bed, his chest pressing hard against her own, his tongue inside her mouth, making her tremble as the chills chased up her spine. I love you, I love you, she thought, but all she could do was respond to his insistent kisses as his hands began to caress her neck and throat. He lifted his head for a moment and smiled at her. "I love you, Ian," she managed to whisper finally. His coal-black eyes narrowed into a cold glint as sharp as a knife. "Save that chatter for Percy. I know the real you, Julia. You can't hide from me anymore. It's passion, girl. Remember, I saw it in your painting. Save your pretenses for Percy and the other silly boys. For I know what lies beneath your angelic face, pretty Julia. I know what you want and in a moment you shall have it." He began to laugh that hideous laugh again as he reached to unbutton her nightgown.

"No! Stop! I lied! I love you! Please, Ian!"

"Miss Julia, Miss Julia! It's just a dream! A nightmare. You're safe. It's Kathleen, I'm here with you. . . . It was just a bad dream."

Julia felt Kathleen's strong arms holding her and began to hear Kathleen's words through her sobs. A dream. It had been just a dream—but it had seemed so real. Ian. How he hated her! "Oh, Kathleen," she whispered between sobs. "It was such a terrible dream. He looked at me with such contempt—"

"Who did?" Kathleen asked. She would not embarrass Julia by telling her that she already knew.

"Ian. Ian Woods!" Julia's throat tightened as another wave of sobs overtook her. She allowed herself to cry as Kathleen held her. She had to talk to someone or she was going to go crazy. She shifted, having forgotten about her ankle until the pain shot through her. It was almost a welcome relief.

"Do you want to talk about it?" Kathleen asked in her pretty singsong voice.

Oh, how she did! And surely she could trust in Kathleen's confidence. Moreover, Kathleen had come from the "real" world, as Julia thought of it. The world outside that was harsher than her own but perhaps more knowing as well about matters of life and love. "Do you swear that you will never repeat what I tell you? Cross your heart and hope to die?"

"I do," Kathleen uttered solemnly, hoping she would be able to offer Julia some comfort. But what did she know that would be able to ease the heart-wrenching tears that had dampened Julia's satin gown? Well, she could listen. That much she could do.

After Julia had told Kathleen everything about Ian from the moment that their eyes met in the church, she sat and waited for the pretty freckled-faced girl to answer. Kathleen's green eyes were darkened and she slowly shook her head in what seemed to be wonderment. "What are you thinking?" Julia asked. "Tell me honestly."

"I'm thinking," Kathleen began slowly, "that I never realized that rich folks have the same problems of the heart as us poor ones do. I don't know why I expected that it would be different. I'll tell you what I think, but I certainly wouldn't swear to knowing what was best. And I wouldn't want you to mind what I say too much. But in a strange way, your . . . eh, problem reminds me of this friend of mine who lived in the same building as we did before I came here. Colleen was her name, and a pretty little thing she was. She was supposed to marry this boy—an arranged marriage, you know? But she was in love with this other boy, Johnny O'Hara. Oh, he was a real rebel. He had ambitions. Even though he pushed a broom in a saloon. He was a boy with dreams, and all the mothers thought he was dangerous—all his blarney talk is how they called it. But Colleen loved him. And she believed in him."

"What did she do?" Julia asked.

"She ran away with him. To Boston, some said. No one ever heard a word about them again."

"That's all?" Julia asked. For how was this half-story with no resolution to help her?

Kathleen blushed. "That's all. Except that I saw her—I never told no one, not even my sister—when she and Johnny was sneaking out down the stairwell. It was a hot night and I couldn't sleep so I sat on the staircase near the air vent, hoping for a breath. Anyway, those two walked right past me and they just stopped and smiled. But never have I again seen such happiness in two sets of eyes as I did that night. I don't *know* what happened to them, but I believe that with the good Lord's help, they're still smiling at each other with those same shining, loving eyes. And I bet that Johnny's probably made something real good out of himself too! . . . But I guess my story doesn't really help you much, I'm afraid. I mean, your world's so different and—"

Julia hugged Kathleen tightly. Then she pulled away and smiled. "I think your story was wonderful and helped more than you'd guess. But I've kept you awake long enough. I think I'll be able to sleep now. . . . Thank you for being such a good friend, Kathleen."

Long after Kathleen had gone to bed, Julia lay awake thinking. If only she were as free to follow the pull of her heart as the young Irish girl Kathleen had spoken of. But she had committed herself to Percy, whom she'd known most of her life. What did she actually know about Ian? Mostly bits and pieces of impressions, rumors and judgments that didn't add up to anything. Was he a bounder as Louise and Mamma believed? Hadn't he told her himself that he had taken up with Mary Hoffman? Yet she didn't believe that he really cared for Mary. She didn't see evidence of it in his eyes when he spoke her name. Still, was that not yet worse—the liberties he was taking with Mary? Men were known to take lovers, young actresses, foreign girls on the Continent, American girls of lesser means and vaguer morals. Yet even in 1898, a man was expected to do so with great discretion and certainly not with a *jeune fille a marier,* a young lady suitable for marriage. Yet he had indicated so to her. . . .

Carefully Julia turned on her side, but still the slight movement of her leg pained her. She thought of the prideful, foolish words she had spoken to Ian. She remembered the shocked expression on his face before he'd burst into hateful laughter. Might he have not said and done what he did as a rejoinder? Papa believed Ian not only a talented and ambitious architect but also a man of character. In fact, Julia suspected that Papa was trying to throw the two of them together. He'd seemed as delighted to see Ian carry her into the house and to her bedroom as he was upset about her injury. Twice now it had been Papa's doing that had left her and Ian unchaperoned. Could it have been merely a coincidence? For she had never known Papa to be devious, and yet . . . Mamma had been furious with Papa for leaving Ian with her tonight, as much as Mamma tried to hide it.

All these pieces of a puzzle she did not yet understand. Most of all she didn't know for certain whether Ian was indeed the man of her dreams, or just a reflection of a frightening force within herself. A force that he called passion. Like an unbroken stallion, unless she held its reins fiercely, it could be her undoing. Her dreams shamed her, but to think that she had allowed herself to act against all that was moral and proper, and still secretly savored those moments, terrified her. It was as if a flame inside her had been lighted and merely his touch could arouse it into a raging fire. She would guard herself carefully. Perhaps it was already too late for her to do anything to change his impression of her that she had so forcefully helped to create. But she would conduct herself like a lady again even if he thought her a . . . She couldn't even think the word.

Was it just a few weeks ago that her life had been so innocent and uncomplicated? Somehow, no matter what happened, she knew that it would never be so again.

The second dose of medicine that Kathleen had given her was finally taking effect. She pulled Ian's ivory scarf, which she had hidden beneath her pillow, to her cheek and cuddled her face against it. As her eyes closed, she remembered his strong hand gently stroking her face, his lips nibbling her own, his mouth upon hers. Reluctantly she hid the scarf beneath the pillow again, her hand holding tightly onto it, and finally she fell into a deep, dreamless sleep.

Chapter Nine

"But a commission like this estate will get us started in the black," Ned argued. "We should take it just this once."

"And then next time some millionaire wants us to build a ridiculous castle to glorify himself and make his wife the envy of society, you'll have another excuse why we can't pass *just* this one up!" Ian yelled. "When we decided to become partners we agreed that we would build skyscrapers of great beauty. We agreed that we would not succumb to the checkbook of some oil magnate! You said that if we had to struggle for a while, so be it, didn't you, Ned?"

"I did," Ned answered quietly. "But no one is pounding on our door offering us those commissions. What harm can it be to do one estate in Newport when we have little else to do?"

"That's not so! If the commodores of business are not coming to us yet, then we must go to them. Isn't that so, Charles?" Ian said, calling Charles to his defense.

"Yes. I agree." Charles puffed on his pipe for a moment. Ian's fuse was so lit that what he had to do was calm him down before the boy said something that would irrevocably fracture his and Ned's friendship and partnership. He wished that Ned had told him of the offered commission for the Dickerman estate before he had thrown it with such innocent glee at Ian. For while Ned was a fine architect and a sincere young man, Charles sensed Ned to be a pragmatist by nature. While Ian's boldness and vision had captured Ned's imagination, the reality of their first commission, and a handsome one at that, did not strike him as a capitulation of their dreams. Charles understood both young men, especially Ian. For he had been much like Ian himself, yet he had allowed his life to follow another path. "When do you have to let them know, Ned?" he asked.

"Two, three weeks. We should submit preliminaries by then," Ned replied, much of his enthusiasm punctured by Ian's anger.

"And what about the meetings you had with Norfolk and Conway, Ian? You took them to the site of Louis Sullivan's Bayard Building down on Bleecker Street. Were they impressed with the construction they saw?"

"I think so. They came back to the office and I showed them some sketches of ours again. Norfolk hedged a bit. But Conway was here most of the afternoon and called for some sketches to be sent to his office. And I'm to meet with Stewart of Stewart and Weatherby on Tuesday. I see no reason for us to be running scared after being in business less than a month," Ian answered as evenly as he could, for he saw that his earlier outburst had upset Ned rather badly, although he hadn't meant it as a personal attack. He understood that Ned was anxious for them to begin designing. Not only for all the obvious reasons, but in the past few weeks Ned had spent all his free time with Betsy Livingston. Ian had no doubts that if things continued to go well between them, Ned would be ready to settle down into a life as husband and father. Ned was not the type of man, either, to be satisfied to live off the income earned by his grandfather and tendered by his father in Chicago. Love meant compromise, as Ian had always known. If he had been deluding himself on that fact because of his feelings about Julia, here was the living proof before him. Ned would have to come around and see things his way, or he would have to find another partner or go it alone, with or without Charles's continued support. But he had not compromised his ideals or his dream yet and he had no intention of allowing a fat commission to prostitute him.

"So. What do you advise, Charles?" Ned asked anxiously.

"I advise that you both continue along for the next few weeks. I see no harm in you doing some work on preliminaries for the Newport commission, while Ian presses on with the corporate people. After the first of the year you can see where things stand and make a decision at that time. That's how I see it."

Ned brightened. "That's fine with me. And you, Ian?"

Charles was right. If he pressed further he might be needlessly alienating Ned. Ned could be pushed only so far before his stubborn streak would come to the fore. Ian had seen it happen when they worked for Louis Sullivan. Most likely Conway would award them the commission for his proposed fifteen-story office building—which would be the tallest yet to be built in New York. Then it would be a moot question, this Newport commission. "I can live with it."

Ned sighed, then smiled. "Swell. Does that mean that we can end this meeting?" He looked at his watch. "I'm starved and I have a luncheon engagement in a half-hour." Ned rose and walked to the drafting table.

"Would I be off the mark if I assumed that your engagement was with a lovely young woman named Betsy?" Charles teased.

Ned's grin was enough of an answer. "No. You wouldn't be," he replied, his smile growing broader as he stroked his mustache.

"Well, then, I can see you will be properly taken care of. What about you, Ian? Have you luncheon plans?"

Ian, already fiddling through some notes, looked up distractedly. "What? No, I'm sorry, Charles. I thought I'd get to work on—"

"He rarely eats unless I drag him out," Ned answered.

Charles was pleased to see the two men smiling at one another with genuine affection once again.

"You sound like my mother," Ian teased. "It's just that I tend to get busy and forget."

"Well, then, today I insist that you dine with me!" Charles looked at his watch. "I have a meeting at my office at three, so we can have a leisurely, hearty meal. Nothing gives me indigestion faster than racing through a decent meal in less than an hour. But the pace seems to get quicker each year, doesn't it, now? I guess indigestion is one of the prices of progress, but I don't have to like it!" Charles rose. "So it's settled. You'll come with me, then, Ian."

"I don't know, Charles. I really should stay here and—"

"And risk insulting your favorite and only patron?" Charles teased.

Ian and Ned laughed. "Never," Ian answered.

"Well, at least the boy knows which side his bread is buttered on," Charles said in a stage whisper to Ned.

"You two. Honestly. Have you considered working as a team in vaudeville?" Ned grinned. "What restaurant are you dining at, then?"

"None. We're going to my house. Julia's been housebound with her sprained ankle and she's getting pretty grumpy. So I thought I'd surprise her by coming home for lunch. Henrietta and Daphne are in a tizzy with Daphne's engagement party tomorrow night. When Louise comes over, it just gets more confused. My poor Julia has been spending the last two days hiding away from it all in her studio. Bringing Ian along will give her a nice double surprise."

Ian smiled, trying to hide his confusion. He was beginning to wonder if Charles was intentionally throwing him and Julia together. But that didn't make sense. Charles seemed pleased about Julia's engagement. Moreover, Charles, who knew him so well, might admire his talent and ambitions, but certainly he would have more sense than to want his favorite daughter involved with a man like himself. Surely Charles had heard all the rumors about him from the "paragons" of society. If Charles had the slightest inkling of the liberties he had already taken with Julia—of the magnetism that seemed stronger than their wills—if Charles even suspected how much he ached to hold and kiss Julia again, how much he wanted to awaken her passion and watch it unfold like the blossoming of the most delicately beautiful but vital flower . . ."Charles, I think it would be best if I stayed at the office. I have much work to accomplish. Besides, Julia might not welcome an unannounced visitor."

"I'm sure she would be delighted." Charles realized that he was pushing too hard. That was the wrong tactic and he did not want to arouse Ian's suspicions. "But perhaps you're right. Why don't you get on with your work. Then if you'd like to, why not drop in for tea? It's Friday and it won't hurt you to leave the office earlier than usual."

"That's a good idea," Ned agreed. "Betsy and I will be there to visit with Julia. It would be swell."

Ian didn't know what to say. Not only did he have to fight his own desires, but he knew he was now risking truly offending Charles's graciousness, which he wouldn't dream of doing. He smiled. "That does sound very nice. All right. But I'll tell you now that I wouldn't be able to stay for dinner in the event that you intended to invite me. I have an engagement with Mary for dinner and the theater."

"Good, because I had no intention of extending an invitation," Charles responded, but his twinkling eyes gave him away. "Are you bringing Mary Hoffman to Daphne's engagement party tomorrow night?"

"Yes, of course." Ian thought again how relieved he would be when the holiday season was over and he could break it off with Mary. As much as he wished he could do it tonight, he had allowed her to accept holiday invitations and had invited her weeks ago to Daphne's party. He would do his best to be a companionable escort for her yet at the same time resist further attempts toward intimacy that she might make. "So, I'll let both you hungry gents be on your way and see you at tea. Will you be coming back to the office, Ned?"

"I certainly will, if I ever get out of here!"

"Then let's get going, Ned," Charles said. "I'll have my driver drop you wherever you're headed. See you later, Ian."

Ian watched the two walk into the outer office.

"Where are you taking the lovely Betsy for luncheon?" Ian heard Charles ask Ned as they disappeared from view. "I hope Delmonico's or someplace equally impressive."

Ian chuckled. He had been overly sensitive about Charles, he thought, as he listened to Charles go on prodding Ned about Betsy. Charles was not scheming as he'd begun to suspect. He and Ned had become like the sons that Charles never had, Ian suspected. He was concerned about their personal happiness as well as their business success. Ian's stomach growled. Perhaps he ought to stop and have a lunch after all. He picked up the Conway file and studied his sketches. The phone rang a few times before he realized that their secretary was still out to lunch. Distractedly he answered.

"Mr. Frank Conway to speak with Mr. Ian Woods, please."

This was the call he had been waiting for! "This is Ian Woods. How are you, Mr. Conway? I was just looking at the sketches we submitted to you."

"I'm fine, Mr. Woods, but it's been a hectic week. I called to tell you that we've already posted a letter to you. You should receive it on Tuesday, but since you spent so much time with me last week, I felt I owed you a personal explanation."

"Explanation?" They weren't going to get the commission after all. Ian felt his heart sink.

"Yes. I really wanted to go with your firm. I think you and your partner are true innovators. Unfortunately I wasn't able to convince my board members. They want a traditional building. I'm really sorry, but maybe in the future?"

"Yes, of course. And it was a pleasure meeting you, Mr. Conway."

"Likewise. If I can do anything to help, please let me know. And I certainly will turn any business your way that I can. I'm truly sorry. If it had been Granddad's day, he could have done as he pleased. But with corporate boards these days, it's a different game."

"I do understand. Thanks for calling, Mr. Conway. A Merry Christmas to you, as well."

After Ian had hung up, he realized that he hadn't asked who'd received the commission. But he could guess. Either Richard Hunt or McKim, Meade & White.

Ian pulled out the Stewart and Weatherby file. He walked with it to the window that looked out on Broadway. The wind blew briskly and the sky was heavy with the threat of snow. Businessmen held onto their hats as they passed quickly up the street. Ladies, further up Broadway, in the shopping district, stepped quickly in and out of their hansoms and carriages. The electric streetcar clanged to a stop, depositing riders on the corner of Fourteenth Street and picking up others while a few motorcars skirted around the streetcar. Only a blue-uniformed policeman at the intersection prevented the onslaught of horse-drawn, electric and motor vehicles from halting to a dead stop in this clotted congestion. The city was becoming more crowded and chaotic each year. Still, Ian had to admit that he liked the vibrancy of downtown.

The ringing telephone brought him back to his desk. He wondered what bad news it would bring as he lifted the receiver.

"Mr. Ian Woods, please," the man's voice said.

"This is he."

"Mr. Woods, this is Ben Robins. I have the information you asked me to find about the birth of Timothy Cornell Hollis."

Robins was the investigator Ian had hired. "Good. When can you bring it to me?"

"Right now, if you like. I'm just a couple of blocks from your office."

Ian glanced at the clock. Ned probably wouldn't be back for at least an hour. "Then why don't you come right up. I'm here alone, or perhaps my secretary may be back, but that's no problem."

"Swell. I'll be there in five minutes or so."

Ian lit his pipe. He was sure that the information Robins said he could acquire was going to confirm what Ian already knew. That Timothy was his son. What he was going to do about it was the question that tore at him.

The sharp ringing of the phone for the third time in five minutes caused Ian to wonder, as he lifted the receiver, if Mr. Bell's invention was a curse rather than a blessing. He was surprised to find it was Charles on the phone.

"Ian, sorry to bother you, but I believe I left a folder on the couch."

Ian glanced and saw the leather portfolio lying against the armrest. "Yes. It's here."

"That's what I thought. I'd better send my man over to get it."

"Do you need it for your afternoon meeting?" Ian asked.

"No. But it contains papers that I've got to look over for Monday—Tuesday, actually, since Monday's Christmas."

"Why don't I just bring it with me when I come for tea, then?" Ian offered.

"Why didn't I think of that? Dang, this hasn't been one of my better days."

"Nor mine. Conway called just before. We didn't get the commission." Ian tried to hide his sharp disappointment.

"Damn, I'm sorry. I know you were feeling pretty

147

good about that one. Well, you know how it is. You lose some and you win some. I'd try not to be too down-in-the-mouth about it if I were you."

"Sure," Ian replied with false heartiness. "We've just begun and all that."

"Ian, we'll talk about it later. Right now my lunch is getting cold and I've got to head out to my meeting, which has been changed from my office to his club. Thanks about the folder and I'll see you later."

Julia was curled up on the couch in the family music room, reading a book. She laid the book down and sighed. She just couldn't concentrate. While her ankle no longer pained her, the three days of being carried from couch to couch and bed had left her restless. Papa's surprise arrival at luncheon had cheered her, but now she was alone again. Kathleen was upstairs doing some sewing. Mamma had gone with Daphne and Louise for some last-minute shopping for tomorrow's party and the house was finally quiet. Julia had been amused by all the fuss about the party and the arguments about the silliest of details. Yet now she found herself wishing that she was again in the midst of all the frenetic activity rather than alone with her thoughts.

She tried to raise her spirits by thinking about what fun it would be at tea with Betsy and Ned, Daphne and Harold and the rest of the family. And of course Percy. Percy had been visiting her two or three times a day since her skating spill. Usually she and Percy spent their time in a flutter of activity, but these past three days, due to her immobility, they had spent some time playing parlor games and talking. Percy had tried to explain the world of stocks and bonds to her but she'd found that her attention wandered. Rather than displeasing Percy, he seemed to find her lack of interest amusing. They had been momentarily alone in the family drawing room when he gave her a quick kiss and laughingly agreed that the world of high finance was one that naturally mystified women. Julia had felt an irritation rise within her. For he was suggesting, however benignly, that she wasn't *capable* of understanding. She had started to answer that she wasn't mystified but just disinterested, but suddenly felt foolish, for perhaps her disinterest did originate in a woman's inability to comprehend such matters. Just at that moment Daphne had entered the drawing room and the conversation fell to other subjects.

Later that night Julia had wondered just what she and Percy would talk about when they were married. He had no interest in art or books and just a glimmer of interest in philosophy and the relatively new subject called psychology that so intrigued her.

She had read an article about an Austrian doctor, Sigmund Freud, whom they called the father of psychoanalysis. Dr. Freud believed that dreams spoke of what was going on in the mind. She wasn't sure if she believed it, for almost everyone thought dreams to be nothing but fancy. What with her dreams about Ian for the past few weeks, she hoped that Dr. Freud was indeed as well-meaning but misguided as his critics quoted in the article claimed. Yet she suspected that the doctor's theory was profound. That his idea of the unconscious, if she'd understood it at all, was correct. There were too many feelings that didn't seem to go away in the light of clear thought, and she couldn't be the only person to feel so. Look at Betsy, for example. No matter how much one tried to convince her that she was pretty, she just didn't seem to believe it. Or Louise. Louise had all that life could offer, yet she seemed to *need* to gossip and speak badly of others to feel better about herself. And even Papa. So often she had sensed that there was a whole other person inside Papa whom he never showed. Maybe she was just too introspective, maybe all of it was fancy, as Mamma and Daphne had suggested when she'd discussed the article with them. But Julia had only to look at the plays of Shakespeare, for weren't his plays about what Freud called unconscious motivations?

Julia lifted her novel again, but after reading the same sentence for the third time put it down. She was as restless this afternoon as she was fatigued; a most disconcerting combination. She had avoided thinking about Papa's casual announcement at luncheon that Ian would be coming to tea as well. While she had shown no outward reaction, inwardly her heart had jumped with anticipation and apprehension at the same time.

Sleep, which she used to take for granted, had become elusive. Night after night she would lie awake thinking of Ian, their kisses and touches. Each night she asked the Lord to relieve her of these sinful desires, but despite her prayers, in the dark of the night her mind would bring the image of Ian to her. When she awoke, already tired in the morning, he was the first of her thoughts. It was a violent crush, she repeated to herself in a litany. In time it would fade. Each time she thought of him, she would try to turn her thoughts to Percy. Most often she did not succeed.

"Stop it, Julia!" she whispered impatiently to herself. "You've got to stop it!" She knew that it was just a matter of will, and it pained her that for the first time in her life, her willpower seemed to fail her.

"Miss Julia," Annie, the parlor maid said, as she entered the room. "Mr. Ian Woods is at the door. He has brought something for Mr. Davenport. Would you like me to show him in?"

Julia gave herself a quick mental perusal. She was wearing a blue silk afternoon dress and as her hands felt the back of her head, she could tell that her hair was in order. "Certainly, show him in. And could you bring us some tea and refreshments, please?"

Julia pulled herself upright and smoothed her gown. Papa would be displeased if she had turned Ian away without a welcome, she told herself. But she knew that the surge of nervous energy that filled her had little to do with politeness. She wanted to see him. She had not anticipated that she would have a private moment alone with him. Suddenly she had the urge to apologize for the misunderstanding the other evening. To confess to her foolish and apparently successful attempt to paint herself as the kind of girl she wasn't. If they could clear the air, then perhaps they could become friends. If she could get to know Ian, the person behind the handsome face and appealing physique, then perhaps her silly crush would naturally dissipate.

"I hope that I'm not disturbing you, Julia," he said as he entered the room. "But I promised to deliver your father's portfolio, and after I spoke with him I discovered that I had to make a trip and would not be able to come for tea later." He glanced at the book that lay on the small table beside her. "I am disturbing your reading. Then I will just leave the portfolio with you and be on my way—"

"No. You're not. Honestly. I've tried to concentrate but I just don't feel like reading. Please, won't you have a cup of tea before you leave, unless you're too hurried, that is?" She didn't want to obligate him, especially after the other night. But in her heart she knew that she didn't want him to leave. All the anger she'd felt toward him, though less than she'd felt toward herself, had vanished and she was flooded with a deep pleasure at the possibility of being with him.

Ian knew that he shouldn't stay. The mere sight of Julia, the genuine, warm, artless expression that filled her beautiful face, the light that glowed from her bright blue eyes, called him to her, as if she were a calm harbor for his turmoil. "I would very much like to join you for a cup of tea. I don't have to catch my train for an hour and a half, actually." He turned to the door to assure that they were alone. He walked to a chair set just feet from the couch. "But first I must apologize for my inexcusable behavior the other night," he said softly.

Julia met his black eyes, which shone with atonement, and knew that however it embarrassed her, she must now acknowledge the truth of her own misleading talk. "It is I who owe you an apology." She forced herself to meet his eyes, even though she felt herself flush and felt her hands tremble. "I was so embarrassed for—"

"No. I think I already know what you're going to say and it isn't necessary. Truly." He sat and leaned toward her. "I meant to alleviate your discomfort, but instead led you to believe other than what I'd felt, and—"

"Ian, please. I need to confess and I do wish you'd let me speak! For it is very difficult to expose one's foolishness and false pride."

As she spoke in her soft lyrical voice, he saw that her color had heightened in obvious embarrassment. He smiled. "I'm sorry. I will let you say whatever you wish to, or I can see that we will soon be fighting about who owes whom an apology." He was pleased when she laughed in response. "You speak, then I will."

"Here's your tea, Miss Julia," the parlor maid said. She placed the silver tea service and plate of little cakes on the rosewood inlaid table before them. "Shall I pour?" Annie asked.

"No, thank you. That will be all, Annie."

"Fine, then. And Kathleen will be down in about five minutes. She said that she knew you wanted her to finish mending and was certain that you wouldn't mind."

Julia hid her smile. Dear Kathleen obviously wanted to give her some time alone with Ian. "No, that will be fine. Please tell her to join us whenever she's finished." Julia could tell from Annie's glance that the older woman wondered what Mamma would think about her receiving a gentleman guest unchaperoned, even if it was the familiar person of Mr. Woods. "Thank you,

Annie. I'll be just fine." Annie forced a smile, glanced at Ian again and left the room.

As soon as Annie was out of the room, Julia looked at Ian and found that she was unable to refrain from grinning. He laughed and smiled broadly in kind. "As you were saying, then?" he prompted her.

Julia took a deep breath. "I truly hope that we may become friends. I can't explain my behavior to you that night . . . when we . . . we sat on the park bench. But contrary to what I indicated later, it was not something I've done before, not in that way, I mean . . . Anyway, I'm sure I led you to believe from the way I acted and then spoke that I am different from how I really am." How difficult this was, Julia thought, as she stopped for a moment. His warm eyes that held only sympathetic attention made it the more difficult. For even as she spoke, she knew that she felt the same emotions that had so overwhelmed her that evening that she had boldly kissed him. "What I said about passion . . ." She had to look away, for she felt so naked. "They were words I was quoting from a silly novel I once read," she confessed, and laughed despite herself.

Ian's laughter halted her own. Was he laughing at her? She looked at him, and to her relief she realized that his laughter was as kind as the warmth radiating from his eyes. "So I do hope that we can put that behind us and be able to become true friends. For I have the feeling that there are many topics in which we have a common interest. Papa is more than fond of you, as you well know, and he is a wonderful judge of character. I also believe that you would like Percy, and

154

he you, as you get to know one another. So, do you accept my apology?'' It was out and she was done with it! Julia sighed with relief, which made Ian laugh again in response.

"No, I don't," Ian declared. He watched Julia's expression change to alarm as her eyes widened. "I don't because it is I who owe you an apology. I behaved like a callow youth. You are what? Twenty-three?" Julia nodded with a confused look. "But I will be thirty-one years old this summer. I said inexcusable things to you. May I light my pipe?"

"Of course," Julia answered quietly. Ian's eyes held a deep and almost mournful expression and she sensed that it was equally difficult for him to reveal himself to her. How she wanted to know him!

"I think that in these brief private moments I would like to tell you some things about myself that I usually don't speak about. In fact, I never do. . . . I'm not even certain where to begin. But I'm afraid that I'd better plunge into the most relevant facts first. I'm almost certain you've heard stories about me that make me sound like a cad of sorts."

Julia nodded. "I have heard stories."

He was struck once again by her forthrightness. For he had expected her to plead polite denial. "In some cases, perhaps I have behaved badly. In others, merely unconventionally by society's standards, which are not always my own. My devotion, my passion if you will," he said, having to smile as she reacted to the word that had passed between them so intimately, "is for my work. That you have surmised. But I am only human.

155

Still, a mutuality, perhaps, exists between us." He thought the words "magnetism," "passion," "lust" and "love," but dared not utter them, for both their sakes.

"I think I know what you mean and I feel it too," Julia said. She saw him fighting a battle within himself and wanted to help him for both of them.

"Good, thank you." He glanced to the door, then back to her. "Our moments of intimacy," he said, his soft voice diminishing to almost a whisper, "were very real and meaningful. But since I cannot offer myself to you the way an honorable man would be more than proud to do, I ask for your forgiveness and understanding, if that is possible. And I do offer a genuine pledge of friendship. I find myself most intrigued, wanting to learn of your thoughts and attitudes about life and . . ." He sighed, then puffed on his pipe. "I'm afraid I'm sounding pretentious. I'm trying to say, rather badly, that I'd like to have the pleasure of getting to know you. I have many acquaintances but few friends." He laughed sardonically. "I believe I truly need a good friend."

His coal-black eyes darkened as if he were fighting back tears. Indeed, he looked so like a lost, lonely little boy that Julia felt her heart go out to him. She reached out her hand and watched as he hesitated, but then reached and clasped it. He held her hand tightly and Julia felt her eyes fill as she smiled.

The tenderness of her smile and the tears that filled her eyes frightened him, for suddenly Ian felt the strongest urge to cry. He hadn't cried in years, and the surge of feelings he felt for Julia were overpowering.

"I am your friend and you are mine," she said. "Would you like to take the knife and become blood brothers, as best friends did when we were children?"

Ian laughed, knowing she was teasing him to lighten the intensity of what had transpired between them. She withdrew her hand and leaned toward the tea service.

"Allow me," he offered. "It's better for your ankle if you don't move about."

"Nonsense. I'm tired of feeling like an invalid. I can certainly pour the tea. Tell me about your trip, why don't you?" His hearty laugh made her look at his face.

"I'm sorry. But that's the *one* subject I can't talk about. Other than to say I have to go to Boston and may not be back in time for Daphne's engagement party tomorrow evening. However, Mother and Flo will be attending, and I do hope you will explain to Daphne that had I been able to arrange my trip at any other time, I surely would have. I hope she will forgive me."

"Daphne will be disappointed, but she will understand. She is a very sweet girl."

"And I flatter myself a bit, for she will be so busy that she probably won't have a moment to notice my absence anyway."

"You're probably right," Julia agreed, and they laughed again. It pleased her how easily they laughed together. She handed him his tea and he reached forward and ate a biscuit. Then he reached for another. "Why do I have the feeling that you have not had luncheon?"

"Because I haven't," he answered, and grinned.

GILDED HEARTS

"And I'm suddenly hungry." His grin, like that of a mischievous boy, amused and pleased her. There were so many aspects to this complex man.

"Then put that cake down and I will have Cook fix you a proper meal—"

"No, I couldn't impose and this is quite—"

"If I could jump up, I would pull it from your hand, but I can't, so you'll have to obey me, Mr. Woods!"

"Good day, Mr. Woods," a smiling Kathleen called from the doorway.

"Kathleen, I'm so glad you've come down. Would you please do me a favor and ask Cook to fix Mr. Woods a proper lunch. He hasn't eaten and will make himself sick on these sweets."

"Certainly, Miss Julia. And would you like some coffee as well, Mr. Woods?"

"Really, Kathleen, none of this is necessary," Ian insisted. Julia's stern, motherly expression made him laugh. He was starved and realized that he might as well acquiesce gracefully. "Yes, that sounds wonderful. And please tell Cook that whatever happens to be around will suit me just fine."

"I will, but she won't hear of it, I warn you," Kathleen said, and chuckled. "I'll be back with your luncheon in a few minutes, Mr. Woods."

"Thank you very much, Kathleen," Ian answered. "She's lovely, isn't she?" he said to Julia after Kathleen hurried out.

"She's more than that. She's wonderful, and a real friend to me. I love her very much."

"I can see that she feels the same about you. It's easy to see the difference when a servant is treated as an

158

object rather than a person and responds in polite deference because she has to keep the job."

"I of course know that Kathleen works for us, but I can't think of her as a servant. The very word makes me feel funny. The idea of people being seen as less because of class and circumstance, when they may truly be so wise and loving and . . ." Julia felt silly. She'd voiced this sentiment before and it had been responded to with puzzlement or impatience. Even Betsy, who usually understood her, had become uncharacteristically defensive.

"I know what you mean. I've always felt vaguely uncomfortable at being waited on. In Paris and Chicago, living on my own was a blessed relief even if it meant tending to my own needs. Now, of course, living again at home, I have the attention of all the servants, but fortunately, as a man I am not required to have a butler as you are required to have a maid to chaperone you."

"Oh, how I envy you, as much as I love Kathleen! Sometimes I fantasize how it must be to just go off alone, shopping or for a stroll or wherever one wishes to go. It's only in the country that I can do so. Which is perhaps one of the reasons I so treasure our time in Lenox, when I can ride in glorious solitude or take a walk through the gardens or in the woods. I have often wondered why we are allowed to go off for a ride with a male friend or beau in the country, while in the city they seem to worry . . ." Julia caught herself and felt embarrassed. For indeed, what she'd intended to discuss so innocently held suggestions of their unlicensed intimacies.

159

Ian debated whether to change the subject. But if he and Julia were to overcome their uneasiness with one another, they could not constantly have to worry about the possibility of a subject that naturally alluded to the intimacy they had shared. "You are embarrassed needlessly. What you were going to say is that you've wondered why a girl's virtue was at lesser risk in the country. I too have wondered about the logic behind this assumption. All I can assume is that the common wisdom suggests that the rigorous activities one participates in, such as riding and hiking, suggest the diminution of other . . . eh, energies, shall we say?" Ian grinned.

"Now who's being evasive?" Julia's easy laugh shocked her as much as her outspokenness. "You mean passion, don't you?" Her voice had automatically modulated to a whisper.

"Yes." Ian was surprised but pleased with her catching him. "Passion is what I meant, and I think we should change the subject!" he whispered back.

"What is so funny?" Kathleen asked as she entered the room with Ian's lunch on a tray and found Julia and Ian giggling like children. Kathleen was sorry that she had asked, but neither seemed to mind.

"We were speaking of exercise," Ian told her with a wide grin. But Julia's rising blush suggested that the conversation was more personal than that. Despite her desire to see Julia and Ian happy together, Kathleen sensed that she had left them alone quite long enough. If Mrs. Davenport knew how long, she would be furious. However, Kathleen suspected that Julia wasn't going to mention it to her mother. Kathleen tried not to grin, but she couldn't help herself.

"And what are you grinning about like a sly cat?" Julia asked.

"Oh, nothing. Just a private joke of my own. . . . I've got my knitting basket up in my room. I'm going to get it and then I'll be down," Kathleen said. She smiled at Ian. As she turned from him to Julia, she gave Julia a quick wink and then strode from the room.

By the time she returned, Kathleen saw that their conversation had taken a turn. She listened a bit as Ian explained his disappointment today. Kathleen didn't understand a lot of the words he used, such as "commission" and "skyscraper." Moreover, she'd never felt comfortable eavesdropping on Julia's conversations. She sat in a large gold chair by the window, across the long room. Before long, Kathleen was knitting and comfortably lost in her own thoughts.

"I understand your disappointment, Ian. But I also understand Ned's point of view. Perhaps you have not explained it carefully enough. Or I have just missed understanding why designing an estate in Newport would *so* compromise your principles," Julia said. "Perhaps it's a subject a woman can't understand very well?" she added.

"Why did you say that?" Ian asked, frowning. "Do you believe that your mind does not conceptualize as well as a man's?"

Julia found herself flustered. She had made that remark by second nature. Did she believe so? . . . No, not really. Some men were smarter, most better edu-

161

cated, but surely someone like Betsy thought as clearly and quickly as any man she had known. And herself? Was she not blessed with a quick mind and cursed, in effect, by a troubling introspection? She had been gazing across the room at the mantelpiece of the fireplace. She returned her eyes to Ian's face. He was waiting patiently for her to gather her thoughts and speak. The only other man who had treated her in such a manner, as if it were worth the wait to hear what she thought, rather than jumping in with another thought, was Papa. "I don't believe it, although almost everyone does. There are bright, capable women as well as men. Obviously there are those of both sexes who are quite stupid." Julia laughed with relief at Ian's responsive smile at her bluntness.

"When I was working as an apprentice in Chicago, there was a young woman, younger than myself in fact, who was also an apprentice. She was as good as the best of us, and better than most."

"Really?" Julia was intrigued. Although she knew that there were some women doctors and women in other professions, they were not within her society. She remembered how fascinated she had been, and proud, when she had been twelve or thirteen and Nellie Bly, a reporter for the New York *World,* traveled alone on a round-the-world trip. Julia could hardly wait for each report that had appeared in the paper over those two and a half months. Miss Bly had succeeded in breaking the record she'd set out to beat, that of the time in Jules Verne's fictional journey in *Around the World in Eighty Days.* If Julia remembered correctly, Nelly Bly had made the trip in seventy-two days.

GILDED HEARTS

Julia repeated her thoughts to Ian and was delighted when he responded with excitement and told her that Nelly Bly had been one of his heroes, or he guessed the word was heroines; that he had met her shortly after her return at a party given by a college friend's father who was editor-in-chief at the *World*. Julia made him recall every bit of conversation with her that he could, although it had taken place almost ten years ago.

Sitting with her knees pulled to her chest, Julia leaned her head against her arms and sighed. "Oh, how I wish I could *do something* in life. Do something *more* than just being somebody's wife and mother. Be more than an 'heiress' and an 'ornament' or whatever!"

Ian looked at her sharply. "Is that how you see yourself?"

"Isn't that how I'm *seen* and therefore *am!*" Julia was more shocked at the intensity of feeling that her voice carried than her statement itself.

"It *is* how you are *seen*. I agree. Not just you, but all girls, all women of society. Only those of the working class lack the 'luxury' of wasting their lives idling on a marble pedestal. Of course there are those women in our society who have jumped off or who have been tossed off for all kinds of circumstances. Some have gone on to productive lives, often in Europe. Others have come to less fortunate ends."

Julia felt as if she understood only half of what Ian was saying, yet as she listened, she found herself eager to absorb each word, as if she were a starving child presented with morsels of bread.

Ian stopped for a moment and gazed into her bright wide eyes and animated, intent face. Was he stepping out of bounds? For he could see that he was awakening another passion that had lain dormant within her. Hadn't he done her enough harm by already awakening the first? Yet, how could he not respond with all he had learned, for there were so few like *themselves* in their society. He needed for her to awaken as much as she wanted to. "I have diverged from my point, and since it is such an important one, let me get back to it. I agreed with you about how you are *seen*. But that is not who you *are*, nor especially who you might *be*."

Why did she suddenly feel frightened of what he was to reveal to her, yet as eager to know it as she had ever been to know anything else in her life? How extraordinary this moment was, she realized as a part of herself viewed them from a distance. "I don't know that I understand . . ."

"But you do," Ian insisted, leaning toward her. "That's why there is fear and excitement on your face. You see, you have always known, deep inside, that you could be more. That you *were* more than a decoration for some man's arm—I speak bluntly, not to flatter you at this moment, but to be very honest. You are blessed with great physical beauty. You know, for any mirror tells you so, as do the admiration and attention you receive from men and women alike. At first I jumped to the erroneous conclusion that you, like other beauties, lived in and through your allure. But there was something about you, even that night at Clarice's wedding dinner—an insecurity, if you will—that suggested a much deeper person. Then, when your father brought me to your studio and I saw your paintings, then I knew for certain. All you would not reveal in public was said in your work. My awareness of it so frightened you that you lied about your self-portrait."

Julia laughed as she felt the heat rise to her cheeks. Why she had so foolishly lied had never made sense to her; now she understood. "Yes, I didn't even know why at the time. I just had to, and I pride myself upon my veracity, most of the time anyway."

Ian's gaze was so full of sympathy and emotion, his eyes bright and jeweled black, that she felt wrapped in a strange warmth and understanding that she'd never experienced. She wanted to speak but didn't know what to say. It seemed that her words were not necessary.

"So you see, Julia, the reason you listened to me talk about my dreams of building skyscrapers, creating something new and purposeful, yet a true work of art as well, with such true sympathy, was not that you are a polite, caring person, which of course you are . . . but that my goals and dreams struck a chord in you, perhaps an unrecognized chord until this conversation, but a strong chord just the same. I saw the passion, and please don't blush, because this is too serious a conversation for us to veer to . . . well, you know. I saw that passion in the highest, most profound sense, in your self-portrait that afternoon. Just as I see it radiating from your eyes at this very moment. Your gift in painting and your passion for it are no different from mine for architecture. What is difficult for you—far more so than it is for me—is to openly recognize who you really *are* and could become, and then act upon it."

The striking of the grandfather's clock startled them,

so intensely lost in their conversation had they been. They both turned to look at the time.

"Oh, goodness! Your train. I can't believe we've been talking for over an hour. You must hurry if you're going to catch it."

Ian had already risen. It was so hard for him to tear himself away from her! He reached out for her hand and felt the shock that passed between them. Quickly, for both their sakes, he hardened himself. "Please, excuse me for running this way. But I can't miss this train." Kathleen appeared with his overcoat, which he quickly put on.

Julia felt herself moved to tears at his departure but tried to disguise her sentiments with a bright smile. "Kathleen," she said. "Please tell the driver to be ready to take Mr. Woods to Grand Central Station at once."

Kathleen scurried out of the room without a wasted word. Ian, his back to Julia, reached for his leather case. "Ian?" Julia called.

"Yes?" He smiled but Julia could see that he was already distracted. The sudden distance saddened her, even as she told herself she was being silly. "May we talk again sometime, about all of this?" she asked shyly.

He wanted to take her in his arms and kiss her. Instead he smiled. "We'll talk again. That I promise you."

Why did his almost brotherly smile disappoint her as much as his words comforted? "Hurry off, then. And I hope that your trip accomplishes what you wish."

"Good-bye, Julia," he called from the doorway. "And thanks for everything."

Hurry back to me, was what she wanted to say, but didn't. She forced a bright smile, which proved unnecessary, for he didn't turn around. She listened until she no longer heard his footsteps on the marble hallway. She sipped at her tea, for her mouth was terribly dry. Kathleen reentered the room.

"He's on his way. I certainly hope he makes it to the station in time. Miss Julia, are you all right?"

"I'm fine, Kathleen. Why do you ask?"

"Oh, I don't know. It's just that you had the strangest look in your eye . . . It's gone now. Perhaps I just imagined it, with the sunlight shining behind you."

"I'm sure that's it. . . . Kathleen, could you ask James if he would do me a favor and carry me up to the studio? Oh, I *hate* having to be carried around. I can't wait until next Wednesday when this stupid bandage comes off and I can walk as I please again!"

"Oh, I know how much you hate it, but Wednesday will come sooner than you think. I'll get James. But are you sure you want to go to your studio? You'll have to be down for tea in less than an hour and you know how you hate to be torn away once you begin painting."

"That's true, but I'm not going to start any work. I just want to sit up there and think."

Kathleen studied Julia. Once again she had the oddest expression in her eyes. Like she was off someplace, far away. Kathleen remembered that her father used to have that expression in his eyes sometimes. When she was little she'd asked her Mamma about it.

Mamma had said it was something special about the Irish. That when their souls became too weighty with earthly worries, they took a trip back to the green rolling hills of Ireland like rich people took a holiday. Well, Mamma was very wise in matters about the heart and spirit, but Mamma had been wrong about one thing, Kathleen thought as she studied Julia. It wasn't just a gift of the Irish after all. Julia, who traveled whenever she liked to, anyplace she wanted to go, had that same expression in her eyes that Kathleen had so often seen in her Papa's. Kathleen wondered where Julia's soul was off to. Perhaps Ireland? Someplace . . . Kathleen caught herself. She had no time for such fancy, and thinking of her dead Mamma and Papa made her sad. "I'll get James right away," she said, but Julia didn't seem to hear her.

Chapter Ten

IT FELT TO JULIA THAT THE DANCING SHE WAS FORCED TO watch from the damask couch in the ballroom had been going on for hours. She stifled a yawn and was glancing at the multitude of guests dressed in their finest evening clothes when Mamma approached and sat beside her. It would have been impossible for anyone to imagine that Mamma had been in a state of tearful frenzy all afternoon, for she looked rested and elegantly lovely in her lace-trimmed green silk gown. Mamma's choice of the ruby pendant and matching earrings Papa had given her for last year's birthday was perfect, as always.

"How are you feeling, dear? You look a bit peaked to me."

"I feel fine, Mamma. It's just this endless sitting that tires me." Julia didn't wish her to know that she had lain awake until dawn this morning, thinking.

Mamma patted her shoulder. "I know, dear. But it will be all over on Wednesday. By next Sunday evening, at the Livingstons' New Year's party, you'll be waltzing the night away as usual. . . . Where has Percy gone to?"

"He's dancing with Mary Hoffman." Mamma's frown made her laugh. "Don't worry, Mamma. I don't think she's stolen him away from me yet."

"Joke about it if you like, but I don't trust that girl. It's bad enough that she's taken up with Ian Woods. It's disgraceful the way she blatantly throws herself at him—I've not missed it." Mamma looked around, seemingly to ascertain that no one was within earshot. "That young woman thinks that she will land a husband with her large bosom," she whispered, "and that silly giggle of hers. And since Ian isn't in attendance, I've watched her attempt the same action with Percy since dinner."

"Oh, Mamma," Julia said, trying to reassure her, as silly as she was being. "You're being unkind. Mary is quite lovely and looks especially so tonight in her red gown. She and Percy have been friends since they were children. There's nothing more to it. Besides, I thought you didn't 'approve' of Ian, although you try to hide it for Papa's sake."

"I *don't* approve of him. I'm not speaking of his professional abilities, for I know nothing about architecture, nor do I wish to. It's true that his background is impeccable, but even the finest of families have been cursed with a black sheep. I just think that if he's going to take up with anyone, it is *just as well* that she is Mary Hoffman. For she is as shrewd a young girl as she is wealthy. And with a shady reputation like her own, she is obviously not some naive young lady who is being taken advantage of by—"

170

"Really! Why do you so believe all the gossip you hear?" Julia tried not to allow her annoyance to rile her, but she couldn't just listen to all this tripe and keep her silence.

"Julia. I realize that you are twenty-three years old, but you are an innocent, well-bred girl and don't understand—*fortunately,* I must say—anything about such matters. I have *also* noticed that you have not been paying the kind of attention to Percy that you should be. Especially last night. He is a fine young man, but still he is a *man.* I tell you that even with the allure of your beauty and sparkling personality, his head can still be turned by a girl who knows how to flatter him, stroke his feathers, make him feel as if he were the most charming, handsomest, cleverest man on earth. Mary has learned that lesson well."

Julia burst into laughter.

"You may laugh now if it amuses you, but I know what I'm saying. Someday you will too. For *once* listen to your Mamma, who wants only the best for you."

Her expression was so serious, her tone so earnest, that Julia's laughter and anger died. She knew Mamma meant well. "I'll think about it, I promise." Julia wished to change the subject. "The room looks very beautiful."

Mamma's face lit and she glanced about. "Do you really think so? For a moment the other day, I wasn't sure that I'd made the correct decision about the poinsettia plants and Christmas tree. But I do think that the scarlet leaves and yellow flowers of the poinsettias work wonderfully with the scarlet and gold ribbons on the spruce."

Julia's eyes followed Mamma's to the tall Christmas tree that stood against the back gilded wall, almost reaching to the Venetian, high ceiling. Behind the tree, through the arched windows, Julia caught a glimpse of the lighted garden covered with a thin layer of newly fallen snow. "I think it looks wonderful and everyone seems to be having a swell time."

"Oh, I hope so!" Mamma smiled with gratification. "And please don't use those slang expressions. It's unbecoming."

Julia laughed. "Everyone says 'swell' these days. But I'll try to speak properly if it makes you happy." Julia's broad grin made Mamma smile despite herself.

"Oh, there are the Johnstons! I don't think I've said more than a hello to them all evening."

The thought of idle polite conversation with people she hardly knew, when she was so weary, held little appeal to Julia. "Why don't you go over to them. I really am tired and Percy will be back in a moment, I'm sure. He's probably still dancing with Mary because he doesn't want to interrupt our chat," Julia added, knowing that would do the trick.

"I hate to leave you sitting alone, but if you're certain? . . . " Mamma answered as she rose. Julia watched her glance at Mary flirting with Percy as they waltzed past them. "I think you might be using good sense for a change," Mamma answered. With that she leaned over and kissed her on her cheek. "Sometimes it's so tiring being a hostess." Mamma sighed.

Julia refrained from chuckling until Mamma crossed the room. Her chuckle turned into a genuinely warm smile as Daphne danced by with Harold. Daphne, glowing in her yellow silk gown that radiated the gold flecks in her shiny brown hair and bright eyes, looked so very happy tonight. For despite her last-minute bout of nerves about the evening, Daphne seemed to have relaxed and was apparently enjoying her own party. She was most obviously as madly in love with Harold as he was with her. Wishing that she felt the same way about Percy, Julia again vowed to herself, as she had done as dawn broke this morning, that she would learn to. She thought of Mamma's warning about Mary, but as she watched Mary and Percy dancing, she felt no sting of jealousy. She had felt more than a sting at Clarice's wedding ball when she'd seen Mary in Ian's arms, just as she had the night of the skating party. But those feelings she'd had no right to.

After Ian had left to catch his train yesterday, she'd sat in her studio for an hour, thinking long and hard. It had taken her awhile to recall their entire conversation and find her way through all the doors he had opened and shut, all the sensations and thoughts he'd evoked within her. While he had acknowledged that their attraction had been mutual, he'd told her that all he had to offer her was his friendship. At first she'd tried to believe that he neither wanted nor offered any deeper hopes. For he was courting Mary, wasn't he? But although she'd professed sympathy for Mary to Mamma, in truth she suspected that Mamma's evaluation of Mary was correct. She'd heard gossip about Mary's tendencies to allow men to take far greater "liberties" than were proper, from friends who lacked the inclination toward idle gossip. She wished she could believe Ian too "noble" to take advantage of such a situation, but men were different on that account, she'd long been told. Regardless of his relationship with Mary, Ian *had* offered her a pledge of friendship she believed to be most sincere. For all their sakes, Julia had come to the conclusion that friendship was all that could ever exist between them. Only with this acceptance would she be able to find peace within herself and commit herself to being the wife Percy deserved.

She was more than fortunate to have such a fine man as Percy in love with her. And she did *love* him. The feelings that Ian evoked within her were different. They were so fiery and unsettling that surely they were not the building blocks upon which a lifelong marriage could be constructed. He had awakened a passion within her she hadn't known existed. And he had offered a channel for some of those passions that she'd never allowed herself to seriously consider. She had taken a cold, objective view of her paintings that afternoon. Perhaps she *was* blessed with a genuine talent. The possibility that her art could become more than a personal outlet had frightened her as deeply as the sensual aspects of her nature that he had brought to light. To contemplate declaring herself serious even to herself was more than she could consider at the moment. She had been relieved when Percy appeared and carried her down to the family drawing room. From that moment, until Papa carried her back to her room at midnight, she'd tried to push all thoughts of Ian and their talk from her mind.

Ned and Betsy had already arrived for tea, as had Harold. Mamma and Daphne had returned from their shopping trip earlier. When Papa returned, Julia told him of Ian's visit and extended his apologies to Mamma and Daphne. Percy, upon learning that Ian might not return from his trip to Boston in time for tomorrow night's engagement party, offered to bring Mary Hoffman along with him and to see her home if Ian didn't arrive later that night. Despite Mamma's surreptitious glance of disapproval, Julia appreciated Percy's characteristic thoughtfulness.

Tea had turned into dinner and then into songs and games in the music room. Julia forced herself into a gaiety she didn't feel, and if her attempt was less than successful, she saw everyone attribute it to her injury. She flung herself into the parlor games to prevent her mind from drifting to Ian. She truly enjoyed Betsy's brief piano recital—though certainly not more than Ned seemed to, for he was aglow as he watched Betsy play. But then, he had shone each time he glanced at Betsy all evening. Betsy had returned the same affection in her own shier manner. Julia was certain they would soon become engaged.

Despite her finest efforts, Julia hadn't been able to dispel her feeling of loss at Ian's absence. Papa had slipped over to her, a look of concern in his eyes belying his bright smile, and asked if she were feeling well. She told him that she was filled with lassitude due to her lack of activity. When he commented that it was a shame personal business had taken Ian away, Julia smiled and agreed so neutrally that Papa hadn't been able to disguise his puzzled expression.

Even now, as she sat alone, momentarily and appreciatively watching the activity in the ballroom, she found herself longing for Ian's conversation. Never had she experienced such a deeply personal talk with a man. She reminded herself that what she must do was attempt to speak equally openly with Percy. For he was not a shallow man and if she allowed him to know her true self better, there was no reason why she couldn't share matters of the heart, soul and mind with him. Percy offered her a good life. A secure, happy, protected life. The life she was expected to have—that she wished to have.

"Julia," Betsy said, sitting down beside her. "I know I told you before, but I've got to say it again. Even sitting so quietly, you are, as usual, the most beautiful girl in the room!"

Julia laughed at Betsy's earnestness. "Oh, Betsy. You're just prejudiced. I bet Ned would never agree with that at all!" Betsy's embarrassed flush made her laugh harder. "Nor would Harold. Don't you think that Daphne has never looked more lovely?"

"Yes, I do. She glows, she really does. But that doesn't change what I said. You look like a pink confection!" Betsy declared. "Mr. Worth should pay *you* to wear his gowns. And I truly love the effect of the blue silk forget-me-nots strewn against the pale pink chiffon. As if that weren't enough, the touches of pink lace and satin—honestly! I've never seen a lovelier dress."

"Thank you again, and I will pass the compliments to Mr. Worth. You're welcome to borrow it whenever you like."

"Do you think I'd let myself be compared in a dress that you've worn? You're my best friend, Julia, but even I have my vanity."

"And will that vanity allow you to admit for *once* that you look beautiful!" Julia challenged.

Betsy stared at her seriously. "Well, I'll go as far as 'pretty.' How's that?"

Julia poked her. "It's a start, you silly girl!" As they both began to giggle, Julia felt her sadness lift. "And are you and Mr. Ned Barrington having a terrific time?"

"Oh, we are." Betsy leaned closer. "He says he has something serious he wants to speak with me about at the end of the week," she whispered.

"And I wonder what that might be," Julia teased. "I can remember, just a few short weeks ago, the girl who sat across from me after Christmas shopping and proclaimed that no man would ever love her," Julia whispered. "Whatever did happen to her, I wonder."

"Oh, Julia. Isn't love wonderful!" Betsy exclaimed. "Isn't it wonderful that we're all in love. You, Daphne . . . and, eh . . . yes! Even I! And I think Mary Hoffman is too. I was talking with her awhile ago and . . ." Betsy stopped and stared at her. "Why do you have that peculiar expression? . . . Oh, Julia, you're jealous! You thought I meant that Mary was in love with Percy, didn't you!" Betsy began to laugh but then grew serious again. "No, you didn't think that, did you?" she questioned sharply.

Julia had hoped that Betsy's uncharacteristic euphoria would make her less observant, but it hadn't, though

Julia had tried to hide her feelings. But she should have known better, for Betsy was one of the few people she could not easily fool.

"Julia, what's wrong?"

"Nothing, Betsy, really. You were right the first time. I became jealous because I thought you meant Percy. For Percy *insisted* that he bring Mary to the party whether or not Ian came, and—"

"I may be behaving a bit flighty tonight, but you're no longer fooling me for a moment!" Betsy frowned. "In fact, I'm angry that you'd even try," she said softly. "I thought you trusted me."

Julia put her arm around Betsy's shoulder. "Of course I trust you, and really, nothing's wrong. I'm just out of sorts because I hate having to sit here and watch everyone else dance." Julia felt Betsy's shoulder stiffen. She glanced across the room and saw Percy heading their way. If Betsy suggested anything to arouse Percy's concern, it would just make matters worse. Julia retained her smile but quickly whispered, "You're right, Betsy. I do need to talk to you, but now isn't the time. For tonight just pretend that everything's fine, because Percy's walking over."

Betsy nodded with a concerned, puzzled expression and then quickly rearranged her face into a bright smile.

"Hi, girls!" Percy said. "Have you two been talking so seriously again?" he asked.

"Oh, we were just trading girlish secrets that are none of your concern, Percy Martin," Betsy answered in a teasing tone.

"And might the secrets have been about a certain

178

very handsome architect?" Percy asked. He stared at Julia, who forced herself to continue to smile as her throat tightened. Finally she realized that he was talking about Ned, not Ian! She was losing control under the continued strain, to have jumped to such a conclusion! Percy turned to Betsy, much to Julia's relief.

"Could be, or maybe not. We certainly won't tell *you*, will we, Julia?" Betsy teased. Betsy, who claimed that she couldn't make social conversation, was bantering with ease. It was all due to being in love, Julia thought.

"Are you going to dance all night with Mary, Perce?" Julia said in a pretended jealous tone, then gave him her brightest smile.

Percy did seem to react like a proud rooster, just as Mamma had suggested, Julia thought, hiding her grin of devious satisfaction. "Move over, Betsy, please," he asked, and sat between them. "There! I'm sitting between the two prettiest girls in the room and one of them's my very own!" He threw his arm around both of their shoulders as Betsy giggled and Ned approached.

"I got here just in the nick of time, I can see," Ned joked. "One lovely lady is not sufficient for you, Mr. Martin?" he said in jest. He reached for Betsy's hand. "May I have this dance, Miss Livingston?" he asked, and took a deep bow that made them all laugh.

"Why, certainly, Mr. Barrington," Betsy replied, allowing Ned to help her up.

"Have I been neglecting you, my dearest Julia?" Percy asked when they were alone.

He looked at her with such love that Julia was certain

she'd made the right decision this morning. "Just a bit. But I think it's very gallant of you to see that Mary is having a good time."

Percy frowned. "And I was hoping all the time to make you green with jealousy!"

"Oh, but you did! I'm just trying to hide it!"

Percy laughed happily. "You hide things too well, Julia."

"Where is Mary, anyway?" Julia asked, turning the conversation.

"I brought her back to Mrs. Woods and Flo. They're admiring the Christmas tree. . . . Actually, I think that if I am to behave as a truly gallant gentleman, I should ask Flo for another dance, for I'm afraid no one else will. I'll get Ned and Barry to do the same."

Julia gave him a genuine smile. "That's very kind of you. Flo is a nice girl. It's a shame that she's always overlooked."

"That's one of the things I love about you, Julia," Percy said softly, his expression serious. "Not many girls like yourself would think twice about a wallflower like Flo Woods. It's a shame that her brother has all the charm and looks, especially since those are assets more essential to a girl. . . . Mary is certainly taken with Ian. She was telling me tonight, hinting actually, that she expects Ian to ask for her hand. That he's given her reason to expect it. . . . Don't look quite so shocked," Percy said.

What had her countenance showed him? "I'm not shocked. It just seems rather premature, for they hardly know one another. Ian only came back to town about a month ago, and I just . . ."

"Are you telling me you don't believe in love at first sight?"

"Infatuation, a crush, maybe . . . but love is a weighty matter. True, enduring love, that is."

"Dang, I don't know. I fell in love with you on first sight, years ago. While you were still engaged to what's-his-name—no, don't remind me."

"I didn't know that." Julia was truly surprised

"Well, I couldn't show it. I mean, you were engaged and I was an honorable young man. But I was the happiest chap in the world when I learned you'd broken off with Robert . . . Ah, I gave myself away, for of course I remembered his name." Percy laughed.

"But you couldn't say that you actually *loved* me then, could you?" Julia knew that her questions had less to do with Percy than she was willing to admit to herself. "Wasn't it merely a crush?"

"No. Do you believe that Ned and Betsy are merely infatuated with one another?"

Julia was finding herself uncomfortably challenged. "Well, no, I mean . . . that first meeting, yes, but soon after that . . ."

"You told me yourself that evening that you believed they would wind up a couple, didn't you?"

"Yes . . . but I'm not sure I meant it in more than a hopeful way, and—"

"Julia!" Percy laughed and held her hand for a moment. "You're taking this entire conversation far too seriously. You've seemed so serious lately. So full of private thoughts that sometimes, when I look at you, I feel as if I don't quite know where you are or what you're feeling."

"Oh, Percy. I'm sorry. Have I been troublesome to you?"

"No, not at all. I just have to admit that I don't always understand you. To tell you the truth, I think you're a much deeper person than I. I just take life as it comes, while you . . . But it's one of the things I love about you." He leaned closer. "I sometimes think of you as my 'mystery lady,' " he whispered.

"Do you?" Julia answered with true astonishment. "Would you like to know what I'm thinking when you get that feeling?"

Percy grinned. "Not really. I like to think of you as my 'mystery lady.' "

Was he saying that he really didn't want to *know* her? "But, Percy—"

"Julia, dear." Julia looked up. Standing before her were Mrs. Woods and Flo.

Julia smiled warmly. "Hello again, Mrs. Woods. Flo. Are you enjoying yourselves?"

"Florence," Percy said. "We were just speaking of you. I was about to come over and ask if I might have the next dance. And the orchestra has just struck up another tune, so, may I?"

Florence blushed. "That would be very nice, thank you, Percy."

Mrs. Woods beamed. "Go on, then, the two of you. I used to be quite a dancer in my day, you know."

"And so you were, Josephine," Papa said as he joined them. "May I have the honor of this waltz with you?"

"And I shall sit with Julia," added Mary Hoffman, who seemed to come from nowhere.

GILDED HEARTS

"Julia, this party is wonderful!" Mary cooed as she sat down. "I thought for sure that I should have a lonesome time without Ian, for I can't *bear* to have him away from me. But I've hardly missed him. Promise me you won't tell!"

"Of course I wouldn't." Why did she think that Mary's seemingly innocent remark carried a deeper message? A subtle warning of sorts? "Even if I were someone to betray a confidence, I would hardly be in a position to do so with Ian."

"Oh, now, don't be modest. I know that you and Ian have become good friends. He's told me what a fine painter you are and how much he admires your talent. I think it's lovely that platonic friendships can exist between men and women, don't you?"

What was Mary getting at? "Of course. But Ian and I don't really know one another except through Papa's involvement with Ian and Ned." She gave Mary an easy smile.

"Yes, but he likes you. Don't be modest, for I am not jealous! I *shouldn't* tell you and you must cross your heart and *swear* that you will not tell a *soul!* Do you promise?" Mary didn't give her a chance to answer. "But I've heard said that you and Percy will probably soon become engaged. Well, I think that society will soon see *another* engagement as well!" Mary turned so that her mouth was against Julia's ear. "Ian's and mine! He has suggested such already, just the other night." She pulled away. "Are you happy for me, Julia?"

Why did Mary's smile appear a gloat? "Well, of course. I mean, I do hope that it all works out . . ."

"Admit it, Julia. If you weren't in love with Percy,

183

who is the most *wonderful* man in the world, you'd be jealous! For have you ever *seen* a more powerful, handsome man than Ian? And that moodiness of his . . ." Mary's mouth came to her ear again. "He is as *passionate* as all the heroes in those wonderful French novels!" Mary pulled away and smiled most wickedly. Then she giggled and her eyes widened in that false manner of hers. "Of course we've never gone beyond the bounds of propriety." Her voice lowered to a whisper. "And if we had, I certainly wouldn't admit it, for a girl has a reputation to protect, doesn't she?"

Julia tried to smile as Mary giggled. "I don't know what to say," Julia admitted more honestly than she'd meant to.

"Your eyes say it all. You are *such* an innocent, Julia, and I think that's *utterly* charming."

Julia felt her face flush and the anger rise within her.

"Julia, I'm not sure why, but you and I have never become close friends. But I hope to change that! Especially since it seems that we are *destined* to become intimates. What with Ian's business arrangement with your father and Ned. So I'm going to tell you our *first* secret, for close girl friends are allowed to share confidences, aren't they? But only if you *swear* never to tell anyone. Do you swear!"

"Yes!" Julia was befuddled. She didn't want to hear whatever it was Mary was about to say, but she'd found herself giving her word, when all she wished for was Mary's disappearance.

"I've got to make a telephone call to a certain man, who should have *just* arrived back in town. If he has, then I'm going to plead a sudden headache. And I'll need your help. For I must make sure that Mrs. Woods and Flo *remain* at the party and that Percy doesn't insist on seeing me home." Mary took a breath and continued in a whisper. "For I will not be going *home*. Ian and I have it all planned." Mary frowned. "Unless he couldn't catch the afternoon train. Do you promise to help me?"

Julia felt her stomach lurch. She might be naive, but what Mary was telling her was perfectly clear. Julia forced a smile that wouldn't give her hurt away. "I don't care for fabrications, so I won't lie for you. But I will try to get Percy to allow you to take a hansom, which I imagine is your intention?"

"That's swell, Julia. I knew I could count on you!" Mary rose. "I must hurry to the telephone. When I return it will be obvious to *only us* whether or not the party has arrived back in town." Mary gave her an intimate smile. The kind of smile that Julia would have naturally returned to Betsy or Daphne. She merely nodded, but Mary rushed off so quickly that she didn't seem to notice.

Julia felt sick at heart. Not only had Mary forced her to accept that she and Ian were "lovers," but Mary had forced her into unconscionable complicity! Mamma had been more than correct about Mary! But Julia knew that it was not Mary's scruples that upset her. She began to remember Ian's mouth upon her own, the feel of his cheek, the sweetness of his hot breath . . . No! She could *never* again think of those moments of intimacy. If she did it would drive her mad. Ian was a new friend and nothing more. Julia smiled with relief when she saw Percy approach.

Julia tried to concentrate as Percy, Mrs. Woods, Flo, Ned, and Betsy chattered. She was actually glad to see Mary when she returned with her brow knit and her hand held to her forehead. At least now the suspense was over. She almost marveled as she watched Mary both direct and star in her little play.

". . . What do you think, Julia?" Percy asked toward the climax.

What would Mary's face look like if she insisted that Percy see Mary home? But Julia knew the price of that moment's gratification would be to make Mary her enemy. She didn't give two straws about that, but she knew that Mary would be clever enough to venture a guess as to Julia's real motivation. *That* Julia didn't dare risk. "I think that I shall be very lonely without your company, Percy," she answered.

Both Mary and Percy smiled. She had made them both happy with one small lie. Had she made Ian happy too? Had Mary informed him of her role in their duplicity? Perhaps she'd misjudged Ian! For what kind of man would consent to allow her to become a party to his illicit affair! Even Mary remained innocent in the sense that she could not have known of the intimacies that had passed between Julia and Ian. The Ian she'd responded to yesterday did not seem the kind of man who could be so insensitive. Or so she had believed. Julia was grateful when the others walked Mary to the door and she was left alone to think. Perhaps Ian didn't know that Mary had involved her—

"Julia." Mary's reappearance startled her. Mary bent and kissed her on the cheek. "I just wanted to thank you. I made an excuse that I'd left my flowers on the couch. Ian thanks you too, though he'd be too shy to say so. I'm so glad that you and I are becoming the best of friends! Good night!"

As Mary dashed off, she took the last of Julia's hopes with her.

Chapter Eleven

Ian hadn't "tied one on" in a long time, but if there was a night for getting smashing drunk, tonight was more than appropriate. Shortly after eight his train had arrived at Grand Central Station, but Ian had walked home rather than call their driver or catch a hansom cab. Flo and Mother were already at the Davenports', as he'd assumed, so the house was empty except for the staff. He'd declined dinner, pretending he'd already dined. Then he'd secluded himself in the library, where he'd lit the fire, poured a stiff drink and watched the logs blaze as he swiftly finished one drink and went on to his second and third. Other than his bedroom, which Ian had stripped to a stark simplicity, the library was the only room in the mansion in which he could find comfort. He was pleased by the library, with Father's massive desk angled between the two walls of shelves holding leather-bound volumes ranging from Shakespeare and Dickens to Herbert Spencer and the works of Charles Darwin, as well as Ian's own recently added mass of art and architectural books. The room had not been altered since his father's death over twenty years ago. Sometimes Ian almost felt his father's presence, like a hovering force, as he sat at his father's desk late into the night. Ian had loved his father—idolized him. He wondered if he would have felt the same if his father had lived rather than died at the apex of his manhood.

Suddenly Ian heard a strange noise at the window. He rose a bit unsteadily and listened to the rapping sound. He drew back the heavy brown curtain and looked into the garden. But the light from the library's lamps caused him to see only his own reflection. He unlocked, then raised the window, for someone was out there. The possibility of its being a scoundrel fleetingly crossed his mind, for he recalled some conversations about the increase of crime in Manhattan—

"Ian . . ." the voice called in a petulant whisper. He recognized it at once as Mary's, but why would she be skulking in the garden? Automatically he looked to see if her maid were behind her, but she appeared to be alone.

"Mary?" he called out into the snowy night air.

"Shush!" she whispered.

"What are you doing out there?" he asked, finding himself whispering in compliance.

"Freezing to death, for one thing," she complained. "I've been trying to get your attention for what feels like an hour!"

"Why didn't you try ringing at the front door?" he asked with a laugh. Mary's hyperbole, which usually so irritated him, humored him at the moment.

"Must I stand out in the frigid air and freeze as I

explain, or will you let me in through the conservatory door?—for if I'd wanted to be announced I'd obviously have rung!"

Ian was amused by how much anger could be conveyed in a mere whisper. He wanted to tell her to go away. He'd had enough of the wiles and treacheries of the female species exposed to him today. But he was afraid that she'd make such a fuss that it was easier to just let her in and find out what charade she was performing. Besides, she did look rather pretty in her fur hat and cape, her muff drawn to her face. He guessed that her nose and cheeks were more than their normally rosy tint, for he'd been so lost in thought that she'd probably been trying to get his attention for a few minutes. "Come around, then . . . No, wait!" The image of what he was about to suggest made him chuckle. "Just come closer to the window and I'll lift you in."

"Careful, I think my cape is caught. Oh, I'm going to fall . . ." Mary protested as she awkwardly maintained her balance on the ledge and then tumbled into his arms. Ian laughed so hard that he almost lost his balance, for as enticing a red-haired little bundle as she was, grace was not her forte. "Ian! Have you been drinking? I can smell it on your breath and your eyes do look rather red and blurry!" she whispered. She straightened and pulled her hands from her muff.

Once again, rather than irritation, she evoked his mirth. He bowed and let her pass, he guessed correctly, to the warmth of the fireplace. "My apologies, my dear Mary. Had I known that you would appear at my window at almost . . . What?" He glanced at the face of the grandfather's clock. "Ten, is it? My, how time does fly when one has the pleasure of such stimulating company."

"Ian, you're drunk!" Mary complained as she pulled her hat off so impatiently that it caused the knot of her hair to undo itself and her crimson locks fell prettily down the back of her black cape. Mary started to unbutton her cape.

"Please, allow me," Ian said as he walked to her. Mary turned and waited. Ian reached easily over her shoulders to the top button, which was already open, and then to the second, which fell at the rise of her breasts. Teasingly he feigned difficulty. Her face was to the fire but he didn't doubt that her countenance matched his own sly grin, for as his fingers lingered, Mary's shoulders relaxed beneath his forearms. She tilted against him, subtly at first, then so completely that if he were to step back abruptly she would tumble. Feeling like a naughty boy, he had an impulse to do just that, but quickly rebuked himself. For silly, seductive Mary was not the object of his rage. It had been Betty, not she, who had used him so cruelly eight years ago.

He felt his mouth tighten as he remembered the truth he had finally extracted from Christine Cornell Barkley, Betty's older sister. Remembering Christine's taut face and embarrassed tears as she'd told him the story in obviously painful starts and stops, he knew, as he had known when she swore so, that Timothy was *not* his son. Nor was he John Hollis's. For all the while that Betty had professed her undying love to Ian, which he'd returned with the naive devotion of a smitten boy, Betty had been having a clandestine romance with a

191

married man. Who he was, Christine could not be entreated to reveal, other than that he'd been in their social circle. He supposed Christine had been correct—it all *was* ancient history.

"Ian . . ." He felt Mary's hand caress his cheek as she stood turned before him. "You were a million miles away and looked so terribly sad . . ." He held her cape. "Poor Ian." She stroked his cheek and then ran her fingers across his face. When Ian looked into her eyes, he saw that her usual artifice was gone. Her green eyes shone with genuine concern. His surprise caused him uncertainty. Mary stood on tiptoe and placed a gentle kiss on his lips. "How I wish I could make you smile," she said softly.

Ian stepped back and let the cape fall onto the ottoman. His eyes took her in for the first time. They started from the red curl in the middle of her forehead and slowly traced down her pretty face, along the curve of her neck to her soft pink bare shoulders and her full jutting breasts that rose against the constraints of her red velvet gown. He watched as she breathed deeply, narrowing her waist and causing the pink globes of her almost naked breasts to rise higher, begging for his touch. "Pretty dress," he said as he felt the lust rise within him. "Think I'll have another Scotch. Can I offer you something while you tell me what brought you here?" He walked to the highboy.

"I'll have a sherry, please," she said boldly. She didn't see his eyebrow arch. First she'd appeared at his window so furtively; now she was openly asking for an alcoholic drink, which a young lady did not do—not a proper young lady. But then, Mary had already allowed him liberties far more "shocking" than a proper young lady permitted. As he poured her wine, he remembered the night after the opera that she had placed his hand across the creamy mounds of her breasts and had boldly explored his mouth as his fingers moved beneath the fabric of her gown and played with her nipples, which hardened as she moaned into his mouth. Ian poured himself another Scotch. A stiff one.

When he turned, Mary was seated—"arranged" was the more apt description—against the corner of the damask couch. He didn't try to hide the glint that he suspected played in his eyes. Mary blushed but returned his bold stare as he approached. Her eyes fell from his face to his crotch and he slowed his pace as he felt himself harden and recalled the Parisian whores whose similar boldness had cost a pretty penny. He returned her lustful gaze by staring openly now at her breasts. The gaslamp, which stood on an end table beside her, made her breasts glow all the more rosily, and the thought occurred to him that the seductive backlighting was due to design rather than happenstance. In either case, its effect was not squandered.

"My lady," he said, and handed her the glass of sherry, which she accepted with a pretty smile and a steady hand. Only the swiftness of her swallow, as if she were drinking spring water, belied her composure. She patted the sofa seat beside her. Ian smiled and matched her drinking with a large gulp from his glass. He felt the sudden desire to toy with her as fully as his rapidly growing lust wanted to vanquish her. He smiled innocently and pretended to settle himself on the other side of the sofa. Her startled, disconcerted expression struck him so funny that he could not help but laugh drunkenly, yet, he was laughing at himself as much as at Mary.

"Ian—"

"No, my sweet . . . not yet." He heard the slur of his words and knew that another drop of alcohol would carry him past the point of ardor to drunken oblivion. "For you have aroused my curiosity as much as my— shall we say—attention." Mary giggled in response and extended her hand to him, which he refused. "Not until you tell me why you chose to enter through such an inconvenient passage. And tell me why you are not dancing the night away at Daphne's engagement party."

Mary, evidently feeling that two could play the same game, smiled slyly and daintily finished her sherry. She handed him the glass. "Another?" he asked with genuine surprise. She merely smiled and nodded. Ian shrugged and walked to the highboy.

"Have you dismissed the servants for the night?" she asked.

"Yes, except for the doorman and the parlor maid. But I told her that I did not wish to be disturbed." Ian saw Mary glance toward the library doors. "They're locked," he said. "Mother and Flo, even if they should soon return, know better than to bother me, for they do not care to incur my *wrath* should they inadvertently disturb me in the middle of my work."

He strolled back to the couch and the routine was repeated, although the alcohol was beginning to make him as groggy as he was aroused and titillated. "So unless someone else should knock at the window, we are quite alone." She smiled and took the glass of sherry from him. Ian reached down and stroked her cheek with the back of his hand, which he let drop to her bare shoulder. "Are you not afraid that I might choose to take advantage of you, here all alone, unchaperoned?"

Ian wasn't sure whether the manner in which she licked her lips with her tongue was a sign of hesitation or another studied effect. "I am certain that you would never behave as less than a gentleman," she replied in a playful tone. "Despite what all the others say about you."

He watched as she sipped, more slowly. This time he sat just inches from her. He smelled the sweet scent of her perfume that he usually disliked, but tonight the candied odor pleased him. In a graceful move, she fell into his arms, her breasts against his chest, her head against his neck. She drew his face to hers, his mouth to her mouth. As she nibbled at his lips, he pulled her onto his lap so that he could kiss her more easily. He felt his erection harden against her rounded buttocks. She traced his lips with her tongue but as his hand caressed the mound of her breast, she pulled away. His hand fell to her lap, meeting his other, which was slipped easily around her waist.

"I have a confession to make," Mary said.

"A confession?" he asked, teasing her with his voice as his hands teased her thighs. "I was merely hoping for an explanation of your strange, albeit most delightful arrival."

"Are you glad I came, then?" she asked with a shy smile. "Are you not angry at me for my boldness?"

He stroked her shoulder and neck, and despite the warmth of the roaring fire, he saw the goosebumps rise on her skin. "Do I seem angry?" The effects of the liquor and his ardor diminished his desire for conversation. For what did it matter how she connived to arrive at his window when her soft voluptuous body was against his now hard, hungry body? This time it was he who pulled her face to his and took her mouth with his own. When she pulled away again he felt the frustration rise within him. Obviously she'd come for exactly what they were doing, he defended against the niggling voice of his conscience. For as much as he did *not* love Mary, he desired her. Who wouldn't?

"Please, let me confess," she whispered as she ran her fingers across his mouth. "I was so terribly bored at the party because I *missed* you so. I called and asked for you. The servant who answered said you were indisposed, so I guessed that you were home sulking or losing yourself in your work." Her triumphant grin made him laugh. "I pleaded a headache, and here I am. Are you sorry?" She looked up at him with her big green eyes, so wide with the expression of a little girl confessing to having stolen a cookie from the jar that he felt a genuine surge of tenderness. Perhaps he had misjudged aspects of Mary's nature. "Well, tell me, are you?" The heightened color of her cheeks and her downcast eyes convinced him that she was genuinely suffering embarrassment for her impulsive behavior.

"I will not tell you." Her perplexed look made him laugh. "I thought that I should show you instead." Mary sighed with apparent relief and he caught her sigh as he pulled her mouth to his and kissed her in a long, lingering kiss that set the fires burning within him to a blazing pitch. He pulled her closer. As his tongue explored her mouth, his hand gently nudged her raised thighs farther apart, as he moved her so that he could almost feel the heat of her feminine core pressing against his throbbing hardness.

"Ian," she moaned. He withdrew his mouth from hers just long enough to lift her from his lap and raise her to a standing position. He rose and wordlessly pulled down the slide fastener on the back of her gown. The dress fell to the floor and he turned her so that she stood before him in her laced corset and petticoat.

The knocking at the door woke Ian and for a moment he was disoriented, thinking himself in his bedroom. As he lifted his head, a surge of painful dizziness struck him. When he saw Mary's startled face, he remembered and somehow forced himself to call out, to what he recognized to be his mother's voice, in an even tone, "Yes, Mother, what is it?" He quickly rose. A glance at the grandfather's clock told him it was almost midnight.

"I just wanted to be sure that you were all right, dear," she said through the thick door. "May I come in?"

The sight of Mary scrambling into her clothes was so comical that, despite his hangover, he had to use all his willpower to suppress a hearty laugh that would arouse his mother's suspicions. "I'm fine, Mother, but right in the middle of a rendering. Will you excuse my rudeness if I most abjectly apologize and ask if we may talk tomorrow morning?"

"I suppose so. . . . As long as you're at home and

well . . ." Ian could picture his mother's pursed mouth and mournful shaking head at her misfortune to have borne such an odd son.

"Say good night to Flo, then, too, please. I shall look forward to hearing all the details of the dinner and party in the morning. And thank you, Mother, for being so understanding."

"I *try,* son, I do." Ian knew that despite her words, she was most probably smiling.

Ian poured himself another drink. When he returned his attention to Mary, she was fully dressed and sat with a small mirror on her lap, fixing her hair. Neither spoke until the silence outside the door lingered.

"Do you think they've gone upstairs for the night?" Mary finally whispered, her hair already in a tidy upswept knot.

"I believe so. Besides, the walls are thick and everyone in the house is accustomed to hearing murmurs from me speaking to myself, eccentric that I am said to be," he said, only half-jesting. He sat beside her and kissed her cheek. "Say, I'm not sure that I'm straight enough to understand any conversation, or quite frankly, remember it in the morning, but how *did* you manage to leave the Davenports' unescorted? For I would have expected Charles or one of the young men, especially your friend Percy, to insist upon seeing you home."

"Oh, he did. Percy, I mean. Actually, it was sweet Julia who helped me."

Ian tried not to reveal how Julia's name and Mary's cryptic remark about her tore at him. "How so?" he asked in an offhand manner. Mary's hand caressed his own and he dared not offend her by pulling away, although he now desired her touch as little as earlier he'd lustfully reveled in it. Mary's hand rose to a lingering strand of hair on her neck. "Let me get you a glass of water, for I believe you've had all the sherry you need for tonight." Mary's appreciative smile made him feel worse. Already he regretted having given in to his sexual appetite. It would be so much more difficult to break with her now, yet that was still exactly what he intended to do. At least, to his groggy, vague recollection, she had not been a virgin—no, certainly not a virgin, as he remembered how her tongue had thrilled him with no instruction required. Through his blur he remembered her mouth so artfully taking him until he had pulled her beneath him again and taken her with a physical urgency that could not be delayed. But he wished to forget those temporal earthy moments, for just the evocation of Julia's name had made him feel that he had betrayed his lovely Julia. No! Not *his*. Not yet, anyway, he sharply reminded himself. "You were saying?" he asked Mary again in a desultory manner as he handed her the goblet of water. "Something about Julia helping you?"

Mary took the glass and sipped slowly as he tried to hide his impatience. "Oh, yes. You may not know it, but she and I are becoming the *best* of friends. She was forced to sit through the party, and since I didn't wish the company of the various men who asked me to dance, I spent a great deal of time with Julia—that is, when I wasn't paying proper attention to your mother and sister, as I knew you would want me to."

She could babble on endlessly. "I still don't understand how Julia helped you," he interrupted evenly and smiled to encourage her.

"Well, we began talking the way girls do. She told me how much she loved Percy and suggested that she would soon be announcing their engagement. She told me that I looked as if I, too, were in love and *begged* me to reveal with whom. When she *forced* it from me, and I said your name . . ." Mary blushed and lowered her eyes. "I guess Julia suspected all along. For she told me that she thought it was wonderful and that we were a *perfect* match! She said how lovely it was that the *right* persons always seemed to find one another. Then she blushed and looked embarrassed. Finally, once I *swore* that I wouldn't misinterpret what she was hesitant to say, she told me that although she found you terribly attractive, you were certainly not the kind of man she would *ever* consider marrying. She insisted that she meant no offense, but she admitted to being far more parochial than I. Although your reputation and 'strange' ideas fascinate her, as travel around the world does, they are too foreign and unorthodox for her taste."

Mary's words cut through him like a knife. How could he have *believed* that he and Julia had shared such a *mutual* empathy that transcended anything he had ever—

"Do you wish to hear what else she said? For your expression makes me think that I've badly explained her intent, which was *not* derogatory, truly! For as a friend she likes you with great sincerity and respect." Mary laughed kindly. "Oh, Ian, beneath that cool exterior of yours I've always suspected that you were so sensitive—too sensitive. For you look so stricken." Her laughter dissolved into contrition.

Dammit, he had given more of his reaction away, but how much?

"It *is* my fault," Mary insisted. "Julia meant no ill will and I have *already* done my new friend a disservice by my inadequate reporting! Shall I keep quiet, or do you wish for me to try to recall the rest of what she said?" Mary's perplexity would have moved him were he not numb.

"Go on," he answered with what he hoped was a detached air.

Mary sat silently for a moment, obviously thinking through her conversation with Julia to the point at which she'd left off in the retelling. She looked up at him finally with a puzzled expression. Then colored. "What does 'prepossession' mean?"

Ian had no difficulty guessing Julia's further disavowal of him, but he didn't let on. "In what context was it used?"

"She said she found you redoubtable, but insisted that her sensations were more a reflection on herself—her *prepossession* . . ."

"'Prepossession' means a fixed conception that's likely to make impossible objective judgment of anything that counters what one already believes in," he explained, as each word of his offhand definition struck like an ax at his hopes, which he hadn't fully admitted to himself, until Mary's recounting razed them.

"Thank you. I *do* intend to read more widely and improve my vocabulary," she answered with an eagerness to please. "You still appear upset, Ian, though you have no need to be. For Julia assured me that the two of you have enjoyed talking about subjects such as art. She said she hoped I didn't *misconstrue* your new friendship for more than it was. And, dearest"—she smiled prettily—"I can assure you that I am not at *all* jealous, I am very *modern* about such things. Besides, Percy and I are devoted friends. Why I *tried* to assuage his jeal—" Mary's hand flew to her mouth. "Oh, never mind. I have said far too much already!"

"You started to say 'jealousy,'" Ian said more sharply than he'd intended. "Go on and explain. What possible reason would Percy have to speak of jealousy in connection with me?"

"None! Which is exactly what I *tried* to explain to him when he told me that he felt you were playing a bit upon Julia's lack of worldliness, what with your unchaperoned visits she'd told him about. But Percy is a good egg! Once he understood that your visits with Julia were as *innocent* as his and mine, well, he actually apologized for his previous statement that he wished you'd stay away from Julia, since they were practically engaged. He even blushed! I didn't really understand his concern, for as I said, I am *very* modern about such things. So you may take that worried expression from your eyes. All is well. Julia is your friend, a true friend, and I don't want you to worry that I've misconstrued any of it!"

He finally found his voice again. "You are as perceptive as you are charming, Mary." She glowed in response. He regained his unwanted loss of composure. "But you still haven't told me how Julia helped you with tonight's surprise visit."

202

GILDED HEARTS

Mary smiled happily. "Actually, *she* planned the whole thing! I told her how *very much* I wished that I could see you. She suggested I call the house to see if you'd returned, and if so, plead a headache. She said she knew that Percy would insist upon seeing me home, but that she would pretend a fit of jealousy and *insist* that he just see me to a hansom. I *hate* to admit it, but I believe Julia is far more clever than I. For I would never have conceived of such a scheme on my own! I guess you have her to thank for our wonderful evening." Mary planted a kiss on his cheek and then fell into a gush of embarrassed giggles.

Ian felt his heart harden though he smiled with what he hoped was the proper effect. "That I do," he said, and stroked Mary's cheek. "And believe me, I will thank her, when the time is right—most discreetly, I assure you."

"Oh, good! For I feel guilty. You see, I promised *never* to tell you the truth! Julia said that you'd be *so* impressed with my cleverness that there was no need to admit that it was her scheme. But I guess I can't help but blabber the truth. That's just how I am."

"You're a sweet girl, Mary," he said sincerely. She might be irksome and silly, but she was so simple and open. Even when she tried artifice, she was not clever enough to carry it off, which made him smile at her more genuinely than he ever had. For he'd had his fill of bright, beguiling, treacherous women. After Betty, he'd thought he'd never fail to recognize another one, but he had. He'd taken Julia's Dresden-doll beauty, her quickness and display of talent, and created a girl who existed only in his imagination. At least with Mary

203

there were no surprises, other than the kind tonight, which had brought him the pleasure that she'd eradicated by her guileless revelation of the true Julia.

"Ian, you have done it again. Drifted off somewhere," Mary complained, but her tone was neither strident nor sullen.

"I'm sorry, my dear. I don't mean to do it and it was not a reflection on you—at least not a negative one." He thought quickly. "I was remembering the pleasure you gave me tonight," he whispered with an air of seduction he did not feel.

Mary climbed into his lap and threw her arms around him. She kissed him gently, then rested her head against his shoulder. "It was you who gave me great joy. A joy such as I have never *known,* but only dreamed of," she whispered.

Her apparent declaration of his skill as a lover pleased him but did little to alleviate the pain that stung to his core. Distractedly he stroked her hair. The one chime of the clock, which called out the half-hour, brought him back, as it apparently did Mary.

"Oh, goodness! It's twelve-thirty! I must get home! I don't know how I will explain to Mamma why I was out until all hours of the night and why I am arriving at the door unescorted—I didn't even think that far ahead when Julia suggested the plan. I—"

"Don't fret," he told her as he stroked her furrowed brow. "I shall see you home, right to your door. I will apologize to your mother for keeping you so late and tell her that I told my driver to continue on for I wished to walk the short distance home. Do you think that will save you?" he teased gently.

"Oh, Ian, would you?" Mary exclaimed with such obvious relief that he couldn't help but kiss her again lightly upon her red lips. He lifted her off his lap and rose. "Let me get your wrap," he said. Mary didn't answer, but her smile and glowing eyes warmed him, despite himself. Mary's declarations of love during their shared passion had obviously been more heartfelt than he'd ever imagined at the time. She really *was* a sweet girl, and it pained him to know that he would break her heart. He truly wished he loved her. He cared for her, more than he'd realized, and the knowledge that he would be the cause of her inevitable pain, perhaps as deep as that he felt right now, saddened him. Would he ever learn that the only sane way to live was by limiting his expectations of people and finding whatever gratifications he sought through his own ambition and toil?

"Mary, I do think that arriving home at nearly one in the morning is unseemly for a young lady. Even if you were properly escorted by Mr. Woods," Mary's father stated after Ian had left.

"Oh, Father," Mary replied, and planted a sweet kiss on his cheek. She was happy that her mother had gone to bed earlier, for despite Mamma's drab, reticent nature, Mary was never able to hoodwink her as easily as Father, whom she had always wrapped around her little finger. Men were such fools. Taken in so easily that sometimes it wasn't even terribly satisfying. She'd thought Ian would be a harder conquest, but he'd proved easier than the others. However, if it hadn't been for Percy's open conversation from which she'd figured out what was going on between Ian and Julia, while poor, silly Percy didn't even realize what was happening right under his nose, she might not have achieved the first part of her plan as quickly.

". . . Mary, why do I suspect that you aren't listening to me?" Father asked, recapturing her attention. Mary detected a worried look in his eye.

"Of course I've listened to *every* word you've said, Father." Mary gave him her most captivating smile. "It's just that . . . Oh, should I? . . ." She made the excitement grow in her voice until Father was intrigued and smiling. "Let's sit down right here on the stairs. For I know I *should* wait until it's all properly done, but I *hate* to vex you so, when I have news that will delight you! And I *do* love to see you happy, Papa," she said, reverting to her childhood appellation for him.

Once seated, she gave him a big hug. "Papa, tonight the reason I was so late is that Ian and I had a long talk in the Davenports' conservatory, which we continued when his driver rode us about the city and through the park. I cannot tell you all that was said . . ." She cast her eyes downward and forced a blush. "But I do suppose that by New Year's, Ian will be asking you for my hand. And you will say yes, won't you, Papa!"

Rarely had she seen her father smile so widely. She even saw a twinkle in his eye. "Mary, dear, I will be most honored to accept Ian Woods into our family if he is the man you love and wish to marry. I've heard talk at the club—and it may surprise you that it doesn't bother me that he's something of a rebel. For he comes from a fine family, and with his inheritance and your own, I need not worry about your comfort when your mother and I pass on."

"Oh, Papa, I love you!" Mary hugged him and planted another kiss on his cheek. "Let's wait, since I've confided in you, to surprise Mamma with my large engagement ring!" she whispered.

Father laughed. "Whatever you say, dear. However, I do have one request. Your mother went to bed with a devil of a headache because you were not yet home. She worries about you. She's not as 'modern' as I am—up with the times, you understand?" Mary nodded. "I realize that times have changed from when I courted your mother, but I also know that doesn't give her justification to worry so. For you are a proper young lady and behave as one, of course, even if you do seem a bit impulsive at—"

"Oh, Father," Mary interrupted in mock horror. "Does Mamma worry that I might act with impropriety? I mean . . ." She lowered her eyes.

"Of course she doesn't worry about *that!* How could you dream that she would doubt your . . . eh, virtue?" The blush rose up his cheeks. He patted her shoulder. "I just think you shouldn't worry her by arriving home at a late hour or going out unchaperoned. You understand, I'm sure."

"Oh, I do, Papa! And I suppose I am sometimes being innocently impetuous . . ." She looked at him with wide eyes. "Why, for all I know, I may have given some nasty-minded people an excuse to gossip—"

"Now, Mary. Don't get carried away. I'm certain that isn't true, so don't let it even worry your pretty little head. I am very happy for you, Mary. Now I think it is time we both went to bed, don't you?"

"Yes, Father . . . and thank you for being the best Papa in the *entire* world!

"That will be all, Nancy." Mary curtly dismissed her maid.

"Yes, Miss Mary. Have a good sleep."

Mary didn't answer. She glanced in the mirror at herself in her satin nightgown and blew a satisfied kiss.

Curled beneath her quilts, Mary lay in the dark, smiling. It was all advancing *exactly* the way she'd planned. And she'd even rather enjoyed her lovemaking with Ian. He was the fourth and best of all, although she believed the joyous lovemaking described in the French novels was greatly exaggerated. At least Ian hadn't repulsed her. In fact, he was terribly handsome, his shoulders so broad and his body hard and lean, that she liked cuddling in his arms and rather enjoyed the kissing. He had helped her plan along without even realizing it. She had intended to get him drunk, but little had she known she would find him already inebriated. When she next talked with him, it would be impossible for him to deny with conviction that she had *not* been a virgin until the moment he'd entered her.

Actually, he'd been quite affectionate after she'd told her lies about Julia. She wondered if the stirrings she'd felt after the sex could be love. She'd never *loved* anyone before. How wonderful it would be if she and Ian actually fell in love. . . . But even if that didn't happen, he would be the perfect husband!

The bonus was having manipulated Ian to reject that uppity, smug Julia. She'd always been like the princesses in the fairy-tale books. Everything good and worthy flowed to Julia without her lifting a finger. Mary knew that except for her large bosom, she was pretty in only a conventional way. Men thought her inconsequential and silly. Once she was Ian's wife and the mother of his children, she'd show them all. Despite all the criticism she'd heard about Ian, no one denied that he was as talented as he was handsome. Mary fell asleep wondering if their children would have red hair like her own and green eyes, or black eyes and hair like his. She hoped she had only daughters, all of whom looked like him.

Chapter Twelve

JULIA PAID SCANT ATTENTION TO BETSY'S CHATTER. SHE merely glanced at the stream of sallow-faced passersby in the growingly dingy neighborhood of fading brownstones and storefronts as the hansom cab continued west across Fourteenth Street toward Madam Rosa's. On this Wednesday noon after Christmas, the crisp air and sky, bright blue and cloudless, accentuated the decline of the area.

Kathleen and Ellen spoke little as they sat behind Betsy and herself. Kathleen's silence was a sign of her disapproval of their adventure to the fortune-teller, whose apartment was above a saloon near the corner of Eighth Avenue. Not only was Kathleen worried about the consequences should Mrs. Davenport find out, but also the notion of someone foretelling the future terrified her. She'd confessed before they left the house that she was certain the Church would find the act itself a sin. Julia had tried to persuade her that she needn't feel obliged to accompany them. But as strongly as Julia had insisted that Kathleen spend the few hours amusing herself in the shopping district replete with rows of women's ready-made clothing stores and then meet the three of them at an appointed time and place, Kathleen had held fast in her refusal to allow Julia to go to Madam Rosa's without her. In fact, Kathleen had reminded her that she had no intention of letting Julia out of her sight until they returned home safely. The grim determination that steeled Kathleen's face convinced Julia not to attempt to cajole her.

Julia envied Kathleen her concern that would vanish once their adventure was completed. She wished her own anxieties could be as easily allayed, she thought as she glanced down once again at the brilliantly faceted diamond engagement ring Percy had surprised her with Christmas Eve.

Betsy lifted her hand and smiled with a happiness devoid of jealousy, which belied her teasing words: "I'm so envious, Julia! The ring is absolutely exquisite. I haven't been able to take my eyes off it since Christmas Day! Why is it that I seem more excited than you?" Betsy asked, sobering as she studied Julia's face.

"Oh, I noticed your eyes wandering from my hand to the face of Ned Barrington quite often Christmas Day, as well as last evening at the theater," Julia teased, in hopes of diverting Betsy.

Betsy grinned but became serious again. "It won't work, Julia. Something's been bothering you for weeks. It's as plain as the nose on your face, even if you don't want to confide in me."

Julia had promised to talk to Betsy. And she had meant to, until Mary had stunned her by revealing that she had not *only* been as naive as Mamma had claimed, but also totally wrong about Ian's feelings and concern for her. She'd barely slept a wink that night or any since. Regardless of Ian's moral deficiencies and his now apparent toying with her for whatever reasons, she'd decided that she had to break her intended engagement with Percy. For she did not love him as more than a good friend. Her shattered heart, her tears through that night each time she thought of Ian and Mary together, had deprived her of the last vestiges of rationalization about her feelings for Percy as well as her last vestiges of dreams about Ian.

Forcing herself from her bed the morning before Christmas, she'd written a note and sent one of the servants to deliver it to Percy's home. The note simply requested his company for an afternoon stroll. She'd decided that it would be easier on both of them if she broke the news to him in the brisk winter daylight. As usual, Kathleen would stroll far enough behind them so that they would have more privacy than they might in either of their homes. Julia had dressed simply and waited for a reply. To her chagrin, the boy had come back saying that Mr. Martin had not been at home but that he'd left her letter for him with the butler. Julia became cross with herself for not having used the telephone, but she hadn't wanted to deal with such a personal matter on such an impersonal machine. To be honest, she'd been afraid that her voice might give her away in a manner that her carefully penned script wouldn't.

She'd spent all morning in her studio trying to lose herself in her work. Kathleen had brought her luncheon on a tray, but upon seeing her face, she had led Julia to the couch, where she cried as if a dam had burst within her. Finally, since she'd already confided in Kathleen, she began to tell her the events that had caused the tears to roll down her face, even as she recounted them, beginning with Ian's visit Friday afternoon.

"Perhaps you shouldn't act so rashly," Kathleen said when Julia finished. "I see in your face when you are with him that you *do* care a great deal for Mr. Martin. In fact, he makes you laugh and smile brightly. Mr. Woods has made you cry and lose more nights of sleep than I even want to know—"

"But I loved Ian! With all my heart and soul, in a way that I could never love Percy!"

Kathleen shook her head sadly. "I know. It seems so often that the love that should bring sunshine and joy brings tears and sorrow. I'm not smart enough to know why, but I've seen it before. It hurts me to see you so unhappy." Her eyes filled with tears.

Julia hugged Kathleen tightly. When she pulled away, she saw tears on Kathleen's cheeks. She gently brushed them away and then wiped her own as well. They gazed at each other quietly for a time, with the ease of intimates. "I can't marry Percy. It would be unfair to him. He is a wonderful young man who deserves someone who loves him as desperately as I love . . . I mean, loved, Ian."

Kathleen nodded. "He does. And as sad as it is, I guess I agree with you. For if I was you . . ." Kathleen laughed self-consciously. "I can't even imagine that, but if I *was* you, I believe I would do the same. But I don't think you should tell him today, for you'll ruin his Christmas. My Mamma always said bad news can always wait, for it will hover over your door until it gets you one way or the other. It's joy that's as fleeting as a butterfly. I think it was an old Irish saying, or maybe she just made it up."

Julia thought about Kathleen's epigram. She would have liked to know Kathleen's mother, for this wasn't the first time that Kathleen had recounted some of her mother's sayings. While many in Julia's society might have seen Mrs. Connor as nothing more than a scrub-woman, just as they saw Kathleen as little more than a pleasant-faced maid, Julia thought again that Mrs. Connor must have possessed the soul of a poet. Kathleen certainly possessed more sensitivity and wisdom than most people she'd ever met. Once again Kathleen was correct: Julia had no right to ruin Percy's Christmas. The news could wait until Tuesday, even if it meant that she would be forced to suffer under this terrible strain until then.

"I will wait until Tuesday," Julia said softly. "Have you more good sense to offer me?" she half-teased.

"Yes, I think I do," Kathleen answered, then hesitated.

Julia was surprised and yet something in Kathleen's manner suggested that Kathleen was about to say something she'd rather not hear. "Well, then?"

"I think that you should arrange a private meeting with Mr. Woods. For your judgments about him *did* come from a secondhand source and—"

"I can't! I won't! He beguiles me so *easily* that he would just *twist* it all about so that I would become even more confused. Or worse yet, he'd deceive me again!"

"You don't know that for certain," Kathleen countered calmly.

"But I do. For what reason would Mary have to lie and expose her indiscretions to me?"

"She's in love with him, isn't she? Why wouldn't she want you out of the way?"

Kathleen's question stumped Julia for a moment. "But she knew Percy and I . . . Yes . . . I see what you're saying, but . . . Wait." For a moment Kathleen had given her a glimmer of hope. But as it fled, her eyes filled with tears again. "Mary is not a friend of mine. If Ian hadn't spoken to her about me, then she'd have no way of knowing about the friendship Ian and I had begun, would she?"

"She strikes me as a shrewd girl who has the knack for finding out whatever she wants to know. Maybe even from Mr. Martin?"

"No, that doesn't make sense. Percy's not a gossip. In fact he would have no reason to speak with her about Ian, since Percy is so oblivious of undertones of feelings. . . . Poor Percy. How I despise hurting him. . . . No. Any knowledge Mary had could only have come through Ian."

Kathleen played with her apron edge. "I wouldn't swear to that . . . but I do know how you can find out."

"How?" Julia asked tentatively, unwilling to allow her hopes to rise and plummet again.

"Tonight, when Ian is at the Christmas Eve celebration, you must find a moment to speak to him—"

"No, I told you I don't dare!"

"I mean just a *moment* alone," Kathleen repeated calmly. "For you only have to find out one answer to one question."

"Which is?"

"Which is whether Mary was speaking the truth when she said Ian thanked you for helping arrange their . . . eh, meeting." The color rose in Kathleen's gentle face. "If he did, then the rest is probably all true. For as you said, what kind of decent man would do something like that? Even the boys I was raised up with would never have involved a pure girl in such goings-on!"

"You're right, Kathleen. But what words do I use?" she asked.

"Well, you're the one who speaks so fine, not me. You'll find the words as long as you remember the question."

"Is that another of your Mamma's sayings?"

Kathleen broke into a broad smile. "No. It's my very own!"

". . . do you, Julia?" Betsy asked.

"I'm sorry, I didn't hear—I was thinking. What did you ask?" Julia said apologetically to Betsy.

"Oh, never mind!" Julia was taken aback by Betsy's irritation. "Oh, Julia, I'm sorry for snapping at you. I don't know what's plaguing you," she whispered. "But just remember that I'm your best friend and am always at your call if you need to confide . . . ."

"I know, Betsy," Julia answered with a hug. "I just can't yet, but I will soon. I promise."

"We're almost there!" Betsy said with a smile. Julia

appreciated how Betsy tactfully changed the subject. "I know exactly what I'm going to ask Madam Rosa!"

Julia laughed despite her melancholy mood. "*I* know exactly what you're going to *ask* and I can tell you the answer. . . . There is a fine young man," Julia began in a silly imitation of a gypsy's accent, "who builds great structures . . . He has a mustache, I can see it clearly . . ." She pretended to wave her hands over a crystal ball. "He will ask for your hand before the last of the snow falls this winter—"

"Oh, Julia!" Betsy began to giggle. "Madam Rosa doesn't have a crystal ball—at least I don't think so. I told you that Carol Butler said she reads tea leaves and palms. And you have to drink the tea first."

"Oh *no* you girls don't!" Kathleen interjected indignantly. "I won't have you drinking it, right, Ellen? There could be something harmful—"

"A sleeping potion," Julia teased.

"Poison!" Betsy continued.

"A devil's brew!" Ellen, Betsy's maid, sallied.

"You can tease me all you like, all of you," Kathleen rejoined heatedly, as she looked from one to another. "But I *still* say that you don't know what's *in* there—or even if the teacups are properly washed! I still think we should take this cab back home—you girls could go for lunch to Sherry's . . . you both *love* going to Sherry's . . ."

"Not on your life," Ellen argued. "This is a real adventure! I'll go first, if it will make you feel better, Kathleen. Then if I don't keel over in a dead faint you'll know it's all well and good and that the Lord hasn't struck me down!" Ellen laughed contagiously.

"It's not the Lord that worries me . . . although I'm not sure he'd approve and I just know that when I go to confession on Saturday, Father Clancey will give me at least fifty Hail Marys and—"

"Oh, please, spare me," Ellen interrupted, making Julia and Betsy laugh harder.

"Ellen Mary Donahue! May Jesus forgive you for such—"

"'Tisn't Jesus I'm worried about. It's Mrs. Livingston. For if she ever gets wind that we let the girls put us up to this, even Jesus won't help us keep our positions."

Julia smiled affectionately at Kathleen, whose dander was raised. "Enough! All of us have teased Kathleen enough. Kathleen, I don't want you to fret. Remember, Carol Butler and her friends came here weeks ago and they're just fine."

"What she means to say, politely, is that they lived to tell about it," Ellen said dryly. "So stop being a silly goose and ruining everybody's fun! Nobody's going to make you drink the tea or force open your hand to be read by the lady—what's her name?"

"Madam Rosa," Betsy replied.

"All right. I've said my piece. I won't open my mouth again until we've found another cab to take us home!" Kathleen set her face so firmly, her jaw clamped shut, and appeared so comical that Julia couldn't help but laugh. Neither could the others. Despite Kathleen's apparent determination, Julia detected the slightest of smiles at the corners of her mouth.

"Missy, we're almost there," the driver called to Betsy, who had been the one to hail the hansom. "Dang this traffic! It gets worse every year! It's a mad scramble by five."

"Thank you, sir," Betsy replied.

Julia felt her smile lingering as she fell back into thought. She hadn't laughed so heartily in a long time, she realized. Certainly not since Ian Woods had come into her life. Well, he was *out* of it. Other than a polite hello and good-bye for Papa's sake, she would have nothing further to do with the man! By the end of the Christmas Eve party, she'd finally seen him for what he really was. He might be a gifted architect, but he was a man of contemptible character!

She recalled with painful vividness how he had virtually ignored her the entire evening. By the time he had arrived, having called earlier in the day to extend his apologies to Mamma for not having "arrived back in town" in time to even stop in at Daphne's party, and then going on to say he wouldn't be able to make dinner but would arrive for the evening's festivities shortly after eight, Julia's nerves were frazzled. For Percy had not called until almost dinnertime. He'd explained that he'd been out doing last-minute shopping all day and had just returned home to find her note. Julia had assured him that of course she wasn't angry and that her voice was merely tired. She'd vowed to try to be as cheerful and warm to Percy as she could without behaving in a manner that would make Tuesday's explanation to him any the more difficult.

The rituals of Christmas Eve, which she'd cherished

since she was a child, were merely a blur in her mind when she thought back about that evening. Not even the clatter of bells in the drawing room and Papa's appearance as Santa Claus, his sack full of presents, had elicited more than a weak smile from her. When she opened Percy's small package, wrapped in gilded cloth and red velvet ribbon, she burst into tears. Everyone assumed they were tears of joy as she stared, stunned, at the huge diamond ring. Even after Percy had knelt and placed the ring upon her finger and kissed her gently on her lips, she was still unable to speak, as the tears closed her throat and blurred her vision. Mamma had handed her a handkerchief, and once her eyes had cleared and she'd found the courage to look around the drawing room where her family and Betsy, Ned and Ian were gathered about the tree, she saw that almost everyone was aglow. Except for Papa, whose smile did not convince her; and Ian, who had the audacity to face her with a smirk on his face and a sardonic glint in his eyes. Quickly she looked back at Mamma's thrilled expression and then to Percy's sweet, proud, smiling face.

Somehow she'd managed to maintain her composure through the rest of the evening. Everyone seemed to attribute her reticence to lingering surprise, for Percy had announced that he and Julia had planned to wait until after the New Year, but that he couldn't resist surprising her with the most perfect Christmas gift he could think of. Assiduously she had avoided glancing at Ian again. When they moved to the music room, Julia pretended to have forgotten something and turned back as they met at the drawing-room door. She called down the hall that she would be right along and when she was assured that she was alone, she sank onto the couch with a sigh.

"Oh!" she exclaimed when she looked up and saw Ian standing before her. He looked down at her with a pleasant countenance.

"I didn't mean to startle you," he apologized evenly. He watched as her left hand clasped her right, hiding the opulent diamond from view. He didn't know if it had been a considered or automatic reaction. He didn't know *anything* about her for certain anymore. "I only came back so that I might have a private word with you," he said. She seemed to blanch.

"About what?" She tried to reply in the same even tone he used. Somehow, her rapidly beating heart did not reflect in the modulation of her voice.

"Well, first I should wish you the best on your engagement once again." He waited but she merely smiled. "And then Mary told me I have reason to thank you for both herself and me," he stated as casually as he could manage. Please, Julia, he prayed. Let me see a genuine expression of bafflement cross your face. Ask me for what. Please! he thought.

"You needn't mention it," Julia finally answered, refusing to give him the satisfaction of loss of composure, or worse yet, the tears that pushed so hard at the back of her eyes that they ached more than her convulsing stomach. "I hope you and Mary are as happy as . . . I hope you are very happy. But I don't think we should mention the incident again, do you?"

She stared into his eyes that glinted with a strange expression. As she stared at him, the anger grew within her until it was almost as strong as the hurt.

He felt the hurt rise in him but determined that he would not allow her to detect it. Why, Julia? he thought. You knew I loved you and yet you lowered yourself to concoct such a demeaning scheme? He wondered why she gazed at him as if he were the one who'd wounded her. But he was probably misreading her, as he had done all along. He forced himself to smile broadly. "No, of course not. I just felt it *only* good manners to thank you. Of course, when I slip away shortly to be with Mary . . ." he whispered, and smirked. Her blush gave him a bitter satisfaction, for at least he'd broken through enough to embarrass her despite her hidden but brazen nature. "You will not take offense? You will help me as you helped Mary last evening?"

"Certainly." She returned her best social smile and rose. "But I must slip away to the powder room *this* moment. Please, join the others and I shall return in a few minutes." She turned away before he could see the tears she could no longer hold back. She used the last of her will to walk, head raised high, from the room rather than run up the stairs. Nor did she allow the sobs to break through her until she was in the second-floor bathroom and had turned the water spigots on to their fullest force. Never had she felt so eviscerated.

"Damn her!" Ian muttered as he felt the bile rise within him. He wanted to run up the stairs and slap her for what she'd done to him. No! He wanted to race up the stairs and pull her into his arms and kiss her and touch her with all the passion that his fury would not dissipate, until he forced her to respond, made her admit that since their eyes had met, since they'd touched and danced and kissed, she could no more be in love with Percy than he was with Mary.

When Julia returned to the music room, Betsy was at the piano and everyone was singing "Oh Holy Night." Julia hoped her eyes appeared less reddened in the soft glow of candlelight that lit the room. Ian was already gone. After the singing, Papa whispered that Ian had explained that he'd promised to see Mary to church. The irony almost made Julia laugh aloud. Instead she merely smiled and kissed Papa on the cheek. She crossed the room and sat beside Percy.

Church, she thought to herself again, four days later, on the way to Madam Rosa's.

"Did you say church?" Betsy asked.

Had she spoken aloud? She looked at Betsy, whose face was puzzled. "No," she lied. "I guess I just cleared my throat—"

"We're here, ladies," the driver called out. "Are you sure this is the address you meant?" he asked, eyeing them with confusion as he pulled the horse up in front of the large saloon.

"Yes, this is it, sir," Betsy said with such a pretended air of sophistication that the other girls burst into a flurry of giggles as the driver just shook his head and took his fare without uttering another word.

Julia and Kathleen sat in rickety old chairs in Madam Rosa's waiting room that was in reality a narrow, dark hall decorated with a faded imitation Persian rug and a shabby table on which some ordinary magazines rested. The walls were decorated with unframed Eastern prints. A curtain of beads was meant to conceal the door that led to the room into which Betsy and Ellen had followed the short black-haired woman, who, except for the eccentricity of her dress—sarong-type apron over a sequined dress with matching head garb—could have been mistaken for a charlady. Ellen had accompanied Betsy into Madam's room. At the last minute, Betsy, despite her bravado, had gotten cold feet, and implored Ellen with her eyes more than her words to come with her. They'd been inside for only about five minutes, but Julia was already becoming sleepy. She glanced at Kathleen and was about to speak, but Kathleen sat with her rosary beads in her hand and Julia couldn't bring herself to interrupt her silent prayer.

Julia glanced around the dingy room again. How dark it was. How could anyone live in such gloom? she wondered. It was also stuffy, despite the draft that poured through the outer door. As Julia rubbed her brow, the sparkle of her engagement ring caught her eye. It was the brightest object in the room. She began to study it. She'd intended *not* to wear it today, but she'd realized at the last second that Betsy would immediately notice its absence. Her plan to break the engagement had not altered, despite Percy's presentation to her of the beautiful ring before she'd had an opportunity to speak with him. She'd known that night that the ring would make it all the more heartrending, but she couldn't change her mind to save Percy from embarrassment. Nor to use their engagement as a salve against the pain that kept her awake each night thinking of Ian and trying to understand how she'd believed that he was the man she wanted him to be, rather than the man he was. The Ian she'd loved no more existed than the image of the man she'd envisioned at her side, walking down the church aisle, in her fantasy at Clarice's wedding. It all seemed so long ago now. . . .

As her hands played against the facets of the diamond, Julia realized that it was but a quirk of fate that kept the ring on her finger on this Wednesday afternoon. For Monday morning, Percy had stopped by, on the way to Tuxedo with his mother and sisters. He was driving the motorcar, he explained, because they needed to leave immediately. His mother had gotten word that her brother had suffered a stroke and was not expected to live through the night. Percy said he'd write and that he expected that they would not be back until the weekend, if that soon. He'd kissed her so sweetly and smiled so lovingly that tears had filled her eyes as she watched him race out the door. So she would wear his ring and accept best wishes from acquaintances and friends until she'd had the chance to speak with him. She'd already decided that if anyone had the indelicacy to actually question *who* had broken the engagement, Percy must agree to discreetly allude to the suggestion that it was mutual. Then, if further pressed, to pretend to admit that it was he. She would do the same. In fact, before Percy's presentation of the ring, her plan had been to beseech him to prove whatever love he felt for her by making society think that *he'd* had second thoughts. Now that was less possible, but still she would use his love, which she knew he would not be able to deny, as a weapon against him for his own best interests. Of course she had no intention of raising Ian's name, for truly, Ian was not the issue. At worst he had functioned as a catalyst for her to recognize her deepest feelings about love and marriage.

"Oh! It was so wonderful!" Betsy reappeared before her, beaming. Ellen was smiling from ear to ear as well. "Go on in," Betsy whispered. "She's waiting for you. And remember, you are Miss *Smith.*"

Julia rose and Kathleen reached out for her hand, her face frozen with dread. Julia patted her top-braided brown hair. "It'll be fine, Kathleen. You stay here and I'll be in and out before you know it." Julia leaned down and whispered into Kathleen's ear: "I frankly don't believe in all this hocus-pocus, but I don't want to ruin Betsy's excitement." She was relieved to receive a grin from Kathleen.

Julia found herself oddly tense. She'd been candid with Kathleen before she'd walked into Madam Rosa's sitting room, which was barely larger than the hallway. Except for the window, through which the weak westerly sunlight filtered past the beaded curtains, there was little difference in the decor. A brass incense holder sat on a side table and the burning incense emitted a smell that had at first nauseated Julia, but then mysteriously grew strangely pleasing despite its pungency. Julia sat across from Madam Rosa at a low draped and tasseled round table. Before Julia sat a cup of tea.

"Go ahead, young lady. Do not be afraid," Madam Rosa said in a thickly accented voice that Julia couldn't identify. Julia knew that she should find the woman comical. Obviously she was a charlatan, or at best a woman making her way through the world in the best way she knew. Possibly Madam Rosa even believed that she possessed these psychic abilities. Julia's rational mind reminded her of all these aspects, but there was something about the woman's eyes that evoked Julia's unrest. For her eyes were so large, so dark—blacker than black, fringed with thick lashes. In fact, Madam Rosa had probably been a very beautiful girl and her eyes were at first glance still strikingly vivid. But there was something about them that made them other-worldly. Madam Rosa sat so still that one could have thought her a figure in the wax museum in London. Her eyes seemed to go through Julia and then beyond. Suddenly Julia was anxious to be out of here. She quickly finished the bitter-tasting liquid, leaving the tea leaves damp and settled at the bottom, just as Madam Rosa had instructed. She'd explained that the reason the client had to drink the tea was that the tea leaves themselves held no power of configuration. It was through the client's drinking that his or her destiny was reflected.

Meekly Julia handed the chipped china cup to Madam, careful not to jar its contents, as she'd been told. Madam's smile was more unsettling than her stare, and Julia was relieved when Madam looked away from her face and began to study the soggy leaves clinging to the bottom of the discolored cup. Madam's eyes seemed to narrow and her brow arched, then knitted. She's doing it for effect, Julia told herself as she felt her hands become clammy and her heart begin to palpitate.

"Your palm, please, Miss . . . Smith, is it?"

Julia nodded and smiled, but Madam didn't smile in return as she took Julia's extended hand in her own. Julia tried to recall the details Betsy had related about Carol's and the other girls' experiences. Julia could have sworn that Betsy specifically said that she read the tea leaves, told the girls what she "saw" and then read their palms. Why was she deviating? Julia wondered, suddenly genuinely alarmed. Perhaps she varied just to keep from becoming bored.

"Relax your hand, please," Madam stated. "You have nothing to fear from me," she continued, but her haunting eyes and the intonation of her voice did nothing to calm Julia's mounting tension. Gently the woman traced her short-nailed, stubby fingers up, down and across the lines in Julia's palm. She opened and closed Julia's hand, bending it this way and that, observing it from the side as well. Then she looked back at the cup, and again Julia detected a frown. Madam took her hand again. Julia wanted to question, but didn't dare.

"Miss Smith. I will tell you something that I would hope you would have both the courtesy and good sense not to tell your friend and her maid."

Julia looked at her with surprise, for the story they'd concocted was that they were all friends, not "heiresses and maids."

"*Most* of my clients are rich girls who sneak from their fine homes for a fine adventure into the 'exotic.' Always accompanied by their maids, of course. It is harmless. They are told that they will meet a tall, dark, handsome, rich gentleman. Or they unknowingly give me enough information for me to guess if they already are being courted, and what his physical attributes may be." Julia smiled despite herself, for Madam was revealing the "trade secrets" Julia had long suspected. But to what intention?

"I am revealing these facts to you for a purpose beyond conversation," Madam stated in almost a professorial voice. "For I will tell you something else that you *may* now believe."

Julia felt an ominous chill creep up her spine, and Madam's eyes took on that paradoxically glazed yet penetrating, otherworldly aura. "I *do* have the gift. But it only comes through on occasion. And I will admit to you that those occasions of vision have become less frequent with each year. But I saw it in you from the moment you sat down."

"Saw what, Madam Rosa?" Julia asked tremulously.

"The tea leaves, eh . . ." Madam waved her hand at them contemptuously, almost knocking over the cup. "They are mostly for effect, and while the client drinks the tea it gives me a chance to study her or him. It is amazing how quickly one can discern the basic personality if one is sensitive and practiced. How the cup is held, and so on," she said, and waved her hand again, this time gracefully, in the air. "I do have the gift of vision, but like all gifts, it comes and goes without one's volition or permission."

"You saw what in me, Madam?" Julia repeated, as fascinated as disquieted.

"I saw that you were special . . . Oh, I am not

speaking of your great beauty, for that is mere decoration. But that you were the recipient of great gifts—not the gift of vision, at least not in the sense I have it—but other *intense* gifts. You are a talented artist but you are terrified by your gift and have chosen to veer from it."

Julia felt her cheeks heat in anger. She was being made the center of a joke. Betsy had come in here and told Madam all about her. It had been her silly plan all along!

"Your friend told me nothing," Madam said so simply that Julia couldn't help but gasp. "That statement is only a demonstration of common sense and observation. For you most obviously jumped to the conclusion that you'd been the butt of your friend's joke. For how else could you explain to yourself that I knew this about you?"

Julia stared at Madam Rosa speechlessly.

"Do you wish to leave?"

Julia shook her head.

"Can you accept, even a bit, despite your fine rational mind, that I just might be telling you the truth about myself?"

Julia nodded in assent. She cleared her voice. "Yes, Madam, I think I can. At least for the moment."

"Good." This time Madam's smile warmed her as deeply as her previous smile had chilled her.

"And that what I tell you about yourself is what I see, because in the strangest of ways we are surprisingly alike with our blessed gifts that can feel like a curse?"

"Perhaps." Julia no longer felt herself afraid. She found herself liking Madam.

"So, I will not go through all the hocus-pocus," Madam said, again waving her hand.

Julia had to laugh at Madam's use of the very term she'd whispered into Kathleen's ear.

"I speak of the tea leaves, not the palm. Palmistry is an ancient art. Far older than Western civilization. It goes back to the Orient, to ancient China. We have much to learn from the Chinese about many subjects. In any case, my vibrations were so strong about you. When I was glancing in the tea cup, I was just stalling for time, to see if the impressions remained as strong."

"And did they?"

"Hasn't what I've told you already forced you to admit so? Even a little?"

Julia nodded.

"When I studied your palm, my suspicions were confirmed. I will not go through an explanation of each line and what it indicates. Perhaps you will pay me another visit. I will share with you this fascinating art. *Not* for payment but for the enjoyment one gains from tutoring a bright and eager student."

Julia smiled at the compliment, which she knew to be sincere whether or not Madam was correct.

"Besides, there is something important that I must tell you. For you are at a *crucial* crossroad in your life. What you do in the next six months will determine the rest of your life, and I will tell you that you shall live to be a *very* old woman. Whether you shall live to be a happily content woman, or a miserably frustrated one, is your choice. For ultimately we are given free will. Think of the palm as a road map. Which road one takes is up to the individual. Should one not heed the warning signs, that is still one's choice and not the fault of the map. Correct?"

"Yes, I agree," Julia said eagerly, taken with the woman's perfect metaphor.

"As I said, my sensations coupled with my reading of your palm convince me that you are at a crucial crossroad. You must think *long* and *hard,* for it shall influence the rest of your life. I have but two statements to make to you other than what I've already said. Both are equally important. Both may sound equally cryptic —vague, if you will—at first. But since all the answers are *within* you, when you think on them, you will clearly understand your choices, though perhaps not the complete consequences of each choice—which is as it is *meant* to be. Have you followed me thus far?"

"I believe so, Madam . . . Should I write what you say?"

"No. It is entirely unnecessary. For you will never forget it. It is all within you anyway. I am merely the medium, just as your paints are."

Julia realized that she'd known she was a painter, but it felt almost natural. But then again, most women who dabbled in art painted so . . .

"What you are thinking is true but beside the point and a waste of time. Some sculpt or only draw."

Julia thought she was beyond being stunned by this woman's uncanny remarks, but her mouth dropped open.

"Listen carefully. You must decide to be who you *are* or who you think you *should* be. You cannot continue to straddle the fence, as they say. You understand?"

Julia nodded as her hands turned icy. Hadn't Ian said much the same thing to her that afternoon in the—?

"Think about this later. For we are spending so much time that your friend will become suspicious, and your maid so worried that I am the devil incarnate, that she will come rushing in here to pull you away."

"How did you know that—?"

"Simple observation." Madam laughed for the first time. "I saw her holding her rosaries, heard her accent and quickly knew she was an Irish Catholic who feared that you were committing a blasphemy."

Julia laughed in response.

"The second statement. Are you ready to take it in?"

"Yes."

"Good. You have two conflicting lines on your palm—one of earthbound practicality, the other of great passion. I see from your face that someone else has sensed the passion and brought it to your attention. There are also two men in your life. You love them both—differently, though. One will bring you great happiness and pleasure. The other nothing but misery and sorrow. It is your free will that allows you to choose. Pick wisely."

"But, Madam, you haven't told me which is which!"

"Nor will I. It is *your* life. The answers are all within *you*. The knowledge is all within you, if you find the courage to face the truths and act upon them."

Julia stared wordlessly, even as Madam rose.

"Two dollars, please," she stated, her palm unembarrassedly outstretched.

Julia fumbled in her purse. She pulled out a five. "Here, Madam. Please take it."

"That is fine from the others. But you—do not insult me!" Despite the sharpness of Madam's tone, her eyes softened. "Come back when you are ready to learn more. Come back when you have gotten off the fence— oh, I do enjoy American colloquialisms. They are so graphic rather than philosophic." Madam reached into the bodice of her dress, withdrew a roll of bills and handed three dollars to her. "You can show yourself out."

Julia had taken but a step when Madam's arm touched her shoulder. "Tell them nothing," she whispered. "Make up the usual fortune-telling story— except to your Catholic maid. She will understand, for she is one of us. That is why she is so frightened. You are lucky to have her as a friend. . . . And tell her that love will come to her with the flowers of summer. Good day, Julia."

It wasn't until they tripped down the stairs of the tenement building and ran into the street that Julia realized that she'd never told Madam Rosa her first name.

Chapter Thirteen

"No, I don't think we need have Charles here before we continue this conversation," Ian countered. "You and I shared our dreams in Chicago. *We* decided to come to New York and establish a partnership, if we could get the financial backing we needed. Both of us agreed that we were unwilling to use our families' money or even our inheritances, which is still their money, since they clearly thought—and continue to think—our ambitions are, at the least, eccentric."

"Charles doesn't," Ned said, his usual amiable demeanor gone. "He's been behind us all the way."

"That he has. Charles is a special gentleman, *very* special. He's given us far more than the financial backing we've needed. But he is a *silent* partner."

"You seem to seek his advice quite a lot for a *silent* partner."

"I do, and it's always proven to be more than sound. On that we both agree. But *we* are the architects," Ian stated intently, then lit his pipe and began to pace the room as Ned sat at his desk. "We must continue to share the same goals—uncompromising goals—or it won't work."

"The key word—the only element of our disagreement—is 'uncompromising.' You view the Dickerson commission as a betrayal. I don't. It would be another matter if we'd gotten the Stewart commission, or Weatherby's. But we haven't received *any* of them. Before you tell me again how all the scrambling you've done in the past two weeks—all the meetings you've had with the likes of Coraday and the guy at the steel company—will lead to an inevitable offer or two—"

"They *will*. I'm certain," Ian interrupted, despite Ned's attempt to silence him.

"I know you're certain. And if we *do* get one, it will be due to *your* incredible determination and energy, not mine. I fully acknowledge that."

"The issue is not kudos," Ian said softly.

"I know it isn't. But don't think I haven't been aware that you've been our driving force, and I applaud you for it. I always have." Ned smiled. "Hooking up with you was based on far more than your 'charming' personality, you know."

Their laughter lightened the air. They viewed one another with a friendship weary but sustaining beneath the mounting tensions of the past month. "As I said, the difference between us is that I see the Dickerson project as a little windfall, giving us time and money to get up some more steam, until we *do* receive a commission for a skyscraper, which I have no doubt that we will by summer—"

"By summer—that's ridiculous. I say it will be by the end of this month, beginning of February at the *latest.*"

"And I think your enthusiasm is coloring your judgment. How many commissions has Sullivan received in the past couple of years? And *we're* still untested as independent architects, apart from our work for him. We have *no* choice but to take the Dickerson estate, and if by summer we have not gotten a contract for a commercial skyscraper, we will have to take *another* mansion or estate and thank our lucky stars for the time it gives us."

"And I say that once we take one, it will be another and then another. Before you know it, we will be rationalizing, *just* like every whore on the street does when she tells herself that *next* year, when she's got enough money, she'll quit and marry the nice hometown boy and raise a half-dozen pretty babies!"

"You see it as nothing less than prostitution, do you?"

"That's exactly how I see it."

Ned rose from his chair and sat on the edge of his desk. "Well, I don't."

"I know," Ian said with sad resignation.

"I'm going to be twenty-eight next week. I want a life. I'm in love with Betsy and I want to ask her to marry me. But I can't if I don't have the means by which to support her. Independent of my family, my inheritance, or worse yet, her family and inheritance. I've seen too many young men from our class, both here and in Chicago—especially here—already little more than eviscerated drunks who may live long enough to deteriorate into pathetic roués. It's the curse of being the third generation of great wealth."

"On this we agree. As we did from the moment of our first drink at your club in Chicago, years ago," Ian said with a sense of reawakened respect for Ned.

Ned smiled, but his eyes carried the sadness that Ian felt. "We have great mutuality, as always. But it is the *one* issue on which we differ that may cause the dissolution of our partnership. Despite our respect, confidence . . ." Ned lowered his eyes as his color heightened. He met Ian's eyes. "And love for one another."

"Yes. What you have expressed are exactly my feelings. And fears."

"So?" Ned asked.

"I think we have to decide. If we wait any longer we are just delaying the inevitable decision. For we are speaking of principle. Something that cannot be simply conciliated, despite our wish to."

Ned sighed. "Let us be certain that we are *absolutely* clear on this, then. From your view, taking the Dickerson project and/or any others like it, even when we have nothing else, is untenable?"

"That's correct."

"And if we should not receive a corporate commission as you insist we will within a month? What then?"

"I've thought hard about it. We left Chicago with Louis Sullivan's blessing. More than his blessing, for we've already offered some assistance with the Bayard building on Bleecker. You know that Louis will be doing a building in Buffalo. I believe he is soon to be negotiating the terms of the contract. I would think we should offer him our services, even though it will be his name that will receive the attention, as it should. For it is his basic vision, as always."

"So, you think that we should go back to work for Louis, rather than take simple estates."

"I do. Although I don't believe that we'll have to. But if you're correct and we don't receive an offer during the next month . . . Yes, that's what I think."

"Which would mean pulling up stakes again and moving to Buffalo, if Louis acceded, which, by the way, I don't doubt that he happily would."

"Yes. It would mean a move to Buffalo for close to two years." It didn't take much intelligence to guess how Ned, wanting to marry Betsy and most probably start a family, would feel about such a move.

Ned lit a cigarette. "It seems to me that we both have a hell of a lot to think about. But dang it, whatever the outcome, I want your *word* that it shall not turn our friendship into rancor!"

Ian crossed the room and clasped Ned's shoulder. "You've never been righter about anything than that!" Their embrace was filled with the sense that their courses were irrevocably diverging, unless a commission saved them from the fate they didn't want, but would be forced to accept.

"Excuse me, Mr. Woods," Vivien, their secretary, said. "There's a Miss Hoffman to see you. She says you're expecting her."

What the blazes was Mary doing here? He wondered. "Show her into my office, please, Vivien—but in about two minutes."

"Certainly Mr. Woods," Vivien said, and closed Ned's door behind her.

Ian turned to Ned. "So, tomorrow morning we'll talk, and whatever conclusion we reach, we'll inform Charles jointly?"

"Fine. I think we clearly understand one another." Ned smiled and looked at his pocket watch. "No wonder I'm starving! It's time for lunch."

Ian watched Ned's poor attempt at hiding a smirk. "What are you smirking about?" he asked.

"I'm not smirking."

"Grinning, then," Ian answered, as Ned began to laugh.

"Do you really want to know?"

"I do, although I'm afraid to hear," Ian bantered.

"Well, although you don't talk about your personal life frequently, I'd assumed that you were no longer courting Mary Hoffman. Especially since Julia and Percy called off their engagement last week."

"I am *not* courting Mary. You want a personal bit of gossip? I don't even know why she's here. I certainly didn't invite her."

Ned laughed. "Well, from the little I've heard about Mary Hoffman, that news certainly doesn't shock me. But I'm sure you'll shortly discover the reason. But what about Julia?"

Ian intended to give nothing away. He'd never spoken to Ned about Julia in more than a desultory manner, and infrequently at that, although Betsy and

Julia were best friends. Ian wondered, as he had wondered before, whether Julia had spoken about him to Betsy and she to Ned. He had doubted so, because Julia seemed to be quite private—but then, that judgment was of the Julia he'd thought he'd known. That Julia, the girl of his fantasies, would never have colluded with Mary—worse yet, actually initiated the plan. Not that he was a blameless participant in the event. For had he been sober and less unsettled by his Boston visit, he would have politely ushered Mary from the library rather than following her lead and allowing his drunken lust to overcome his good sense.

". . . is your answer then?" he half-heard Ned's question.

"Pardon me?" His obvious loss in thought was a disclosure he was reluctant to make, in regard to his feelings about Julia.

"Oh, hang it! I asked what about Julia?"

"What about her? I barely know the girl."

"Oh, I see. Well, have a good luncheon and send Mary my regards," Ned responded, tactfully veering from the subject.

As Ian walked from Ned's office to his own, he decided that Mary's visit at lunch hour might be more opportune than he'd first thought. He hadn't seen Mary in almost two weeks—since the New Year's Eve party. Since that night she'd appeared at his window, through the social flurries of the holiday week to which he'd already committed himself to accompany her, he had made sure that they were never alone. Still, he'd been less than honorable, for it was the middle of January and he had avoided her rather than confronting her with the fact that he did not love her and didn't wish to continue to see her within the artifice of courtship. Yes, he could justify his avoidance, just as he had made excuses to decline her various invitations: business, his mother's cold that had turned to pneumonia but was thankfully better the past day or so. Of course, the surprise at Julia's broken engagement was not an issue he would discuss with Mary, regardless of its effect upon him.

"Are you certain that Mr. Woods . . . Oh! Ian! I didn't see you," Mary said after their impact. She'd been storming out of his office, a petulant frown of annoyance on her face, as he'd turned the corner into the doorway. He'd tried to move out of her path, to no avail, and had wound up catching her by the shoulders before she could injure either of them. Her frown had changed first to surprise and then to a brightly artificial smile.

"I gathered so," he responded dryly. He led her into his office, saw her to the leather chair and then sat behind his desk. "What brings you here?" he asked, apparently so gracelessly that her cheeks heightened in tint.

She leaned forward, her elbows resting on her green velvet, ribboned afternoon dress and smiled more brightly than before, if that were possible. "I've come to take you for a proper luncheon! My treat— Delmonico's, Sherry's, wherever you choose! For what with your work, and your mother's illness and the holidays, you've been driving yourself entirely too hard. Since you would never dream of indulging yourself in a leisurely weekday luncheon, I've decided to be your benefactor . . . among other things." Her voice lowered to a whisper and her high color grew to a full blush. "What do you say?" She ended her little speech with a high inflection, too cheery to be natural.

"I say yes, on one condition." He watched her face soften. "That you pick the restaurant, but that you allow me to take you to lunch. Otherwise it's no deal!"

"Whatever you say, Ian," Mary agreed easily. "And I pick Delmonico's!"

"Fine, then I'll just grab my hat and coat and we're on our way." He helped her up and gestured toward the door. He couldn't help but notice the slight undulating of her full hips.

Mary smiled prettily at the drab secretary as Ian took her arm and they headed out the door. She hadn't expected it to be *difficult* to tantalize him, although he'd been avoiding her for a week, but neither had she thought it would be so *easy*. Nor so perfect, if they hurried. For on her way over to his office, after her visit with Percy, she'd passed Delmonico's. And who was being helped out of a carriage but Betsy, and then Julia. Mary turned her head as her carriage drove past, just in time to see the two girls enter the restaurant.

"I do find Delmonico's so delightful," she said sweetly to Ian as they stood alone in the elevator. "And I haven't been there for the longest time." She ran her fingers up his coat sleeve, then quickly stood on tiptoe and planted a quick kiss on his cheek. "This will be so swell, don't you think?" she continued, pretending that she hadn't noticed how he'd tried to pull away from her kiss without risking offending her. Well, try as he might, he wouldn't be able to pull away much longer.

In fact, if it all went as easily as it was already going, in a few hours they would be engaged to be married!

"Julia, I'm so pleased that you finally agreed to luncheon." Betsy glanced around the chandeliered, red-carpeted dining room.

Julia smiled. "Yes, Delmonico's is very pleasant, isn't it."

"Certainly, but I didn't mean for that reason." Betsy spoke softly. "I'm truly worried about you. Why, you don't even look like yourself—of course you're as lovely as ever, but your coloring is so *wan*. Though you've tried to hide it, I see the melancholy in your eye. If I didn't know better, I would almost believe it was the result of your broken engagement."

"What do you mean, if you didn't know better? Do you believe me so cold that I would not feel mournful about Percy?" Julia rested her soup spoon. The attempt to eat required more energy than she felt. Just what was Betsy implying?

Betsy laid her spoon down as well. Julia found it difficult to continue to look at Betsy's penetrating brown eyes. "Of course I know you feel terrible about Percy. But I also know that it wasn't a mutual decision. Nor was it Percy's desire to end—"

"Who told you?" Julia let out, immediately realizing that she'd given herself away. It wasn't that she wanted to keep the secret from Betsy. She'd simply promised herself that after her conversation with Kathleen, she would not speak of it to anyone before she told Percy.

"No one *told* me. Even though you've apparently not trusted me as you used to, enough to confide in me—"

"May I take your soups, ladies?" The waiter's appearance threw them into silence.

"I can see why you'd feel that way," Julia quietly answered, seeing the hurt in Betsy's eyes. "But that isn't so. I just haven't wanted to talk with anyone. I did intend to tell you the whole truth, but I've felt so tired and reclusive—I've done little but take a walk each morning and then paint until dinner. After dinner, I've barely been able to keep my eyes open. For weeks I *couldn't* sleep and now it seems that's all I can do."

The waiter returned, placing their entrées before them. After he left, assured that everything was satisfactory, Julia and Betsy gazed at one another.

Betsy's expression held only empathy and suddenly Julia wanted to pour forth the entire story. Perhaps Betsy would see it from a fresh view and help her, for Julia felt so lost in a miasma of conflicting emotions and thoughts she couldn't escape.

"I've been truly miserable, Betsy. I've barely been able to eat. I choke down dinner in order to appease Mamma. I've upset the entire family, although after Mamma's outburst a week ago Saturday—after I'd broken the engagement with Percy—she's barely said a word to me. At first I thought she was angry, but now I see she is truly worried and confused."

"Julia. Why don't you begin to eat that chicken? It looks wonderful," Betsy appealed gently. "Then we can go back to my house and talk until dinner—or longer—however long you like."

First she couldn't talk; now she didn't want to stop. The sight of the food on her plate repulsed her, but she remembered that Betsy was quite hungry. "I wish that you would begin to eat before your steak becomes cold. I'll try, but if you can bear it, I'd like to continue talking."

"Bear it?" Betsy's eyes looked at her so lovingly that Julia found herself forcing back the tears. She smiled, with a silly embarrassment. "Oh, that's the *other* thing I spend my time doing. Crying. One would think I had shed all the tears a body could."

Betsy laughed, making Julia laugh herself. "I've often wondered the same thing. Take my word for it, there seem to be years of tears in us. But I like to think that we forget to count when we laugh."

"I guess so." Julia smiled, as her eyes cleared. She'd been wrong not to seek Betsy's advice since the beginning of all this misery. Already she was feeling less alone. "So, do you forgive me?"

"Forgive you?" Betsy looked surprised, but then understood. "Oh, I was never truly angry at you. I did feel shut out, but my anger today was just a means of trying to get you to open up . . . and it worked. Why don't you nibble at your food—or at least a roll and butter. You need to eat to keep up your strength, or else you'll just feel worse. I know, for I've done the same thing—while my sister, Catherine, can't seem to *stop* eating when she's unhappy, and that makes her feel worse when her mood rises, for she is, as you know, already more than fashionably plump. Funny how it seems to be opposite sides of the same coin . . ."

"Indeed." Julia had never thought about it, but Louise had always done the same thing. In fact, Louise had gained so much weight since Clarice's wedding that Mamma had bluntly asked if she were with child again.

Now that Julia thought about it, something was upsetting her older sister. She'd been too wrapped up in her own problems to think on it before now. "I was thinking of Louise," Julia responded to Betsy's quizzical expression. "But that's another story and I don't even begin to wish to guess at it right now."

Betsy buttered a soft roll and handed it to her. "Try this."

Julia tasted it and smiled. She was hungry, although she couldn't bring herself to touch the chicken. She sipped at her tea. "Where should I begin—there's so much I haven't told you."

"Tell me, if you can, why you broke your engagement to Percy."

"Do you think it is obvious that it was *I* who ended it? For it was—is—quite important to me that everyone believe it was mutual. Better yet, that it was Percy who had second thoughts. For his sake."

"Well, let me set your mind at ease on that matter. I suspected you ended it only because I've known for quite some time that something was troubling you. I know you are a very private person, as I am. So many other girls *first* confide in their best friends, and then proceed to tell their merest acquaintances the same information!"

Julia laughed wryly, for Mary Hoffman came to mind. Betsy's color rose as she attempted to stifle a giggle. "What's tickling you?" Julia asked.

"It's just that I never dreamed that I would tell my best friend the worst, silliest, most malicious gossip about herself. Let alone know that it would *thrill* her!"

"Tell me," Julia said with more animation than she'd felt in a long while.

"Ned and I were at Jamie Butler's party this past Saturday evening, which neither you nor Percy attended. The whole crowd was abuzz with stories about your broken engagement. If what you intended was to save Percy's pride, that you certainly did. For among the various stories—I will only mention the best—was that Percy broke the engagement, but because he is such an honorable young man, he wanted everyone to *suspect* that you called it off."

Julia found herself smiling.

"One bit of gossip is that he realized you were far too flighty to make a proper wife." Betsy giggled. "Another was that he'd become enamored of Carol Butler."

"Carol Butler? He hardly knows her." Julia shook her head with wonder.

"Oh, I've got an even *better* one. That Percy has been secretly in love with someone who's supposed to have been merely a platonic friend. Are you ready for the name?"

"Of course." Julia smiled, her curiosity building.

"Mary Hoffman! Have you ever heard of anything more ridic—? Julia, what's wrong! You look as if you're about to faint! There's no truth to that—of course there isn't—but it was Mary Hoffman's name that turned your smile into . . . That's it. Now I've finally put it all together!"

As upset as Mary's name had made her, Julia found herself fascinated by the quickness with which Betsy's mind worked. She had no doubt that Betsy had figured most of it out, but her curiosity made her challenge Betsy. "And what have you deduced?" she asked.

"I'm sorry I'm smiling. It's only that it's been obvious all along, so I'm as cross as two sticks with myself! I've been so involved with my own life that I didn't think sharply enough, although I tripped over it a half-dozen times in the past two months!" Betsy sobered. "It's Mary only indirectly," she whispered. "You've been in love with Ian Woods since the night you met him. You've been upset since the night of Clarice's party. And the night of the skating party, when you sprained your ankle so badly, you were skating with Ian, and even before that, that afternoon at your house when I first met Ned . . ." Betsy's eyes drifted across the room, as her mind obviously placed all the pieces together. Finally Betsy's eyes met her own. "Yes. You're in love with Ian. Your love for Percy was a friendly, sisterly feeling. And you couldn't go through with it because you couldn't marry Percy with less than total passion," she whispered.

"You're correct about it all, except for one important element," she whispered back. "I *loved* Ian. But even before I'd broken my engagement, I realized that not only weren't my feelings reciprocated, but that I didn't know him at all! I learned in a hurtful way that Ian is *far less* than an honorable gentleman, despite his social charm. He and Mary are well-suited. That much I will tell you now. Later, I'll tell you everything. But I do know that if Ian is capable of genuine love, it is only to Mary that he reveals these feelings."

"That's ridiculous! I know that Ian has accompanied

Mary to all the parties this holiday season, but he doesn't care two straws for her!"

"I know differently, I'm sorry to say." Julia, tired again, sipped at her tea. She glanced at Betsy, whose eyes were again drifting across the room as she thought. Suddenly Betsy blanched.

"What's the matter?"

"Don't turn around, but speaking of the devil, Mary and Ian have just entered the room." Betsy's expression immediately changed to a social smile through which she whispered, "Put your best smile on, for they're approaching us right this second."

Oh, no! She just couldn't bear to see him. Worse yet, with Mary! She did her best to try to smile.

"Julia, Betsy," she heard Mary's shrill voice before she came into view. Mary planted a wet kiss on her cheek. Then she did the same to Betsy. "What chance! But such a lovely surprise running into you two, isn't it, Ian, dear?"

"Yes, it is," Ian answered quietly, doing his damnedest to hide his discomfort. He smiled at Betsy and tried to look past Julia's eyes as he smiled and nodded at her as well. "How are you two ladies?" he asked, cursing social dictates in his mind.

"We're just having a delightful luncheon, aren't we, Julia!"

Julia forced her brightest smile. "Yes, just delightful!" Go away, please, she thought.

"And since it's getting rather late, I'm certain the two of you are starving," Betsy said so skillfully that Julia wanted to hug her. "Oh, the captain is trying to get your attention, Ian. It appears your table is ready.

So please don't allow us to keep you another *second*. Have a lovely luncheon, you two," Betsy said.

"Oh, you're so sweet, Betsy. But we're in no hurry at all, are we, Ian?"

Ian's gratitude for Betsy's skillful dismissal changed to irritation he could barely suppress at Mary, who was so obviously fawning that it made him lose his appetite. "I'm afraid we are, Mary. For I have a meeting in little more than an hour," he lied. "Nice seeing you, Betsy." His smile to her was full of the gratitude he felt. "And you, Julia."

He hadn't intended to allow himself to gaze at her, but his eyes had forced their way to her face. Her beauty took his breath away. For it had been weeks since he'd seen her and he'd almost forgotten how lovely she was. But it was more than that. She appeared pale—too pale. Something was very wrong with her. Perhaps the rumors that Percy had ended their engagement because of Carol Butler were true after all. He tried to remember his hurt and anger, but they vanished as he stared at her stiff smile that was belied by the troubled expression in her eyes. He wanted so to take her in his arms and tell her how much he loved her— He quickly caught himself. He was reacting like some sorry milksop. He mustn't allow himself to be taken in again, for she had the power to cast a spell upon him—make him believe she was all he'd ever dreamed of.

For a moment Julia thought she had detected a worried look in Ian's eyes. But it must have been no more than a trick of light, for he now looked at her with hard eyes, despite his neutral smile. "Good afternoon,

Ian, Mary," she said, as Ian took Mary by the elbow and began to lead her away. Had she not felt so miserable, she would have had to suppress a smile at how Mary had released herself less than gracefully and stepped back to their table. "I just wanted to suggest that perhaps the three of us could have luncheon later in the week," Mary chirped, looking from Betsy to Julia.

"This week's busy for me, I'm sorry," Betsy stated so quickly that even dense Mary could not have missed the social slur.

"I shall be going out to Long Island tomorrow," Julia said. Not until the words had fallen from her mouth did she realize that was exactly what she wished to do. "Another time, perhaps?" she added. As much as she disliked Mary, she couldn't bring herself to further humiliate the girl.

"When will you return, Julia?" Mary asked, apparently unperturbed. When Mary had spoken of their becoming friends, she'd apparently set her mind to it, Julia realized, with some feeling bordering on awed respect at the girl's audacity.

"I shall stay at least a week. Perhaps two. Then I shall visit my aunt in Tuxedo. By that time it will be mid-February, if not later, and I will be dashing about readying for our European tour." Julia almost laughed at the fact that Mary had forced her to do what Mamma had been unable to get her to do—to decide upon her itinerary until they left for Paris at the end of March on Mamma's favorite steamer.

"And then you'll be off to Lenox for the summer. Julia, you're such a social butterfly," Betsy added.

Ian, who'd stood at Mary's side, wondered with amusement how Mary could remain so seemingly oblivious of the dismissal she was being given. Yet his heart ached at the knowledge that he would soon lose the last comfort of imagining Julia painting in her studio, reading in the drawing room, or lying in her bed, when his willpower failed him, usually in the depth of the night. But then, for all he knew, he might be off to Buffalo in a matter of weeks. "Well, I'm sure you ladies will arrange a convenient visit at another time, for I am quite hungry. So I will excuse us, as you permitted, Betsy." He smiled and firmly grasped Mary's elbow.

Julia couldn't help but remember that moment he'd grinned like a little boy and admitted that he was ravenous as he munched on those sweet cakes. There was no grin on his face before he departed. Obviously he wished to absent himself from her presence as quickly as possible.

"Julia," Betsy whispered. Julia watched Mary and Ian being seated across the room, with Mary facing her. Betsy's expression was fierce when Julia looked back at her. "I don't know any of the details yet. But I can swear to two things. You love him and he loves you just as desperately!"

"Betsy," she replied sharply, "you are the smartest girl I know. But that is the most *ridiculous* remark I have ever heard come from your lips. On both counts!"

Betsy didn't react, but regarded her shrewdly. "Then you're in no hurry to leave the restaurant?"

"Of course not. I have no reason to be. In fact, I've grown a bit hungry after all. I will ask the waiter to

253

reheat the chicken, for it does look delicious," she declared, daring Betsy to defy her.

As Mary babbled, Ian thought about how skillfully she had maneuvered her position so that she'd be facing Julia and Betsy. Actually, he was relieved, for he could not have sat for long and resisted watching Julia. He reminded himself of the purpose of this luncheon and allowed Mary to chatter on as he sipped his drink and decided how to broach the subject. He was determined to be free of her by the time lunch was over. He hoped he could do so with honor, despite the renewed distaste her fawning demonstration had elicited within him. "Mary—" he began, deciding to get it over with.

"Oh, Ian, excuse me for interrupting you. But I *must* tell you something, or else I'll just burst!"

"What?" What tidbit of gossip was she about to expose now?

"Well, I'd attributed it to *nothing* more than hurt, sour grapes, if you will, on Percy's part. Until something Julia said made me see that it was true!"

He became alert. "I don't have the slightest idea of what you're speaking about," he answered evenly.

"Of course you don't." She leaned forward and patted his hand. "That's because I haven't seen you in weeks! Besides, I hadn't intended to mention it, because I can tell that gossip bores you. And Julia is your friend—though she didn't seem that amiable today—but I suppose that can be expected after breaking Percy's heart, the poor guy—"

"Breaking his heart? Aren't you speaking a bit melodramatically, Mary? For Charles told me that

they'd come to a *mutual* agreement that their engagement was not . . . eh, meant to be, shall we say."

"Oh, I know! That was the cover story. In fact,
everyone thinks that it was actually Percy who broke off
with Julia, but to be honorable, he announced it was a
joint agreement."

"I'd heard that through Ned," Ian admitted. He
found his irritation mounting. "So what is it that you
really know? Are you saying that after accepting his
ring Julia changed her mind and broke off with him?"
He knew that despite himself he hoped that Mary
would tell him this was the case—for perhaps all
between himself and Julia had been a huge misunderstanding.

"Yes and no. Poor Percy was almost in tears this
morning when he visited me. He did ask for his ring
back."

Ian felt his heart plunge. Why had he still tried to
cling to the most flimsy thread of hope?

"But he only did so because he discovered that Julia
had been unfaithful to him. Dishonest in her avowal of
love!"

His jaw tightened and he clutched at the glass of
Scotch in his hand. Had Julia been foolish enough to
reveal to Percy the intimate moments that she and Ian
had shared? Luckily, Mary was so eager to continue
her story that he saw no evidence that she'd detected
any sign of disquietude on his part.

"As I said, I really didn't believe Percy, although I
knew that *he* believed what he said to be true. But you
see, the man Percy said Julia was *really* in love with
resides outside of the city. In fact, he is a neighbor of

her uncle's on Long Island. Percy said they'd 'rendez-voused' that weekend Julia visited, *after* she'd agreed to accept his proposal but asked him to wait until after Daphne's engagement party to publicly announce it. Percy didn't name the man. I remember now that Julia behaved strangely those weeks after her return. Even the night of the skating party she seemed less than happy, and she was already engaged—her family and closest friends knew—although of course I didn't. Did you?"

"Yes," he admitted, seeing no reason not to, although his mind was still trying to sort through what Mary was telling him. "Ned had mentioned it to me."

"Apparently Julia had met this man months ago, but he was still married at the time and—"

"Married? You mean she'd gotten involved with a married man?" he asked, truly shocked, yet surprised at his capacity to be further jolted by the deceptions Julia was capable of.

"I don't know, because Percy wasn't sure, and he found it hard, despite his hurt, to doubt Julia's virtue," she ended with a whisper. Her eyes lowered. "Perhaps it is only *fair* to assume that Julia had but a crush on the man. At first. A crush from afar. But apparently, the weekend after she agreed to marry Percy, she learned that this man was about to divorce his wife."

"You mean that he's still married?" Ian couldn't help but recall Betty Cornell, the love of his youth.

"Yes, but in the process of divorce, I think. Percy wasn't clear, and again, since I didn't believe Julia capable of such deception, I didn't listen closely enough to remember all the details. But I *absolutely* don't believe that Julia would have allowed the man to take liberties with her while she was engaged to Percy. I think she acted with integrity, albeit belated, by breaking off with Percy. Don't you?"

"I have no opinion." Ian thought of his moments of intimacy with Julia, the physical and emotional. So, all the time, while she'd played the innocent virgin she'd been affecting the same pose with this married man. Obviously the other man had become just as beguiled. For if it hadn't been for Mary's incessant gossip and talk, he himself would never have doubted Julia. "But I do wish we could change the subject. I am sorry that Percy is feeling so unhappy, but I'm sure he'll somehow survive," he said wryly. "I would like to speak about us," he said directly. Mary's loving, excited smile almost caused him to lose his resolve. She was a silly, irritating girl, but at heart kind and embarrassingly transparent. He knew that she loved him and that most of her improprieties were a reflection of her desire to be liked. Even that one night of unfortunate sexual intimacy between them, vague as his memory was of that drunken night, remained vivid enough to suggest that her sexual prowess had been less a sign of a passionate nature than a desire to please. The waiter's appearance gave him a moment to renew his determination.

"What is it you wish to talk about, Ian?" she asked in a softer pitch than usual.

"I have wanted to talk to you about us, but have been a bit unsure how to do so—I apologize. I should have spoken with you weeks ago—"

To his surprise, Mary reached across the table and

caressed his hand. "It's all right. I know exactly how you feel and what you are about to say," she replied most seriously.

"You do?" Perhaps he had underestimated Mary.

"And I know how difficult it is for you to express your feelings. So, I shall make it easy for you," she continued in the same soft, serious tone.

He was so surprised that he just let her continue.

"The answer is yes. And I think we should do it right away," she whispered, "to avoid embarrassment."

He was confused. "I'm not sure I understand—"

She laughed with delight. "Oh, Ian, I adore that puzzled boyish expression of yours!" She leaned toward him. "I've known since the night you showed me"—her voice was such a bare whisper that he was forced to lean toward her to hear her words—"the magic, revealed the mystery of lovemaking to me"—Mary blushed but continued—"transformed me from a virginal girl to a woman. I've known since then that you loved me and that it was just a matter of time until you asked for my hand in marriage."

His mouth dropped open in astonishment, while Mary smiled and began to giggle.

"Oh, don't look so surprised! For I never would have *given* myself to you," she whispered, "if you hadn't shown your love before in a thousand ways. But I'm certainly *relieved* that you decided to do so today"— her blush deepened—"for I should have gotten my monthly days ago, but I suppose there's no need to worry at all." She lowered her eyes with maidenly modesty. Then she looked up at him with a bright smile. "If it means what I think, which do you hope for? A boy or a girl?"

"Is everything all right, sir?" asked the waiter, who'd just reappeared.

"Perfect, thank you. Everything's perfect!" Ian threw his head back in a hearty laugh. Mary looked at him with shock clearly registered in her green eyes. What was it they said about green eyes? He drowned his drink and raised his glass as he caught the waiter's eye. "Give me a moment to absorb the 'news,' Mary, will you?" he said with a smile.

"Ian, are you all right?" she asked anxiously.

"Mary, I'm fine. Just give me a moment . . ." The waiter brought another glass of Scotch, which he was about to place on the table when Ian snatched it from his hand and downed half the glass, to the waiter's astonished but silent response. The waiter rubbed his balding head and walked off. Ian quickly turned. He caught Julia's stare and blush, apparent even from across the room.

Julia was mortified at the sardonic smirk Ian gave her when he surprised her by turning and catching her gaze. "Let's leave, Betsy," she suggested.

"But, Julia. We've just ordered dessert. But if you really can't bear being in the same room with Ian—"

"We'll stay, and I can do without your sarcasm," Julia said more sharply than she'd intended.

Betsy instantly looked contrite. "Julia, if you really want to leave, then we shall. Right this instant!" She began to rise.

Julia reached for her hand. "No. Please sit down. Let's have dessert."

Betsy settled back into her chair. "I'm sorry . . ."

Was there no end to the trickery and deception of these girls? Ian wondered bitterly. He turned back to Mary, giving her the most unconcerned smile he could manage. He could be duped—far more easily than he'd guessed. He might be a fool, but Mary had underestimated his intelligence if she thought she could really blackmail him into marrying her. For if she had been 'the virgin Mary' that night he had been with her, then he was Jesus Christ himself. He knew just how to beat her at her own game. To think that he had felt sympathy for this conniving red-haired witch! Even disdaining gossip the way he did, he'd heard enough to know for certain that Mary had given her 'favors' to three or four other men she'd attempted to ensnare. But even had he not known so before she'd set him up that evening, he still knew there had been no sign of her virginity, physical or otherwise. For the moment, he'd play along with her. He almost laughed to himself, wondering how quickly she'd try to back down. He reached for her small hand and embraced it with his own.

"Ian?" she asked anxiously. "You're behaving so strangely . . ."

"Have I alarmed you, my sweet?" He gave her as tender a smile as he could manage. "I didn't mean to. It's just that obviously I'm more than a little surprised. First by your perspicacity—"

"Perspicacity?" she asked with a flush that showed her embarrassment. Ian realized she didn't know if he'd given her a compliment or a curse, poor girl. She really should have studied her lessons in school.

"Your keenness of perception, my dear. For I always pride myself on being somewhat inscrutable, but obviously you've read me as easily as a school primer."

Her giggles, he sensed, were from relief. "Well, I do think I'm the kind of *caring* person who has a certain flair for understanding people."

"And that you do, Mary!" He lifted one of his hands from hers and stroked her cheek. "Second, the news about the possible child," he whispered. "Well, of course I'm thrilled! But it does worry me a bit. You see, one of the reasons that I've taken so long to declare my intentions is that our new partnership is less successful than I've let on. There's a good chance that Ned and I will go our separate ways by the end of the week."

"Oh, I see," she said sympathetically, though he knew that she had no idea of the implications. "Shall you get a new partner or go it alone?" she asked.

"I suspect go it alone. Though it is all rather depressing. You see, it has come down to a matter of principle. I believe I've revealed enough about myself to you in conversations for you to be aware that I am a man who must live by his principles."

"Oh, yes," she said with a glow. "And that is one of the aspects of your character that I most respect . . . and love."

"That makes me feel more assured. To continue . . . Mary, are you certain that you are truly in love with me, or could you actually be feeling more of a crush?"

"I have had crushes, Ian. This is the real thing. True, everlasting love! I would follow you to the ends of the earth if you asked me to!"

"What about Buffalo?" he asked evenly.

261

"What *about* Buffalo?" she replied, confused. Just as he wanted her to be.

"Would you follow me to Buffalo, dearest?"

Mary tittered. "That must be the latest joke I haven't heard, but it is witty."

He pretended to be offended. "But it's *not* a joke. That's where I'll be moving, for at least two years—I'm sorry, I should say *we!*"

"Whatever for?" she asked. For the first time today, if not since he'd made her acquaintance, her voice lacked artificiality. She was obviously upset.

"Because Ned will keep the business here, probably with Charles, and I will go back to work for Mr. Sullivan. The money won't be much—we'll have to live conservatively. Could you do that? Would you be willing to live without maid or driver? . . . I suppose we could afford a cook. . . ." He pretended to ponder and looked down at her soft pink hands within his. "For I couldn't bear the thought of these gentle hands becoming reddened and worn." He looked up at her, feigning a lack of attention to her narrowed eyes, furrowed brow and agape mouth. "Anyway, it will only be for two years, maybe three at the longest!"

"Is the move to Buffalo definite?" she asked weakly.

"No, as I said, I'll know at the end of the week. That's why I was staying away, for I could not be with you and long disguise my *amore!*" he said in a seductive tone. "Besides, I realize that I am asking you to make a great sacrifice. Uprooting yourself from friends and family to a provincial town, living in a manner far less comfortable than you've been accustomed . . ."

Mary brightened, to his immediate alarm. "It may not be that horrible! For you may not leave the partnership, which means we'd remain in Manhattan. Even if worse came to worst, what with your family's money and mine, our inheritances . . ."

He clutched her hands tightly and stared deeply into her eyes with the most serious expression he could, while he had to bite his inner lip to keep from laughing. "Mary, remember we talked about principle. I'm determined to make it on my own. I would accept *no* money from *anyone,* nor would I permit *you* to accept any. I cannot compromise on this or I would not be the man you love. Is that not so?"

"Well, Ian . . ." she began, as her eyes clouded and she looked as if she were fighting back tears. She tried to pull her hands from his, but he pretended not to notice in his feigned intensity and grasped hers more tightly.

"Do you sew, Mary?" he sprang at her. Had she not intended to commit such a heinous entrapment of him, he would have pitied her.

"Do I *sew?* Of course not. Why?"

He frowned. "Oh, it was just an idea. I thought that once the baby came," he whispered, "you could take in a bit of sewing to help out *just* in case we needed—"

"Ian, dear." She pulled her hands from him and pretended to arrange some strands of her perfectly coiffed upturned hairdo. "I don't want you to be disappointed. I should have waited, for I may *not* be . . . I mean, perhaps we haven't been blessed with a child yet," she whispered.

"I almost forgot, in my excitement, that it wasn't yet definite," he said sadly. "Well, no worry! Once we're married, I'm sure it will be no time at all until we *are* blessed—I hear they have excellent doctors up in Buffalo, so you'll be under the best of care. Do you mind?" he asked, indicating his pipe.

"No, of course not. But what you haven't told me is why you'd let that Ned Barrington take your business from you. Especially since it appears that you do all the work—I never liked him, not one bit. I'll admit that to you now!"

"Oh, it isn't Ned's fault. It will be all very amiable. You see, he's brought us in some fine business. A commission—a very large commission—for a huge estate to be built in Newport."

Mary smiled, frowned, then smiled again. "Then I don't understand."

"It's simple. I thought I'd explained it all to you before. I don't want to design the mansions or estates of rich men. Why, if I did, Ned and I could *easily* make a bundle. I want to build great skyscrapers. Nothing more, nothing less," he admitted quite honestly. "If it means struggling for the rest of my life," he exaggerated, "well, dang it, I intend to do exactly that. Little did I expect to be blessed with a lovely girl like you to love me and share my life and give me little bundles of joy . . ."

Mary frowned. "We don't know that for certain," she repeated.

"Oh, I keep forgetting. When will you know? For we should marry as soon as possible. We can elope. Maybe take a honeymoon at Niagara Falls so that we can swing down through Buffalo and you can have your first look at our new home!"

"Niagara Falls?" she repeated, but her mouth remained unattractively gaping.

"Why not? You've been to Europe a million times," he said, resorting to her hyperbole. "Although the idea of a safari into darkest Africa appeals to me. What do you think? . . . Oh, we couldn't! For it would deplete what little savings I have left. Another time, perhaps for an anniversary?"

Mary glanced at her little jeweled wristwatch. "Ian. Didn't you say you had a meeting? Well, dearest, you're going to be quite late unless you rush out of here."

"But we haven't even touched our steaks," he said. He withdrew his pocket watch and pretended to be alarmed at the time. "Would you mind terribly if I raced off and left you to finish your meal at a leisurely pace?" He didn't want to overplay his hand, but he couldn't resist the joke. "After all, once we're married it will probably be a long time before we dine at Delmonico's again." He hadn't thought anything could make her blanch paler, but his last remark did just that.

"No, dear. Rush off and I shall have the waiter bring me another steak. I'll tell him this one is *far* too tough for a lady's palate."

Ian began to rise, but then sat down again. He took her hand despite some resistance on her part. "One last thing. Would you like me to come over this evening and ask your father for your hand, now that it's all straight between us?"

"No! I mean, they're attending the opera tonight."

"Oh, that's too bad. Well, then, tomorrow evening!" he said, rose and gave her a peck on her cheek. "Shall I come to visit *you* tonight?"

"No! I mean, I'm going to the opera with them."

He smiled softly. "How sweet you are. You've told me how much you despise the opera. I must rush—I'll call you later!" His final glance showed him a pale, worried girl. He turned away quickly. Noting that Julia and Betsy were still seated, he made his way across the other side of the crowded dining room.

Only when he stood in the cold afternoon air did he allow himself to smile broadly and break into a hearty laugh.

"Fine day, young man, isn't it?" an elderly gentleman passing by said and tipped his hat. Ian tipped his in almost a salute to one of his own sex. Then he strode quickly in the direction of his office.

Mary couldn't believe it. Her plan had worked so beautifully that it had *almost* left her engaged to a maniac! Thank the Lord she wasn't pregnant, for whatever would she have done then? Why hadn't she heeded the talk of how strange Ian was? Well, she would be 'unavailable' when he called. She would write him a letter as soon as she arrived home, then claim she'd written it in the middle of the night. She would tell him that she loved him so, that she could not tie him down and therefore had to let him go free. Damn! But what about her supposed pregnancy? She could write the letter, but she had to wait at least a day before having it delivered. She'd have to avoid him until then. She'd make such a veiled mention of the fact that there was no baby on the way, that even if he ever showed the note to anyone—which she was certain he wouldn't —she would have been elusive enough in her words to protect her reputation. Distractedly she glanced about the room. Why, she'd quite forgotten that Julia and Betsy were still in the restaurant. Julia had been staring at her! Now she was laughing, as Betsy no doubt was as well. They were laughing at her. Well, at least she'd use this dreadful episode to her advantage one last time.

"I'm afraid to tell you," Julia said when she saw Mary approaching them with a wide smile on her face, "but Mary's on her way over here."

"Oh, goodness!" Betsy replied.

"Hello again, girls," Mary trilled. "May I join you for just a minute?" She sat before either of them replied. "I must rush to do some shopping, but I had to share the news with you two—only if you *swear* not to tell anyone just yet!"

Julia noted that although neither she nor Betsy replied, Mary was intent on the telling. Well, what of it? Nothing could be more upsetting than Mary's previous undesired confidence.

"Ian just asked me to marry him! Of course, marriage is a grave step, as you both know—oh, I'm sorry, Julia. I didn't mean to embarrass you. In fact, I think you've been very wise to break three engagements rather than marry a man when both of you weren't passionately in love with one another. But, please . . ." Mary turned to Betsy. "I implore you not to mention our secret to Ned, since he is Ian's partner, for the time being at any rate. For I've got to give it most serious thought before I decide. And," she whispered, "I do have some doubts."

"I won't utter a word," Betsy said coldly.

"Julia, dear. Your friendship and confidence you've already proven to me. I know I can trust your discretion," she said, and patted Julia's hand. With that she jumped up. "As I said, I must run. You can offer your good wishes when it's official . . . though I'm just not *certain* . . ." Mary frowned, then gave them a cheery smile. "Adieu."

Julia had thought nothing Mary could say would ever hurt her as fully as it had the previous time. Once again, she was proven wrong. She turned to Betsy, whose face was unhappily puzzled.

"There has to be a reasonable explanation for all of this," Betsy insisted, hitting her fist lightly on the table for emphasis. "And we're going to get to the bottom of it, I promise you!"

Julia fought back her tears. "It's just as I told you earlier. He doesn't love me, he loves her. Even Mary wouldn't announce to us that Ian had asked for her hand if it weren't so, would she? What with Ned being Ian's partner."

"No, I don't think even Mary's that stupid. . . . I tell you, I just don't understand!"

"That's because you're my best friend and don't want to, any more than I did. But I'm tired of denying the truth. I've got to get away. I'll go to Uncle's first thing tomorrow. Would you like to come?"

"I'd love to, but I've already promised Mamma to go with them to visit our cousins in the Adirondacks. Then, when you're in Tuxedo, I'll be out west for a week . . . but at least we'll be going to Europe together!" Betsy said, and forced a smile.

"Yes, I'm really glad that your mother and Mamma planned that again this year."

"So am I!" Betsy replied with genuine enthusiasm. "We had such a terrific time and we'll have even a better time this season! Already Ellen is chattering about it, and it's two months before we leave! You'll see. By the time we return, you'll be your old self again."

"I hope so," Julia replied, but she didn't believe it. She'd never be her 'old' self again, whether Mary decided to marry Ian or not. And of course, Mary would. Julia had no doubts that Mary's supposed uncertainty was nothing more than show. Why did Mary hate her so? Julia wondered, aware of the fact for the first time.

Chapter Fourteen

BY THE TIME IAN ENTERED THE BAR AT HARRISON HOUSE off Forty-second Street, he'd walked down, up and across a good deal of Manhattan Island.

It had been midafternoon (on his journey from the tip of the island, where he'd viewed the Statue of Liberty from the Battery for some time) when he'd found himself wandering through the swarming mass of immigrants. They spoke in a dozen foreign tongues as they bought and sold their wares, haggled, laughed and engaged in animated discussion in the confusion that was called Orchard Street, on the Lower East Side. When Ian finally left the hub of activity and crossed into a sunless court between two tenement buildings, he encountered some scrappy-looking boys grouped about a row of trash cans. Although they stared at him ominously, he felt no fear. He nodded as he passed them and wended his way, unbothered by their comments in a language he couldn't understand or identify, through a dark, narrow alley and then back out onto the sidewalks that swirled with the tides of city life at its worst. Still, the slum possessed a vitality that intrigued him. For here was life at its most animated, compared at least to Fifth Avenue and his usual environs. Here children ran and played with abandon, men and women shouted, often calling down from the stoops and fire escapes on which they sat, to those in the midst of the open-air marketplace where storekeepers competed with pushcarts, wagons, makeshift stands, all offering a strange and enormous variety of items. Such a vivid reminder of how the less fortunate existed suggested to him that his problems were minuscule in comparison. Moreover, the sense of vitality—for on the whole, despite their wretched circumstances, these people seemed no less happy than those within his own world—renewed him. At least momentarily.

He walked west, down the blocks of factories and warehouses, until he reached the Hudson River, where he looked out to New Jersey. The burly workmen he passed seemed to take little notice of him, despite his clothing that marked him an outsider again. But he realized they were far too busy with their own lives to give him more than a passing glance.

He cut back northeasterly, crisscrossing, until he reached the arch in Washington Square Park. Though tiny compared to the expansive green of Central Park, after his voyage through some of the worst hellholes of Manhattan, the park, surrounded by stately brownstones and a new apartment building or two, was a welcome relief. He rested on a bench for a while, having a smoke, and observed the children playing under the watchful eyes of their nannies or mothers. He noticed a young couple on an adjacent bench, sitting a respectable distance from one another, their glowing eyes filled with love. He smiled, and when the pretty dark-haired girl, in a cloth winter coat, noticed his attention, she blushed prettily. Her beau glanced in Ian's direction with a protective sneer that gave way to a smile and a wink. Ian smiled back and politely looked away, but the couple made him think that love was possible, perhaps. And love made him think of Julia.

Growing tense, he rose and walked back through the arch and began a slower stroll up Fifth Avenue. Thirty, forty years before, lower Fifth Avenue had been *the* address of society, which had gradually moved north through the decades, until the fashionable addresses began in the upper Forties and ran to the Eighties. He studied the changing architecture, from the simple brownstones on lower Fifth to the new brick and limestone housefronts as he wandered across to Madison Avenue. As he approached the corner on Madison, he noted the change to an eclectic representation, from pseudo-Georgian facades with marble porches and awnings to the simplicity of the white-stoned neo-Federal-style flat-front houses. He had taken this walk many times, his eye trained to the most subtle nuances of architecture, but he never failed to see something he hadn't noticed before.

As he approached the stately bar, he realized that he was chilled, for the dusky streets had grown from pleasantly cold to frigid about the time the streetlights went on. His stomach growled, reminding him that he hadn't eaten all day. The first time Ian had visited the Harrison House, he'd been brought there by his old friend Sam Walters. It was here Sam had informed him that Betty's boy might be his son. It seemed fitting to stop in, for he knew Sam frequented the saloon, and he hadn't seen Sam since before his trip to Boston. Harrison House was a noted rendezvous for actors, businessmen and Democrats. In fact, the most influential of the city bosses could be found sitting around a large table across from the bar, above which hung a large painting of appealing nudes by the famous Frenchman Adolphe William Bouguereau.

Ian spotted Sam standing at the bar as soon as he entered. Sam's smile warmed him, as did the heated room and the beers he downed with Sam in succession. Sam eventually led him to the buffet, where he followed suit and loaded his plate high with roast beef and ham sandwiches. They had a couple more beers, some laughs, and Ian was so thoroughly enjoying himself that he was disappointed when Sam said he had to take his leave at half-past eight. Sam offered him a ride home. But Ian didn't want to go home. Besides, he needed to walk again to clear his beer-soaked brain. But being unable to think was a welcome relief from the past few weeks, to say nothing of this dreadful day. Ian drank another beer and then set out into the night. He didn't know what time it was, nor did he care.

Pulling his collar to his neck, Ian wished he had his scarf and gloves with him, for it was clear but frigid, and the wind that had struck up during his respite chilled him to the core. He began to walk briskly, although he had set no destination.

It was after ten when Julia retired from her studio. She was pleased with the landscape she'd almost completed. It had a stronger mood than anything she'd done before. Not only had her work become her most comforting outlet this past month, but she believed she saw a substantial improvement in both her drawing and her painting. Perhaps the old cliché about artists working best when they were most unhappy was true. But then, she wasn't truly an artist . . . or was she?

As she turned out the electric light and started down the stairs to her bedroom, all she knew for certain was that she was an unhappy, confused, heartsick young woman. She missed Percy. He had taken her withdrawal from their engagement far worse than she'd expected. He'd pleaded, cried and then stormed away. He either hadn't understood her feelings or hadn't wanted to. She had written him three letters, trying to tell him how dear he was to her and that she had broken their engagement as much for his sake as for her own. Thus far she'd received no response, which angered her. For if he loved her *half* as much as he proclaimed, then how could he cut her off so, refusing to talk or write? Had she been he, she could never have done the same!

Betsy had insisted that men were different in this way from women, but Julia found that an inadequate excuse. She was hurt and angry . . . perhaps more disappointed than angry, for she'd believed that she knew Percy so well. Did anyone ever really know another? But she and Betsy had a strong empathy, as did she and Kathleen. Betsy had argued that when one talked of romantic love, all rational behavior and explanations held little weight. She'd disputed it, but she knew that Betsy was correct. For how else could she explain to herself that despite all the hurt and indignity, she still loved Ian? That she wished some magic would bring them back to that afternoon in the drawing room and erase all that had happened since.

She walked into her bedroom, lit the gaslamp and then wandered to the window. It was a clear but starless night and very cold, she noted, when she rested her face against the windowpane for a moment. For her one breath had frosted the clear pane. As she had done when she was a child, she quickly doodled a face with her fingertip onto the frosted pane. She breathed again and drew another and then another. Finally she forced herself to stop. She was thinking about changing into her nightclothes when she recognized Kathleen's knock upon the door. She'd dismissed Kathleen hours ago and assumed she was fast asleep by now. "Come in," she called, delighted for some company. Since Daphne had gone for a visit to Harold's aunt and uncle a few days ago, the house had felt especially empty. Well, she might as well get used to it, she thought, for once Daphne married in June, it would always be this way.

"Why are you frowning?" Kathleen asked.

"Why are you dressed in your uniform?" Julia countered.

"I was doing a bit of sewing and letter writing, and just when I was about to undress, I heard you go down the stairs. I was feeling a bit lonely, so I thought I'd see if you wanted some company."

"Oh, I do, for I'm feeling the same. But I assumed you were long asleep and didn't want to disturb you."

"Still brooding over the incident at lunch, I expect?" Kathleen asked rhetorically as she sat on the edge of Julia's bed.

Julia shrugged.

"Would you like to play whisk?" Kathleen offered. "Or another game? Or just talk?"

"I feel so restless! I guess because all I've done the past two weeks is sleep. I'm not a bit tired now, but I don't feel like playing cards or anything like that. . . . I know what we can do!" Julia brightened.

"I'm not so sure that I like that grin on your face. The last time I saw it, you talked me into going to that fortune-teller's," Kathleen said guardedly.

Julia laughed. "Oh, this is nothing like that! And her name is Madam Rosa."

"It's all the same to me," Kathleen answered dryly.

"I can't believe that you're *still* upset about Madam Rosa. That was weeks ago. If it's all foolishness . . . what did you call it?"

"Malarkey."

"If it's all malarkey, then why are you still fretting about it? Besides, I should think you'd be *happy* to know that you'll find love when the summer flowers bloom," Julia teased.

"I'd rather not discuss the subject again, if you please," Kathleen said with such formality that Julia burst into laughter, which caused Kathleen to laugh as well.

"You sounded just like Mamma's pretentious secretary, Miss Pendleton, right then!" Julia giggled at the thought.

"May the Lord save me from such a fate," Kathleen said with a sigh and then crossed herself, but her eyes twinkled with suppressed laughter. "Now, what brilliant idea have you come up with to vex me tonight?"

Julia had almost forgotten. "I think we should bundle up and go for a walk!"

"A walk?" Kathleen asked with astonishment. She glanced at the clock on the mantel. "Why, it's after ten-thirty on a *freezing* weeknight. Whatever gave you such a foolish notion?"

"Oh, please, Kathleen! Just a quick walk around a block or two. We'll bundle up. I'll let you wear my fur coat—the one you love best."

"Bribery won't help your cause. And what if your parents arrive home any minute?"

"But they won't. For they were going to dine, after the opera, at Sherry's with a party of people. We'll be back in fifteen minutes, I promise. It will let us both sleep well tonight!"

"And I can wear the fur coat?" Kathleen began to laugh as Julia ran to her closet.

Ian felt like a fool. Why was he standing before Julia's house, staring at her window at almost eleven o'clock at night? Good thing there was no trellis or he'd probably have climbed it already, fallen off in his semi-inebriated state that neither the cold nor his walking had adequately dissipated, and ended up with a broken leg or a cracked skull, he thought. He turned on his heels, intending to walk straight home—

"Goodness, I'm sorry!" he said to the figure he'd almost knocked to the ground.

"If you'd watch where you were go—"

"Julia!" he exclaimed.

"Ian?" she asked, equally amazed.

"What are you doing out alone at such an hour?" he asked sternly.

"I'm not alone," she retorted.

He glanced to her right and saw the worried face of Kathleen.

"And I might ask you a similar question. What are you doing standing in front of our house? For surely you were not intending to pay Papa such a late call, and besides, he's not at home, as you probably know anyway."

"I didn't know," he answered. He wondered if his words sounded as slurred to her as they did to him. "And I was not *standing* in front of your house. I was *merely* taking an evening constitutional," he stated slowly, with what he believed was great dignity.

"Your breath smells horrible! You've been drinking." Julia's face filled with distaste. "In fact, you're inebriated, Ian Woods!"

"Miss Davenport," he said, articulating with care. "You are not only *quite* rude, but incorrect. I am not. Not in the least! Perhaps a bit drunk—but *not* inebriated!"

"Are you two going to stand out here and fight all night?" Kathleen demanded. "It's freezing and you'll both catch a death of cold. Look at you, Mr. Woods. You're not even wearing a scarf or hat. Not even gloves!"

Ian reached to the top of his head. "I did have a hat. Honestly, for how else could I have tipped it at the gentleman this afternoon?"

It wasn't funny, Julia told herself. Ian standing there, weaving and looking for his hat. But she couldn't refrain from bursting into laughter.

"Sshh! You'll wake the neighbors and we'll be in more trouble than you'd be happy about," Kathleen warned. "I say we take him into the kitchen, give him some coffee—at least a potful—and then send him home when your father returns with the carriage. After all, Mr. Woods isn't exactly a stranger to this house. If there's any trouble about it, I'll take the blame."

"No you won't, because he's *not* going to be invited in," Julia insisted. "He only lives a few blocks down. If he's made it this far on his own steam, he can certainly walk the remaining blocks." Julia turned from Kathleen and looked him straight in the eye. Even in the dim light beneath the streetlamp, she could see his eyes were reddened and blurry. "Ian, go home," Julia demanded, suddenly furious at what a pathetic sight he was. She pushed at his shoulders.

"Goodness!" Kathleen exclaimed, as Ian began to lose his balance. Julia grabbed at him from the front and she grabbed his sleeve as he regained his balance.

"Julia, please. Let me come in. I *am* cold. I promise I won't stay long." He took her hand and gently held it between his own. He was going to sit her down, and as drunk as he was, tell her the truth. That he loved her

279

more than he'd ever dreamed it was possible to love. That whatever misunderstandings they'd had could be worked out. He wanted her to be his wife. "Julia, please, I know I'm drunk, but it's urgent that I talk to you."

Julia felt his sad eyes plead with her. How dare he! He asked Mary to marry him today and then he wanted to talk to her? She wanted to take him in her arms and hold him to her breast. She felt his hand's soft stroking through her paper-thin kid glove, and before she realized what she was doing, she curled her fingers against the curve of his palm.

"Oh, Julia," he said with that gentle look that was not drunken, the same look she'd seen the time they kissed, the afternoon they talked so heartfelt and openly. She looked away and glanced down at her hands. With a will of its own, her other hand had fallen upon his. She was more daft than he! She pulled her hands free.

"We have nothing to speak about, Ian. Except that good manners compel me to offer you congratulations on your impending engagement."

"What engagement?" he asked, looking genuinely bewildered.

Was it possible that Mary had fabricated the story after all? "Your engagement to Mary Hoffman. Did you not propose to her at Delmonico's today?"

"Oh, that," he laughed. "That didn't mean anything —not the way you think, anyway."

"Do you take engagements so lightly, then?"

His mind was slow, but gradually the import of what she was saying dawned on him. That bitch Mary! After he'd left she must have proceeded right to Julia's table and made her announcement, just to make Julia miserable. But why would she want to do that unless she knew? . . . Oh, how he wished he were completely sober.

"It appears that the cat's got your tongue! Or is it that you can't resort to your usual charming glibness with so much liquor in you? Or perhaps it might be your conscience—that is, assuming that you have one! Which is doubtful—"

"Julia!" Kathleen interrupted. "I think you're saying things you're going to regret!"

Kathleen's warning registered in the recesses of her mind, but after months of tension and heartbreak, Julia couldn't stop the accusing, angry words from pouring out, even if she'd wanted to. "No. You most definitely don't have a conscience. Or honor. For you wouldn't be here speaking to me this way the *same* day you asked Mary for her hand if you did! To say *nothing* of some of the other things you've done and taken so lightly and—"

How dare she accuse him! When *she* had taken up with a married man, as well as *toyed* with him while engaged. Anger sobered him, and all he'd tried not to ruminate about tonight flooded back at him. "I think *you* should examine your own behavior, which leaves *much* to be desired by any standards of honesty and decency, before you throw stones at me! And if you wish to lecture about the immorality of taking engagements lightly, I suggest you lecture yourself, my dear Julia!"

"How dare you!" She slapped him, to her shock. He

grabbed her wrist. She'd never raised her hand to anyone before.

"I demand that you both stop this!" Kathleen said. She grabbed Julia by the arm and tried to pull her into the house. But Julia was as immovable as a boulder. "Mr. Woods, please!" Kathleen pleaded, but again her words fell on deaf ears.

Ian released Julia's wrist. "Slap me again, if you like, but that won't change the fact that you've deceived, lied, beguiled and cheated more than *any* woman I've ever known. You're even worse than Mary, for at least she's *obvious*. I don't know why I thought I still loved you."

Ian's laugh was harsher than his words that fell like blows.

"You're not worth it. None of you women are! Actually, I'd probably do as well to let Mary ensnare me as anyone else. Good luck with your married friend," Ian whispered.

She was too stunned to speak. He stroked her cheek. Before she could speak, he abruptly turned and strode away. His sardonic laugh echoed down the empty street.

"How could he . . ." Julia started to run after him. For he could not say such lies and turn away, but Kathleen's grip was firm this time. "Please, let me . . ." Julia's throat tightened so that she couldn't speak. Then the tears overcame her, like a violent storm. She turned and raced into the house without stopping until she slammed the door behind her and fell onto her bed.

Ian had gone two blocks, cursing and ranting under

his breath, when he whirled back in the direction of Julia's. He slowed his pace. For he had to think what he would say when the Davenports' front door was answered. There was a possibility that Charles and Mrs. Davenport had just arrived home. Charles would probably not be terribly off-put by his mien, but Henrietta—she would not be likely to react in kind. Still, they would ask him in. If Kathleen or Julia answered the door, or if the butler announced his arrival to Julia, would she see him or slam the heavy front door in his face? He'd said some terrible things to her—he couldn't even remember *exactly* what he'd blurted, but he shuddered as he guessed.

He was as sober now as he had been sloshed earlier. He loved Julia and no one else—this he could no longer deny. He believed he'd even shouted so at her. But what right did he possess to declare his love? Thanks to Mary, his "engagement" plan had thus far backfired. What if he'd misread Mary more than he'd thought? That Mary did *not* love him, he was certain. But perhaps she was genuinely fearful that she might be pregnant. Worse yet, what if it came to pass that she was? Every instinct in him said she wasn't. But look where his instincts had so far taken him! If she were pregnant, and he doubted that she'd seen any other man since his arrival in town, he would have to marry her. He would be paying for his few minutes of lust for a lifetime, but it was *his* debt, and pay it he must. If his gut feelings were correct, then he should receive a letter from her today declaring her "undying love" but nevertheless declining his "proposal."

He was almost to the Davenport house when he

turned back again. For what could he say to Julia? Could he tell her that he wanted to marry her if he didn't *have to* marry Miss Hoffman? Of course not! He heard the wheels of an approaching carriage and darted behind a post. He sighed as he saw the Davenports' liveryman pull into their drive. He slipped back down the street and began his slow trek home.

Long after she and Kathleen had heard Mamma and Papa return, long after she and Kathleen talked half through the night until Kathleen's eyes could barely remain open, Julia lay awake trying to deduce exactly what had happened. The scene between her and Ian was clear enough, but Kathleen had been even more clever than usual by insisting that she stop crying and write down all they remembered of his remarks, forgetting for the moment all anger. Kathleen had softly but firmly insisted that his accusations were clues. For something about the entire "conversation" had struck her strangely.

"I've seen fights lots worse than that in my day, back in the old neighborhood. People yelled things at each other—the women as bad as the men—that would make your ears blush . . . but there was something about the way *you* two were yelling at each other . . . It was like you were throwing things at each other that *neither* of you honestly understood. I don't think Ian knew what *you* meant, any more than you knew what he was talking about."

"I'm not sure I'm understanding *you* now," Julia had answered, wiping her eyes again.

"Let me try to say it more simply. I know what you were accusing him of. But *he* really didn't seem to! That's why he got so mad."

"But he admitted to having asked Mary to marry him, didn't he?"

"Yes, but remember that at first he didn't know what you were talking about when you congratulated him on his engagement—"

"He said . . . 'what engagement,' " Julia interjected.

"Right!" Kathleen said with a proud smile. "Now, why don't you get up and write each thing down. We'll make a list. Then we'll see it in black and white."

Julia hurried to her dressing table, grabbed a box of paper and quickly inked her fountain pen. She wrote quickly but evenly. Then she turned to Kathleen, who hovered above her shoulder. "I've got that down. Now, when I said, 'your engagement to Mary,' he didn't deny it."

"But he said, 'Oh, that,' and laughed, or words like that. It struck me so odd at the time because I was watching both of you, and he was still smiling at first, even after he said that. Then his face changed fast. It was like he realized something that made him real angry."

"He realized that he'd been caught in a lie!" Julia insisted.

"But then he would have looked real sheepish. He never looked sheepish. At first he thought it was a big joke and then he was real mad. Nothing in between?" Kathleen puzzled.

"Wait, I'm starting to remember it all now, too. At

first *I* was so angry and hurt and it was all a blur. But now I do remember—it did seem as if he were amused about his engagement, as if it *were* nothing more than a joke. When he became furious was when it dawned on him that Mary must have told Betsy and me after he left the restaurant."

"Yes, that's it! That's what I was getting at. We're regular Sherlock Holmeses. Did you write it all down?"

"I'm writing as quickly as I can." Julia actually laughed, surprising herself.

And so on they had gone, for hours. By the time Kathleen pulled herself upstairs to bed, Julia had admitted that it was possible that Mary Hoffman was behind much of it, but she wasn't certain how. However, she was determined to find out. In the morning she would pay a call on Mary on the way to Long Island. What kept her awake and tossing was her fear that she might find out just what she *didn't* want to be possible. For during their analysis of the argument, it had dawned on her that perhaps Mary was pregnant, or believed she was pregnant. If Julia hadn't been so distraught and tired, she would have laughed. For Betsy had reached that conclusion within five minutes after Mary's departure from Delmonico's. In fact, Julia realized that Betsy had promised to ask Ned if Ian had indeed proposed. But Betsy hadn't called her, so Julia assumed she hadn't spoken with him yet.

The strongest indictment against Ian was his own words to her Christmas Eve. For if he were the victim in all of this, as well as she, why had he thanked her for "helping" Mary achieve their rendezvous the night of

Daphne's party? That piece didn't fit, no matter which way she turned it about. Julia fell asleep murmuring to herself, "But why? . . ."

Ian quickly lifted the ringing telephone in the foyer as he unlatched the door. Surely his mother and sister were asleep, as well as the staff. Who would be calling at such a late hour? For a glance at the clock told him it was almost midnight.

"Hello," he answered with irritation.

"Ian! Dang it, where have you been all afternoon and night? Didn't you receive any of my messages?" Ned asked, sounding angry.

Ian lifted some papers that lay on the table by the telephone. "They're right here, but I walked in just this minute. How come you're calling so late? Is there some kind of trouble that couldn't wait until morning?"

"Yes and no. Good news and bad news. Before you snap my head off, why don't you hear it?"

"I'm sorry," Ian apologized.

"I've got a question for you first. It's personal, but I swore to Betsy that I'd pry, and I hope you don't mind."

"Go ahead. Don't worry about it. I'll answer if I can, because it would be nice to make *somebody* happy."

"Did you ask Mary Hoffman to marry you?"

Ian laughed softly but bitterly. "Yes and no."

"What kind of answer is that?"

Ian sighed. "An honest one. I had to ask, but I'm certain she'll refuse by tomorrow. Then at least *she'll* be out of my life for good."

"I don't understand."

"I'm not trying to be evasive. Honestly. I'll give you the gory details as soon as it's ancient history, which should be by tomorrow night at the latest. Can you put Betsy off until then?"

"I can try. Now, do you want the good news?"

"It would certainly be a novelty."

"We got the Caramody commission! Well, I mean it will take a couple of weeks to negotiate, and I suppose they could pull out anytime before the contract's signed. But they definitely want us—you. Mr. Caramody stressed, when I called after the afternoon post arrived, how impressed he'd been with you!"

"I can't believe it!" Ian said, attempting to keep his voice down.

"And I can't believe those are your *first* words! Who was telling me how positive he was, just this morning?"

"I know, but still . . ." Ian smiled happily. "This means so much more than just a project."

"It means that I'm not going to get rid of you after all, dang it!" Ned teased.

"Same for you, walrus," Ian sallied, calling Ned by his nickname, given in Chicago because of his mustache.

"It's really swell! We're going to do what we want *and* be renowned as well as bloody rich in our own right!"

"You've never been righter!" Ian agreed.

"And that means I can propose to Betsy!"

"Oh, no . . ." Ian moaned into the mouthpiece.

"Why, I thought you liked her!"

"Of course I do! I think you're a lucky man. I didn't

moan for that reason. Ned, does anyone know about the commission besides you and me?"

"Mr. Caramody and his board of directors, I assume."

He couldn't allow Mary to find out! "I'm serious. It's very important that no one know—for a day or two at most, I would guess. I'll explain why in a minute. Did you tell Charles?"

"I almost called him, but I wanted you to tell him yourself. No one knows but us," Ned replied. "Would you . . . *could* you explain to me what the mystery is?"

"I know it's late, Ned. But do you think I could come over to your flat and talk to you? I need to talk to someone, and maybe you can help me figure some of it out."

"I'll have a Scotch waiting," Ned said warmly.

Ian grimaced. "How about some strong tea?"

"I agree with your gut instincts. Frankly, from what I've heard about Mary—I met one of her *almost* husbands at Charles's club and we got to talking over a few drinks. He was astonished to hear that it was true that you were courting her—or so it appeared to everyone at the time. He said that she was more treacherous than any whore in the red-light districts on the Continent. Worse than the ones down at the docks, who often decide to slit a guy's throat on a whim. He couldn't understand why you couldn't see through her. For he said he was straight out of college and still wet behind the ears when he met her."

"I guess I really wasn't paying attention. . . . And after that night, I felt like such a cad. I mean, I was in love with Julia, yet I'd allowed myself to be seduced by Mary—and very *easily* I must admit, in her defense. What a fool! It's ironic that it happened on the *same* day that I learned how I'd been taken in by Betty."

Ned poured Ian another tea. "So, you're only human, like the rest of us. You were hurt and lonely."

"That's too easy a rationalization, as much as I'd like to cling to it. Besides, it's too late to matter now."

"What I can't figure out is how Mary managed to manipulate both you *and* Julia." Ned drifted into thought again.

"The thing that doesn't make sense is that when I indirectly confronted Julia, she knew exactly why I was thanking her. There's no way of getting around that. And now this story about her breaking her engagement because of a married man—"

"I don't buy it. And that one's easy. You just have to ask Percy if he said that to Mary."

Ian rubbed his brow. "And what if he did? I mean, we haven't been able to put our finger on any direct lie Mary's told. So why would she risk lying about something that could be so easily checked?"

"I don't know. The girl has problems, that's all I know. And Betsy said she obviously hates Julia."

"So we're back where we started two hours ago. If Mary sends me a note refusing my proposal and claims she isn't pregnant . . ."

"Then we're sure she's just been scheming all along."

"Or maybe she does truly have cause to believe she's pregnant. And if she is, I'll have to marry her."

Ned shook his head sadly. "I know. But why dwell on the worst? As you said, we'll know in a few days at the most. I have a feeling it will all turn out the way you want it to."

"But even then, will I be able to win Julia's hand?" he asked, and sighed with despair. "You agree I can't go to her this morning—until I hear from Mary."

"I do. And I'm going to tell Betsy everything tonight, as we decided. For she's too smart to tell me what we need to know unless I level with her." Ned yawned.

"I can take a hint. I think I'd better go. It's almost three in the morning. Is Caramody expecting a call from me tomorrow?" Ned nodded. "I was afraid of that," Ian said, and rose from the sofa on which he'd been sprawled.

"You can sleep here if you like."

"Thanks, but I'd have to go home and bathe and dress in the morning anyway."

Ned saw him to the door. "Good night, partner," Ned said. They embraced.

"I don't know how to thank you . . ." Ian said.

"By getting the hell out of here and letting me sleep!"

Ian laughed softly as Ned closed the door behind him.

It was shortly after ten when Mary sat over a cup of tea, feeling much relieved. For she'd decided to send one of the servants with her letter to Ian's office. She'd thought about it all evening. How many times had she truly believed she was pregnant and then within hours gotten her monthly? So why let this nasty business with Ian go on a minute longer than necessary? For all she knew, he'd already announced their engagement to half the city! He was a fool, and crazy, but she liked him. He'd treated her with more respect than any man she'd ever known. Other than a kiss or a caress, he had never tried to trick her into intimacies, and she knew that he found her appealing. He had certainly been *ardent* that one evening, even if he wasn't in love with her. He hadn't even *pretended* love, or pledged words of love at just the right moments, to have his way with her in the manner that the other boys and then men had. She didn't wish to hurt him.

"Miss Hoffman, you have a caller. It's Miss Julia Davenport," the parlor maid said. "She says it's essential that she see you at once."

Why was Julia here? It was unlikely that she'd pay a visit just to chat. Mary's eyes narrowed. "Send her in, Sarah. Then bring us some more tea." Mary turned back to her morning paper, which she'd barely glanced at, although she rarely did more than glance. She was relieved that Mamma was already out at some charity meeting.

"Good morning, Mary," Julia said.

"Julia, what a wonderful surprise! Please sit down." She gestured at the chair in the sunny family dining room off the kitchen. "I was just finishing breakfast and catching up with the news, but it's so dull. McKinley is such a bore—all of politics is, for that matter, don't you agree?" She smiled brightly.

Julia smiled politely as she sat down, but didn't answer. She thanked the maid who poured her tea.

"I'm as surprised as I'm delighted to see you. I thought you were off to Long Island today and—"

"I am. In fact my driver and Kathleen—Kathleen Connor, my maid and friend—"

"How liberal of you, to call a servant a friend. I do believe I have much to learn from you about—"

Julia hadn't the time or patience to let her chatter on. "Mary, excuse me for interrupting. But I *am* in a hurry. As I started to say, they are waiting for me in the carriage. And this isn't a social call."

"I don't understand." Mary feigned embarrassment.

"I've come to ask you a few questions. I would appreciate honest answers, for everyone's sake."

"I haven't the slightest idea what you mean, but it's no matter, for I always speak the truth. Perhaps too openly and naively, as I've been told." She smiled, but Julia remained somber.

"Ian did propose to you yesterday?"

"He did."

"And have you decided to accept?" Julia tried to keep her voice steady.

"I didn't. I spent the entire night, until the first bird's chirp, composing a letter of explanation."

"I see," Julia said. She was more relieved than she'd expected and would have liked to leave it at that. But she couldn't. "Did you think you were pregnant?"

"No! Of course not! Though I don't think I have to answer such a personal question—"

"You involved me, without my desire, in your intimacies, if I remember correctly," Julia responded dryly.

"Julia! Really! Did you think that I went to Ian's that night to . . ." She flushed and stammered. "Well, I can't even say the word. We sat together and kissed and hugged. I'll admit to that without shame. But I am as much a virgin as you are!"

"Are you certain that I am?" Julia asked, having expected this possible retort. Mary's expression proved that she'd thrown her, just as she'd intended to.

"Well, I just assumed, I mean I never thought . . ." Mary's stammer was genuine this time, as was the heightening of color in her cheeks. "Do you mean that those stories Percy told me were true!"

"What stories?"

"I'm so surprised by your confession that I don't know what I'm saying!"

"I think you do," Julia said sternly, never taking her eyes from Mary's face. "What stories?"

"Julia Davenport! Who do you think you are, badgering me this way!" Mary rose. "Just because you're so beautiful and have always been so popular doesn't give you reason to condescend to me, interrogate me as if I were some naughty child—"

" 'Criminal' would be more apt," Julia said evenly as she rose. Suddenly she was bone tired. She started for the door.

"How dare you!" Mary yelled shrilly. "I hate you, Julia Davenport! I've *always* hated you and all your stuck-up friends who think that I'm nothing more than a silly, big-bosomed, empty-headed, stupid girl! I hate you all! Especially you!"

Julia turned and eyed her sadly. "I know, Mary.

You've made it perfectly clear. I'm really very sorry for you."

"Sorry for *me! You're* sorry for me after *I* took the *one* man you loved *away* from you! It was *me* he made *passionate* love to, time after time. It was *me* he wanted to *marry,* but *I* didn't want *him!* So don't you *dare* say you're *sorry* for me. If you'd only seen how Ian told me about your *silly* crush on him and *ridiculed* you, you'd be feeling sorry for *yourself!"*

Julia felt herself pale. She left as Mary laughed hysterically.

Ian burst into Ned's office at ten-thirty, laughing ecstatically and waving a letter on gilded paper in his hand. "She did it! She refused my proposal!" He tossed the letter at Ned. "So it was all a lie, just as we'd thought. And just before the letter arrived, I talked with Caramody. He's as enthusiastic as we are, so I can't imagine anything will go wrong. I've got to go right now to speak with Julia!"

Ned jumped up and raced to the door. Grabbing Ian by his shoulder, he yanked him back into his office and slammed his door. "You can't! It's too soon! As much as you love her. We've got to wait until I talk to Betsy at lunch. It will be just a couple of hours."

Ian sank into the chair, suddenly disheartened. "I'm sorry. I was so excited that I completely forgot . . . But you're right. Even this letter doesn't answer the key question of whether Mary was somehow manipulating Julia as cleverly as she did me."

"That's why I insisted Betsy meet me for lunch at

noon. I had a strong hunch this letter would arrive before then, and I knew you couldn't stand having to wait until tonight.''

Ian rose wearily. "I think I'll do some work," he said.

"I think, with that hangover of yours and no sleep, that you ought to lock your office door and take a nap on your couch. Tell Vivien to bring me all messages and after I've gone to lunch to just hold them. With hope, you'll need your energy to speak semicoherently to Julia tonight.''

Ian nodded. Ned patted him on the back and they smiled with renewed hope.

"Are you certain she's unavailable?" Ian asked the maid who answered Julia's uncle's phone. "This is the third time I've phoned. Please tell her that if she doesn't call me back this evening, I'll be forced to drive out to see her tomorrow.''

Ian turned to Ned and Charles as he hung up the telephone in Charles's library.

"I'll do what I can, Ian. But I think you've got to give her time to cool down. Julia can be more muleheaded than any man I know, when she wants to be." Charles clapped him on the shoulder. "This will all blow over in time, Ian. Believe me. For now, dang it, the best thing we three gents can do is toast to our first skyscraper. Ned, Ian, sit down while I pour us all a stiff drink.''

"One last question first, Charles. When will she be returning from Long Island?''

"I don't expect them back for about two weeks. I'm

going out myself for a very long weekend on Thursday. But I'm certain you'll hear from Julia before then."

Ian smiled and nodded, knowing he was fooling them no more than himself. Charles handed him a drink.

"Now, I would like to propose a toast," Charles began.

"Please, excuse my rudeness, but I must propose a toast first. To something more important than our first skyscraper." They stared with incredulity. Ian felt his eyes cloud with tears, but he didn't even wish to attempt to hide them. "My toast is to my best friends, Ned and Charles! May I continue to keep you so for all our lives!"

"I'll drink to that!" Charles said heartily, though his eyes misted.

"It's the finest toast I've ever heard," Ned said, tears forming freely in his eyes.

They clinked their glasses and drank, each man slightly embarrassed despite himself, Ian realized. Why was it that women could show their affection—their love—for one another so much more easily? It was a damn shame, Ian thought. He jumped when the phone rang. Charles lifted it immediately.

"Yes, hello, sweetheart. . . . Yes, he's right here. So is Ned. We're having a celebration but I'll tell you about that later. . . . All right, if you insist!" Charles winked at Ian. "We're celebrating the first commission for a skyscraper that Ian landed for us!" Charles's smile dwindled. "Yes, dear, I'll put him on. Ned and I were going to grab a sandwich or something in the kitchen, so you and Ian can speak freely. . . . I see. . . . Yes,

I'll speak with your Mamma later tonight. Here's Ian." Charles handed him the phone with a shrug and a doubtful shake of his head.

Ian watched as the two men left the library and closed the door behind them. "Julia, hello! I'm so glad you called, for I was beginning to fear that you wouldn't. I've got to apologize and speak—"

"Ian, please," Julia interrupted. "This is difficult enough. I only called to entreat you to leave me alone. Please don't call me here again. And please don't drive up here," she said as she wiped the tears from her cheeks as she sat alone in the room that was hers for her stay.

"Julia, are you crying?" Ian asked softly.

"Yes, I am, but pay that no mind, for I cry easily."

"Julia, I love you," he responded with such tenderness that she thought for sure her heart would break.

"Perhaps you do. But I've got to think. I promise to call you when I know what I've decided," she said through her tears.

"I want you to be my—"

"Please, Ian. Don't say it, I beg you. Not until I'm sure about things. I may never allow you to ask, as much as I . . . I've got to go. Congratulations on your skyscraper. Papa is so proud of you. He loves you like a son. . . ." Julia couldn't risk speaking another second. For she knew she would lose her resolve and say what was in her heart. That she loved him even more. She hung up.

Ian rested his head on his arms. He tried to stop them, but the tears came in a racking torrent of disappointment.

Chapter Fifteen

"BETSY, WHAT ARE YOU DOING HERE?" JULIA ASKED WITH astonishment as Betsy appeared unannounced in Julia's aunt's drawing room, where she'd been painting.

"Some greeting," Betsy said dryly. She walked to the easel and gave Julia a hug and kiss. Betsy studied the half-completed landscape. "I think you're getting *so good* it's absolutely incredible . . ."—Julia beamed—"absolutely incredible that you can be so stupid!"

"What?" Julia gasped.

"You heard me. I'm really mad at you this time, Julia Davenport!" Betsy led her to the sofa.

"What have I done! Since I saw you I've secluded myself in this room and done little more than work on my painting!"

"Oh, you've done more than that! You've ruined my trip to the Adirondacks, but that's the least. You've made *everyone* crazy and miserable. Your father, Ned, me and *most especially* Ian. He rode all the way here to see you yesterday and you wouldn't even *see* him?"

"That's not fair," Julia complained as the hurt filled her eyes with tears. "I *told* him two nights ago not to come!"

"And still he did. Didn't that tell you *anything!* Honestly, how can you be so thick-headed? Don't you realize how much that poor man loves you!"

"Maybe he does, but I don't know whom to believe anymore. For your information, I went to see Mary before I left and I've *tried* to call Percy since we arrived, but they said he was away."

"I know you went to see Mary."

"You do? How? Did you go to see her too?"

"No, I was going to, but after Ned told me the whole story Ian told *him* and has been *trying* to tell *you*, I called at Percy's. For some reason I didn't believe he was away, so I went to the house and he was standing in the hallway and couldn't flee from me, though I'm sure he would have liked to."

Julia felt dizzy with confusion. "But why?"

"Because Percy's turned out to be the one who's a liar. Second only, of course, to Mary Hoffman." Betsy laughed. "In fact, what's almost funny about the whole thing is apparently, one of the few times Mary told Ian the truth, or what she thought was the truth, she was *actually* just passing along Percy's lie."

"I can't believe that Percy would say anything truly malicious about me, even if he is hurt—"

"What would you call spreading the rumor about town that you left him for a married man, a neighbor right here in Long Island, with whom you had begun an affair *after* you and Percy became engaged?"

"What?" Julia laughed despite herself.

300

"This was one of the many stories Mary told Ian during that luncheon at Delmonico's. As well as that she believed she was pregnant."

Julia's mouth dropped open. Betsy had been right all along.

"Close your mouth, for it's going to gape open again before you've heard all I have to recount!"

"Madam Rosa," Julia whispered, after Betsy had finished telling her everything.

"What?"

"She tried to warn me! I never told you, because you made such fun of her and she told me to keep my own counsel. But she told me that there were two men in my life . . . that I loved them both . . . one would bring nothing but sorrow and misery . . . the other great happiness and pleasure."

Betsy looked impressed. "Did she tell you which was which?"

"No," Julia answered softly, remembering Madam's words. "She said it was my free will that would allow me to choose. She said to pick wisely, that it was my life and all the answers were in me, if I found the courage to face the truths and act upon them. But I didn't, did I!" Julia castigated herself.

"Now you're being a *little* bit hard on yourself. Were her words a factor in your decision to break your engagement to Percy?"

Julia nodded, for she couldn't speak.

"Well, then, you did begin by making the *right* decision."

"But for the wrong reasons!"

"Well . . ." Betsy pondered. "Maybe it's as she said, that you hadn't yet found the courage to face the truths."

"Are you saying you believe in Madam Rosa?"

"I'm not saying anything about her. But if you give me two dollars, I'll give you something even better, guaranteed to make you live happily ever after."

"And what's that?" Julia asked, knowing that Betsy was teasing but unsure as to where she was heading.

"Where's the two dollars?"

"You mean, after all these years, you won't trust me to pay it to you?" Julia laughed.

"I guess I will." Betsy reached inside her small black purse and handed her a slip of paper.

"What's this?" Julia asked as she unfolded the slip.

"Ian's telephone number. He's waiting at home for your call. Don't tell him I let on, but he's been packed since last night," Betsy said, and giggled.

"But before you call him and he drives up here and you fall into each other's arms and all that sort of thing, I have *one* request to make. For I'm catching the train in a half-hour, to the Hudson Line, and then going on to the Adirondacks."

"What's your request?"

"It's a suggestion, actually. Would you keep in mind the idea of a double wedding?" Betsy slipped off her gloves and waved a beautiful diamond ring before Julia's eyes.

"Oh, Betsy!" Julia cried as they embraced.

Betsy wiped the tears from her eyes. "Julia, enough of this. I'm in a hurry but I can't leave until you do it!"

"Do what? . . . Oh!" Julia rose and with the slip of

paper in her hand she walked to the desk. She lifted the telephone and asked the operator to connect her to Ian's number. She smiled at Betsy, who inched toward the door as they waited.

"Hello?" his rich voice answered anxiously.

Julia smiled and nodded. "Hello, Ian, this is Julia. . . ." Betsy smiled smugly, blew her a kiss and disappeared through the doors.

Never had she been so nervous in her entire life! She heard the motorcar drive onto the circular gravel driveway and raced to the window. Mamma, Daphne and the others had gone for a drive to an antique store, leaving her with Kathleen and the house staff.

"Kathleen," she shouted. "He's here!"

"You don't have to yell, I'm right behind you," Kathleen admonished, but when Julia turned to her, Kathleen was smiling brightly. She moved next to Julia and stared out the window. "I wonder who that fine-looking driver is? Does Mr. Woods have a driver?"

"I don't know. Probably works for his mother," Julia said as she watched them emerge from the motorcar. "He *is* handsome!"

"You mean Ian?"

"Well of course *he's* handsome! But I meant the driver." Julia turned to Kathleen and grinned as she remembered Madam Rosa's words. Well, it wasn't summer yet, but it could be a *beginning*. She pulled Kathleen by the hand. "Let's go out and greet them!"

"That isn't proper," Kathleen halfheartedly protested, but allowed herself to be dragged.

"No one will ever know," Julia teased as they raced for the door.

Standing on the veranda, Julia watched Ian walk slowly up the drive, looking terribly serious. He's nervous, she realized, even more so than she! She grabbed at her skirt and ran down the steps and didn't stop until he caught her in his arms.

They kissed sweetly and held each other tight.

How long I've waited for this moment, Ian thought as he choked back his tears. I think I've waited all my life. Afraid that he was going to cry, he pulled away. He cleared his throat. "Julia, I don't believe you've met our driver. Mr. Michael O'Casey, Miss Julia Davenport."

"Pleased to make your acquaintance, miss," he said in a charming brogue and tipped his hat. His bright blue eyes twinkled and his hair was only slightly darker than her own.

"Why, you must be from County Cork, just like my Mamma was!" Kathleen blurted.

When Julia turned to her, Kathleen had turned beet-red and had clasped her mouth with her hand. Julia refrained from laughing good-naturedly, for she knew it would only mortify shy Kathleen further. A glance at Ian told her he was attempting the same, albeit less successfully, from the looks of his creeping grin. "Mr. Michael O'Casey, this is Miss Kathleen Connor."

Michael repeated his greeting, but Julia saw that his eyes sparkled with interest. Three cheers for Madam Rosa, she thought. "Kathleen, I'm certain that Mr. O'Casey—"

"Michael, miss,"

She smiled. "Michael, then, must be thirsty and hungry too. Why don't you take him to the kitchen, for Ian and I are going to take a little walk. I promise we'll be back before Mamma returns!"

"Certainly, miss," Kathleen answered, her blush rising again.

"May I have the honor of this walk, Mr. Woods?" Julia asked, and linked her arm with his.

They'd come to the top of the small hill that Julia had led them to. Off at a distance was a wintered apple orchard. Although it was only the end of January, the day was so mild that Julia had unbuttoned her jacket and Ian had carried his topcoat over his free arm.

"Isn't it beautiful?" Julia asked as she stretched her arms and breathed in the fresh country air.

"The most beautiful sight I've ever seen!" Ian answered with such intensity that Julia turned to him. She realized that he'd been speaking about her and flushed before bursting into laughter.

Ian pulled her into his arms. Finally alone again, he thought, as he kissed her with a delicacy that belied his passion. But Julia demanded more, as her mouth cleaved to his.

Dear Lord, how wonderful it was to be in his arms, she thought as she felt the heat that emanated from his lean and hard body pressed against her. He smelled so manly—a scent more heady than the finest perfume she'd ever encountered. How long she had wanted to run her fingers through his thick black hair that was as satiny to her touch as she'd imagined! Ian pulled the pins from her own Psyche knot and her hair cascaded down her shoulders and over his chest as he kissed her again, his lips nibbling hers, his hands stroking her cheeks and hair. Abruptly he drew away, startling her. She laughed with relief when she saw him spread his cashmere coat like a blanket upon the hard winter ground. He sat down and pulled her onto his lap. They began kissing again and she felt as if she never wanted him to stop as his hands caressed her beneath her open coat, gently at first, then more insistently until she felt a yearning flame within her, making her catch her breath as his fingers and tongue thrilled her.

"I love you, Julia . . ." Ian whispered. Her mouth answered him in a natural, open manner that fired him beyond words, and he felt himself grow steely beneath her. But more than the lust that overwhelmed him, he felt passion, so much stronger yet. And love, the strongest of all.

"Stop, my love," Julia whispered and withdrew from his arms. Had their rush of intimacy frightened her? he wondered as he studied her flushed face with concern. But her smile, more radiant than the sun shining above them, and her outstretched arm bidding him to rise, reassured him.

"Come," she said, her voice a sweet song. "I have more to show you." Ian rose and quickly stood at her side, following the direction to which her finger pointed. "Look down there . . ." Ian saw a little cabin beyond the apple orchard, standing in a secluded grove of evergreens. It was built from rough-hewn redwood and a graceful trail of smoke rose from its chimney into the cloudless sky. He gazed back at Julia, whose eyes shone brightly, her dimples deep in her cheeks as she smiled.

"I know a shortcut," she said with a mischievous grin. "Would you like to have a tour?" she asked boldly, but her cheeks heightened in color, which gave her nervousness away.

"Oh, I'd love to," he replied brightly. He forced his face into its most serious expression. "But perhaps we should go back to the main house and have Kathleen properly chaperone you?" Julia responded with such a flustered and disappointed countenance that he didn't have the heart to tease her any longer. He swept her into his arms and brought her mouth to his own as she held him tightly around his neck, her legs swaying gently as he held her. His lips kissed, nibbled and teased her own until she sighed and he felt the quiver of desire course through her. "Or perhaps we could explore by ourselves? What do you say?" He stood her on the ground and she hugged him tightly, lifted her face to his and placed a gentle kiss upon his mouth.

"I say we should hurry," Julia declared, and then the laughter gurgled from her throat.

Julia watched Ian gaze about the small, comfortable cabin that she had known and loved since she was a child. She enjoyed the surprise that registered on his face as he saw that it had been converted into a comfortable painting studio, a studio more fully equipped and far less austere than her own. In the middle of the room stood a potbellied stove and before

307

it lay a thick blue Persian carpet. The room was filled with a profusion of vases containing dried bright spring flowers, for her aunt, a competent painter in her own right, preferred to paint flower arrangements above all else.

"I feel as if we've stepped into springtime," Ian said with as much pleasure as surprise.

"I thought you'd love it," Julia answered. She glowed more brilliantly than the bright colors of blue, purple, yellow and red flowers and paintings that filled the room, Ian thought. She leaned her cheek against his own as she sat upon his lap. Ian rose and carried her to the thick blue rug before the open stove in which the wood logs burned strongly. Obviously someone had been sent to the cabin not more than an hour before their arrival to light the fire, he realized. "Are you cold?" he asked her as she snuggled tighter against him.

"No, not at all," Julia replied as he rested her on the rug and lowered himself behind her, his strong hands stroking her neck beneath her flowing hair. "Well, perhaps a little chilled," she teased as his touch sent goosebumps up her spine. She pulled him beside her and cuddled into his arms.

"I see . . ." he answered, his own grin matching hers. "Well, never let it be said that chivalry is dead. It is my responsibility to see that you don't catch a death of a chill, is it not?"

"Most certainly," Julia whispered. He pulled her tightly into his arms, and as he lowered them to a reclining position across the thick rug, his lips never left her own. Gently he rearranged her hair so that it flowed like a wheat silk curtain behind her. He turned sideways, raising himself on his hip and elbow, after he'd released her lips, and gazed down at her.

The teasing expression that had played on his features before had transformed into a solemn gaze. "Is something the matter?" Julia asked. His smile flooded her with relief even before he spoke.

"You're so beautiful. Being next to you, I feel as if I'm dreaming this moment—that I will wake and find myself alone in my bed and wanting you."

"I know exactly what you mean. Since that first moment I saw you, I have never been the same." His hands stroked her face and she reached for his fingertips and kissed them. "I felt . . . I felt a longing that I couldn't even explain to myself at first. I dreamed of you holding me and kissing me . . ." She wanted to continue but suddenly felt shy as her cheeks blazed.

"Did I hold you like this in your dream?" he asked as he drew her to him and she felt the tautness of his body pressed against her and that sweet, heated sensation flooded through her. "And kiss you like this?" he whispered. His mouth captured her own; his tongue danced within her until she answered from some deep well of knowledge.

As he rolled her onto her back, his mouth left hers and began to tease her cheek and neck, making her shudder with pleasure and moan as he played at her ear. She felt his hands deftly open the buttons of her blue velvet dress and the coolness of his fingers as they caressed her breast chilled and heated her at once. She sighed and felt her nipple harden under the touch of his hand. When he brought his lips and tongue to her other

GILDED HEARTS

breast she began to writhe beneath him, so strong were these unknown sensations that thrilled her.

Julia felt as if they were riding the melody of the most beautiful Chopin concerto. She responded to his caresses and kisses, answering with her own, making him sigh with pleasure. Their clothes were magically gone and she looked with joy at his strong, broad shoulders that tapered to narrow hips. As she stroked the soft black hair on his chest she thought again that he was as beautiful as the finest Greek statue, and then she was lost in a world of wordless desire stronger than she'd ever imagined.

His hand gently slid between her legs and nudged them apart as his head moved from her breasts, his kisses tracing down from her stomach until his lips reached the throbbing, vulnerable spot at her core, making her cry out in ecstasy. His hand brought hers to his manhood. Tentatively at first, she caressed its wonderous tip and his gasp of pleasure thrilled her. Again the innate knowledge told her how to please him further, until she could do nothing more than catch her breath as his tongue probed deep within her and she thought that she would swoon. Thought that there could be no pleasure greater or more intense, until he rose and cleaved his mouth to hers again, driving her breath into catches that escaped from her throat into his mouth. As he entered her, the music filled her head as he filled her. The smoldering light in his eyes transformed into a burst of colors as she met his thrust with an urgency that shook her to her core, then lifted her into a sweet oblivion as she rode the undulating waves of pleasure with Ian. She could

310

feel the wild beating of his heart as strongly as her own.

Ian thrust slowly and deeply into her very being and felt her rapture. Her glistening rosy mouth round in a sigh, her jutting hard pink nipples calling for his lips, carried him to an ecstasy he had never known. How he loved her, he thought, until he could think no longer.

Julia rode the crest of the wave, her mouth locked to his, her tongue lost within his mouth, her legs tightly wrapped around his waist as the delight of his thrusting quickened and deepened until she was carried off again. "I love you, Ian," she heard herself cry from some distant place as the rainbow behind her eyes and music in her head rose to a crescendo and she was lost in the whirling urgency that rocked through her. She clung tightly to Ian, her body answering his every move until she felt as if a volcano were about to erupt within her. "I love you, Julia," she heard Ian cry in a deep rumbling voice that came from far away and at the same time deep within her.

As the waves subsided and she floated in the peaceful undulating sensations, she thought that if she died right now, she would have known what it was to have lived and loved. She stroked the back of his neck as Ian arched, cried out and collapsed against her. "I love you, my dearest Ian," she whispered, thinking he hadn't heard—but that was all right, she thought, as she smiled to herself. For she had the rest of their lives to tell him that she loved him a billion times! She felt his heart pounding against her.

Ian kissed the tip of her nose. "I was right about you, Miss Davenport," he whispered, with a grin.

"Whatever do you mean, Mr. Woods?" she teased back as she ran her finger across his lips.

"You are the most infuriatingly passionate temptress that I have ever met! You shall be my ruin!" Julia blushed and looked so flustered that he knew he could not maintain his stern countenance for another moment.

"Ian—" she began with a catch in her voice, but he silenced her with a kiss. "But, Ian, I don't under—"

"You, Julia, will be the death of me! I swear that I will most definitely die in your arms in forty or fifty years!" Her giggle thrilled him. "But how much pleasure we shall share until then. And I can't think of a more perfect way to die!"

"Ian Woods!" Julia declared, and as she laughed, she tried to push him off her, but he swung her on top of him and as they wrestled about like children, he playfully caught her hands and pulled them behind her back.

"Fifty years at the most, my sweet. We haven't a minute to waste!" he teased, and caught her laughter with his mouth. He kissed her deeply and her laughter turned to a sigh once again. Abruptly he pulled away.

"What now?" she asked, wanting to laugh but refraining.

"I knew I forgot something!" he declared. "You will marry me, my love, won't you?"

Julia couldn't restrain her grin. "I'll think about it," she teased.

"Good," he bantered back. His lips nibbled at hers. "Can you think and kiss at the same time?"

"I can try."

"Well, then, I guess we'll just put you to the test," he said, grinning. "I'll just amuse myself, and should you come to a decision, don't hesitate to interrupt. . . ." His hand played from her neck to her breast as he spoke, and she reached for his head and brought his mouth to hers once again. Abruptly he pulled away, teasing her. "Are you certain you'll be able to think clearly?"

"I'll marry you, Ian Woods! I'll marry you!" she yelled as tears of joy and laughter mingled in her eyes.

"Oh, that's a relief!" he said, and drew her into his arms again. "After all, with only fifty or so years—"

"I know," she interrupted as she nuzzled his neck. "We don't have a minute to waste!"

She smiled as he answered her with a kiss.

Tapestry

HISTORICAL ROMANCES

Next Month From
Tapestry Romances

NEVADA NIGHTS
by Ruth Ryan Langan
TANGLED VOWS
by Anne Moore

POCKET BOOKS